# Earth:
## The Elementals Book Two

Copyright © 2020 by Jennifer Williams
All rights reserved. This book or any portion thereof
may not be reproduced or used in any manner
whatsoever
without the express written permission of the
publisher
except for the use of brief quotations in a book review.

Printed in the United States of America

First Printing, 2020

ISBN: 9781952422096
Imprint: Imagine Nation

Chenoa, IL 61726
AuthorJenniferLush@gmail.com

This is a work of fiction. Names, characters,
businesses, places, events, locales, and incidents are
either the products of the author's imagination or used
in a fictitious manner. Any resemblance to actual
persons, living or dead, or actual events is purely
coincidental.

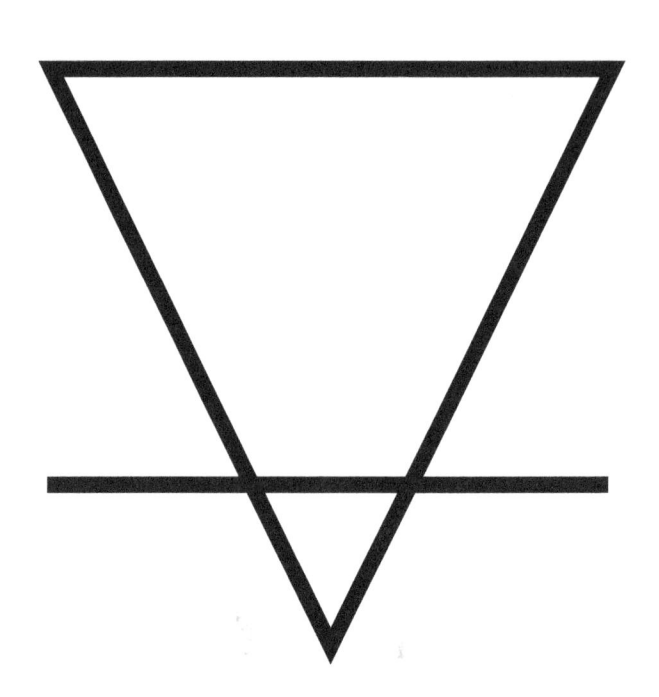

# Chapter One

She ran through the forest stopping to throw her arms around a silver birch tree. Her face lit up with sheer joy from feeling the nature that surrounded her in every fiber of her being. She kicked at the leaves and inhaled the woods like the scent was a drug, and she couldn't get enough.

She should've been more careful was what she would tell herself many times over the next year. She should've paid more attention to whether she was alone. If she had been cautious, she could have avoided the fate she faced. If she had been cautious, she would have never experienced a love so powerful that she would contemplate giving up eternity for it.

Daniel was mesmerized. He watched her appear seemingly from out of nowhere. It was as if she emerged from the trunk of a tree. He knew he must be seeing things. The darkness draping the forest in shadows was playing tricks on his mind. Still, only a tree sprite would dance around in sheer giddiness like this. Of that he was most certain.

He dismounted his horse and walked closer. She took no notice of him. Even through the darkness, he could see her beauty. Her skin was dark light the night, and her long black hair appeared softer than most women of her descent. She was almost close enough he could reach out and stroke it.

Daniel snapped to attention. She was a sprite who had him under her spell. He looked behind him ready to make his retreat before she saw him. It was too late. With a gleeful giggle, she turned and ran straight into him.

He didn't know what to do. He could only stare into her beautiful oval eyes. Frightened eyes. Terror spread across her face, and he sensed that she was about to dart away. He grabbed her arm and said sternly, "I will not bring you harm, but you are in grave danger."

Her eyes searched the forest behind him looking for a way to escape.

Daniel relaxed. "Listen to me, woman. You needn't have worry of me, but you are not safe here. Do you understand me?"

He stood waiting for an answer. From where did this lovely creature appear? He had never seen her before, and someone with skin as dark as his would've been remembered. Daniel began to wonder if she even spoke the same language.

She opened her mouth, but thought twice about speaking. She nodded at him.

"Good. Come with me. I will put you up for the night, and tomorrow I will get you home."

He led her back to his horse, not letting go of her arm because he feared she would run. Too many evils lurked nearby for him to leave her be. "The people here...they're friendly. They don't mind how people like me and you look. Others are not as nice. Wars have been raging. Armies pass through close by. You have to be careful. It's not safe for a woman out here alone."

She understood what he was trying to tell her. He helped her onto his horse, and he sat behind her. They ventured out of the trees to a path that ran along a fence. They followed the fence to a small home. Daniel told her to go on inside out of the chilly air while he tended to the horse.

Worry wracked her mind. She had been here for five minutes before she failed. She didn't mean to, but that wouldn't matter. She needed to find a way out of this safely and proceed with caution for the next year. Maybe by fixing her mistake some compassion would be shown to her when she returned.

The home was tiny. It was perfect for one man. There was a hearth and a table with two chairs. The far wall saw a pile of furs on the floor. She looked around, but her eyes kept returning to the fur. That's where he slept. She sucked her breath in and wondered where she would be laying her head that night.

The door opened behind her, and he walked inside. The two of them was enough to make the room feel crowded. He began taking off his outer garments and hanging them by the door. "Where are you from?" he asked.

She didn't know what to tell him. She had never thought about having to form these human details as she wasn't supposed to interact with anyone for any reason. She wasn't even entirely certain where she had emerged. The weather was cold enough that she could rule out some locations, but she hadn't seen enough to narrow it down much more than that. He took her silence for fear again.

"My name is Daniel. I'm from a small village that requires two months travel by boat to reach. It's a long story how I came to be here," he looked at her and waited, hoping she would contribute.

"Do you have a name?" Still she didn't answer him. "You don't have to tell me anything you don't want to. You have no reason to trust that I am not a bad person. I will deliver you safe and sound in the morning to wherever you desire to go. Then you will see."

He walked to the hearth and pulled a pot from the side. He set it on the table and lifted the lid, stirring the contents. The aroma drifted across the short distance to where she stood, and she felt her stomach churn. She hadn't realized how hungry she had become until she smelled the stew. Or rather, she hadn't realized the gnawing in her midsection was what hunger felt like.

"Are you hungry?" he asked her, and motioned to a chair.

"Yes," she sat down quickly.

"She speaks!" His laughter roared out heartily.

She looked down at her hands nervously wringing them. She should not have spoken no matter how harmless it may seem.

He served up two bowls of stew and placed one in front of her. She began eating it fast, not taking time to taste it. He watched her wondering how such a beautiful woman found herself alone in the woods this time of year far from any encampments or villages. She caught him watching her and stopped.

Daniel leaned back in his chair and stretched. He observed her as she tasted the rabbit stew he had prepared. Her eyes showed obvious approval. She began to spoon one bite in her mouth after another barely having time to enjoy the flavor let alone chew. "Whoa," he told her. "Slow down a mite. There's plenty more if you want it, but eating like that will make you sick."

He broke off a couple pieces of bread and passed her one. Daniel continued to watch her with growing interest as she looked at it like it was something completely foreign to her. He sopped up some liquid from his bowl with the bread and took a bite. She watched him then did the same. He was convinced now there was something altogether unusual about her and was beginning to think she really was a tree sprite.

After they dined, he cleared the table and cleaned up. His father would laugh to see him doing the home chores while a woman sat staring intently at the fire. But, she was also a guest. A guest who it was becoming more and more clear was in need of his help. Daniel finished up and joined her by the fire. He had so many questions, but he was aware she wasn't ready to provide any answers. *'Perhaps by morning,'* he thought to himself.

He looked at the pile of furs along the wall. A pallet bed was hidden underneath. There would be no way the two of them could sleep together without being practically overlapped. He sighed which drew her attention. Daniel knew he would sleep on the floor and allow her the comfortable rest. She was after all a maiden in distress.

Since she seemed to understand him, he explained to her what he had decided about the sleeping arrangements. He took a pile of quilts and furs and laid them out between the bed and fire. His mystery guest tried to insist on letting him have the bed, but he refused.

She laid down on the small bed and covered herself in furs. This man had been exceptionally kind to her. *'He plans on taking me to where I need to go tomorrow only I don't know where that would be,'* she worried. How would she tell him she needs to be somewhere void of people or at least at the edge of them? She needed to devise a plan to leave here on her own.

His bed and blankets were comfortable and warm, and she soon found herself unable to stop the sleep that was overtaking her. Right before drifting off, a voice in the darkness spoke to her and her alone. She turned to the spot where Daniel lay, seeing nothing but a pile of blankets being illuminated by fire. "My name is Anya," she told him quietly, before letting dreams overtake her.

Anya opened her eyes and for a moment she was with the other three on the flat rock filled with excitement of what lay ahead, then consciousness suddenly took over. She shot upright and looked around. The tiny cabin was empty except for her.

The fire was blazing bright, and there was a new tempting aroma coming from the hearth.

This might be her only chance. She quietly crept from the bed. There was nothing to do except leave. The only possessions she had were the robes she wore, and she had worn them to bed. She walked softly across the floor so intent on leaving as quickly as possible that she paid no attention to the chopping noise outside. Nor did she take notice when it stopped.

Anya was about two steps from the door when it swung open nearly hitting her. She jumped back and let out a small cry. There was Daniel carrying an armload of firewood.

"Good morning, miss," he told her with a smile. "I'm sorry if I woke you. I have just a little bit of logs left to cut for the winter, and I've been meaning to get them done before the snow fall."

Anya didn't say a word. She watched him stack the wood by the hearth before bringing the pan to the table. "Let's eat," his words came out like an order. "Then I'll take you wherever you need to go."

Anya nodded and sat down like she had been instructed. He served her some form of a frittata. The herbs danced through the air going in through her breath and having a direct effect on her appetite. It smelled delicious, but she waited for him to ready himself before she ate.

The taste did not disappoint. She closed her eyes savoring each herb that crossed her lips. Sage certainly, and basil she recognized. Anya tried to determine each flavor hoping this might be a dish she could recreate when she was on her own. Herbs grew wild all over the countryside, and Earth could certainly be able to find them with ease.

This time she enjoyed her meal he noticed. She ate the meager breakfast as if it were a delicacy that she would never experience again. He needed to take her home, but where was that his thoughts drifted off again. He had been plagued with worry and hadn't slept all night because of it. Well, that and due to sleeping on the uncomfortable floor. If she had a home, a good home, she would not wish to linger here. What if she had managed to escape a life of cruelty, and he was trying to simply hand her back over?

You have to take her back he told himself as he had a hundred times while lying on the floor last night. If she is found here with you, your punishment will be severe. People of your kind are not tolerated well in these parts. You are welcomed not because of what you contribute, but because you cause no waves in doing it. You keep to yourself, do only what is necessary, and do it well, so no one ever has any reason to point a finger your way.

After they ate, he cleaned up again, but this time she studied his every move as if trying to learn from him. She grew more and more mysterious to him with every passing minute. At one time, he turned and she was directly behind him. She was so close that he bumped into her. Even though her body was fully covered in some crudely styled robe that did nothing for her figure, he could easily feel the curve of her breasts underneath. She stepped back and crossed her arms over her chest. He was about to apologize when he noticed a smile just before she turned her back to him.

This was too much. She was beautiful. Her cocoa colored skin was creamy smooth. She had straight black hair that hung below her shoulders. Her robes were tied with a belt at the waist that showed her dainty size. He had already been preoccupied with thoughts of her and now he had to add the feel of her breast to his overcrowded mind.

He cleared his throat, "I'll be happy to take you

anywhere you'd like to go, Anya. Just tell me where your home is located."

A look of panic shot through her eyes, but it was fleeting. "I can make my own way. Thank you for your kindness."

"That is the most you've spoken since we met. I can't let you leave alone. It's not safe for a woman to travel unaccompanied anywhere, but certainly not in these parts. There are men traveling through this area more wild than any animal you may encounter."

"It's not far."

"Good," he smiled. "I'll get the horse ready, and we'll be off."

He gathered his outer wear and went out into the chilly morning to a small shed at the back of his cabin home. Daniel nuzzled up close to Cora, his mare, and stroked her mane. He took a treat from his pocket and fed it to her. He pulled the saddle over back and fastened all the while talking to her about the short ride ahead and how thankful he was for her companionship. For many years now, this horse had been the only friend or family he had in his life.

He led her around front and tied her loosely to a fence post. Daniel walked back to the cabin to collect Anya. The sooner he had delivered her safely, the better for so many reasons. It was a simple fact of nature that two people left alone for long would soon develop a relationship less than godly. He was already feeling a physical draw to this woman, and he was only human.

Daniel threw open the door, but saw no one. He entered his home and looked around. She was gone. For a moment he wasn't sure if he felt fear or relief. This would save him the effort, sure. It would also be a risk to him if unsavory people saw them on the ride. He would be accused of all manners of impropriety for having a strange woman with him.

The fear for her safety slowly boiled over and took precedent in his mind.

'*Dammit woman!*' he thought, and slammed his fist on the table sending cups and a jug airborne for a second before they landed upright on the table again. He knew he had to at least try to find her. He would never sleep a wink again knowing he had let her go to meet a countless number of ends all of which were worse than death.

He walked outside and surveyed the options. He would've seen her if she'd passed by the shed. She'd probably still be in sight if she had ran across the open field. There were only two prospects and one took her back to where he had found her wandering the woods the night before. He chose to look for her there. It was the closest he had to an idea of where her home may be. She had to be from somewhere near those woods.

He hopped onto his horse and took off. She couldn't have gotten far on foot. If he didn't see sign of her soon, he'd search the opposite route from his home, and that would be that. She had to know the dangers that lurked in these parts. It was her decision to risk it.

Daniel spied her within a couple minutes time. He called her name, but she didn't acknowledge it. He halved the distance between them and called for her again. This time she veered off to the right straight into the trees.

He pulled the reigns up high and his horse came to a halt. He reached down and patted the side of her neck staring at the spot in the woods where Anya had disappeared. As much as he didn't want any trouble, he was intrigued even more. The need to know her and why she was on the run was his only desire.

He dug his heel into Cora's side and made way for the woods. She hadn't made it very far. She was crafty he would give her that. She zigged and zagged trying to lose him the best she could. Daniel raced past her on her side and grabbed a low hanging branch pulling himself off Cora's back. He swung out and jumped down on the other side of the tree directly in front of Anya.

She ran straight into him having no time to redirect her course. He reached out his hand to help her up, but she didn't take it. She righted herself, and Daniel began to speak. "You are more unruly than the children who fight each other in the street."

Anya fled again. He glanced down at her arms for a moment to see if she had been hurt from the fall, and she took the opportunity to run. He caught her within seconds. Daniel brought both arms around her from behind pinning her arms to her side, and they slunk down together to the mossy forest floor. "Listen to me, woman!" Daniel yelled angrily.

The shock of his anger startled her and she went limp in his arms. Fearing it was a ploy, he didn't release her yet. "If you don't want to go home, fine!" he yelled at her. "But I can't allow you to run off on your own like this."

He loosened his grip just a little to test her, and she remained perfectly still. Anya was breathing him in. He smelled of sweat, the wood fire, and evergreen. Somehow the combination was enough to alight all the nerve endings in her body, sending tingling sensations all over. She had no desire to move from his embrace.

"You have to know the evil that awaits you out here on your own. Barely clothed at that! You should be thanking the stars above it was I who discovered you last night because anyone else would not have been this nice. I guarantee you that."

He let his arms drop. She still didn't move a

muscle. Daniel stood and took a step back. If she ran this time, he vowed to himself he would let her go. The risk he was taking by offering to take her back to his home wasn't worth anything she had to offer him in return. He had a feeling expecting help with chores would require training in all departments first.

Anya continued to stay exactly where she was. Part of her wanted to run and knew she should do exactly that. She refused to allow herself to think about the punishment that would already await her for this brief interaction with Daniel. She couldn't move. The closeness of his body, the scruffiness of his beard on her neck, and his smell kept her frozen in place. It was a powerful combination that had awoke a longing deep inside. She wanted more.

"Let's go if you're coming with me," he ordered.

Anya scrambled to her feet and followed him to his horse where she dutifully climbed up for the ride back to his cabin. She knew he was angry with her. He had every right to be. She feared for the questions he would surely ask. She hadn't created a backstory because she wasn't supposed to have need for one. She didn't want to add lying to her list of wrongs, but she knew she'd have to come up with something and quick.

They rode back in deafening silence. Anya leaned into him feeling the warmth emanate from his body. She hadn't realized how cold she was until she felt his heat. Sensing this, he opened his coat and pulled it around in front of her. It smelled like him. Between his heat, the coat, and the stirring between her legs that spread like fire out in all directions, Anya quickly began to warm up. They arrived at the cabin in minutes. Too soon as far as she was concerned.

Daniel helped her down then took the mare back to the barn. Anya went inside and sat in front of the fire. Without him, all the warmth she was feeling faded, and she had begun to shiver again. He came inside and started rummaging around in a wooden box by the table. He slammed a pan down on the table then a knife. He was still angry.

He dumped a gunny of potatoes onto the table and picked one up and set it down. He picked up the knife, but immediately set it back down. Daniel slammed his fist on the table, and she jumped. "You don't want to talk? That's convenient."

He began peeling potatoes, and Anya watched him carefully. She watched the blade of the knife cut through the tuber, stringing the outer layer off in slices. He tossed each one into the pot when he finished.

"At least answer me this. What fate will I face by letting you stay here?"

Anya wasn't sure what he was asking. It was her that would be punished, not him.

"Who will be looking for you?" he asked, his voice softening slightly.

"No one," Anya answered.

"No one?"

She nodded. She got up from the fire and walked over to him. She reached out her hand for the knife. He hesitated, but handed it over. Anya picked up a potato and asked, "How many?"

"All of them."

She began to peel the potato the way she had watched him do it. He eyed her for the first one then took her seat at the fire feeling confident she knew what she was doing. *'No one,'* he thought to himself, replaying her words in his head. It created more questions than it gave answers.

Daniel decided to wait before pressing her for more information. She wasn't exactly forthcoming with details anyway. *'She will see in time that I am a friend,'* he thought. *'She can trust me.'*

He watched her work at the table preparing

what would be their meal to nibble on for the rest of the day. Suddenly he didn't mind having the presence of someone else in his small home. It would do him good to have some company. She would have to continue to help out like this of course, and they would have to scramble now with the autumn weather leaving to make sure there was enough to last the winter for two.

As he watched her peel the potatoes, he noticed that sometimes her robes would move, showing the slightest curve of the side of her breast. He found himself staring at the edge of the robe almost trying to will it to move again and again. She turned to him, and he whipped his head back to the fire immediately. His face flushed hot, and he silently begged that she would think it was due to the flames and not his thoughts.

Anya peeled the potatoes feeling pleased that she was able to contribute. It was the right thing to do. She knew she wasn't supposed to be there, but she was at least learning what it meant to be part of the human realm. To be hungry, cold, warm, nervous, or comfortable. She had lost track of the emotions and sensations she had experienced already in less than a day.

Daniel helped her prepare another stew. It didn't go unnoticed that she followed his lead. When he peeled a carrot, she watched him then copied what he did. He wondered who this woman was who stood before him in rags, but acted like royalty who'd never had to do anything for herself.

Once the pot was on the hearth, he dug through his meager belongings and held some clothes out for her to take. "This is the best I can do. I don't have the means to acquire anything more right now, but it will keep you warm."

She smiled and took the garments from him.

"I'll be in the barn. Come see me when you're dressed. There's work to do."

Anya waited for the door to close behind him before she laid the clothes out before her. She slipped the britches on under her robes even though no one was there to see her. She lifted the robes over her head and slipped on his shirt. It smelled of him. The clothes were much too big. She tucked the shirt into the pants, but they still fell off of her when she tried to move. Anya took the cloth belt off her robes and put it around the pants tying it tight.

She still didn't have shoes or outer wear. She looked around the room. She found a worn pair of boots and put them on her feet. She looked like a small child wearing her father's shoes. There was no additional outer wear to be seen, so she picked up one of the furs and draped it over her shoulders.

She trod out in the cold. Anya couldn't walk in the boots. She had to slide her feet across the ground. Every time she lifted a foot, it would come halfway out of the boot. She finally made it to the barn and went inside.

The barn was cold, but not near as bitter as it was outdoors. Daniel was brushing down his mare. He studied her and frowned when he saw her feet, but he didn't say a word. He gave her a quick lesson in the work that they needed to do. The morning's chores were all done, so she would start helping him tomorrow. Today, her job would be to assist him in preparing some meat to salt. His traps had caught several rabbits and squirrels.

Anya was unsettled by the idea of watching him skin and gut these animals, but knew it must be done for nourishment. He would show her one, then help her do one. Soon, they were working side by side. Daniel moved much faster than she did.

When they were through, they went back inside to make bread. They sat after the loaves were put into the hearth to bake. "You know, it's a luxury?" he asked, nodding toward the fire.

She thought for a moment and tried to remember what she had seen before coming here. "Bread?"

"Yes," he smiled. At least she is aware of something. "I made some good trades last summer for that flour. Of course, I didn't know I needed enough to feed two."

Worry appeared on Anya's face. She hadn't given thought to if she would be a burden to him.

He saw her reaction, "Its okay." He told her. "It was only a jest. We'll be fine." Deep down inside he tried to convince himself that it was true.

That night they dined together again. He tried not to show it, but he had been wrought with worry all day. "I will do my part," he told her. "I will keep you safe, warm, and fed all winter. In the spring when I travel south, I will take you to any destination you wish. I just need you to promise me one thing in return."

Anya met his eyes. She felt her heartbeat race. She knew what directed the heart of most men and feared that would be his payment. "What is it you request?"

"I need you to tell me true. Will there be anyone looking for you? Will there be any trouble in store for me for helping you?"

Anya relaxed. She was wrong to doubt his intentions. He was the honorable man she had thought he was. "No," she assured him. "No one will give you any trouble."

She could guarantee that. No one was looking for her because no one knew her, save for the other three Elements who were doing their own exploring. She had no chance of running into one of them because they were no doubt following orders and not interacting with people unlike her. If someone did give him trouble for any reason while she was in his care, she would be able to make them let matters be and leave. Her powers were weaker in this body, but she was not powerless.

"Good," he smiled. He glanced across the room. "Now then, sleeping arrangements need to change. My back is still sore from my time on the hard ground last evening."

"I can sleep on the floor. That won't be a problem."

"I wouldn't hear of it. You are my guest. A guest who I expect to pull some of the work around here, but a guest no less."

Anya froze. What other sleeping arrangements could he mean? The bed was not big enough for both of them.

Daniel saw the expression on her face and erupted in laughter. He held his stomach with one hand and waved the air with the other. "Oh, woman!" he finally managed to say. "That is not what I had in mind."

He continued to laugh, but went to the bed. He picked up the pile of blankets and furs and laid them on her lap. Daniel bent down and pulled part of the bed toward him and dropped it on the floor. "See?" he asked. "Two pallets. Two beds."

Anya flushed red with embarrassment. He grabbed the pile from her lap and distributed them between the two beds.

"Will this work for you, my lady?" he bowed, teasing her.

They readied themselves for bed with Anya taking the pallet closest to the wall. She didn't know why Daniel insisted, but she would learn during the night when she heard him wake to stoke the fire. It made her feel safe and protected knowing that he was between her and the door. It surprised her because Anya knew she had the ability to protect herself far better than Daniel could.

She lay awake for a long time wrestling the urge to leave as she would for many, many nights to come. She shouldn't be here. She didn't know what she would face for being disobedient. Anya tried to convince herself that her punishment would be no worse if she left now or later. She had failed her orders either way. There was something drawing her to Daniel making it hard for her to go. For now, she was content being the poor tree sprite he had found and decided to wait until he could take her somewhere better.

# Chapter Two

Everleigh sat at the kitchen table of her grandmother's house observing her cousins practice. It was the house where she grew up in and where she still lived, but it belonged to her grandmother who raised her. The room was filled with herbs and candles, and all the basic needs of introductory spell work. It was beginning to feel like déjà vu had struck and taken a permanent hold on her life. Here she was again just like in high school working on the small baby steps of magic.

Step one: light a candle with your mind or your breath. Step two: move small items using only your powers of concentration. Things that seemed so trivial to her now, but were almost overwhelming when she was first learning how they were done. It was exactly like repeating first grade after graduating from college. Only this time, she was one of the teachers.

Magic had always skipped a generation. It had been that way since the first real witch Anya arrived a millennium ago. Each child of a witch would have one child of theirs who would receive the calling to become a witch. For Everleigh, it was easy because she was an only child. There had never been a doubt she would be chosen for the craft. The education of the mystical began when she was very young. She had been raised around magic and often tagged along to celebrations where she watched in awe. Everleigh knew more about herbs before she began her formal education then most people learn in a lifetime.

It was her cousins who were not so lucky. They had multiple siblings, and they would wait with baited breath as their teenage years rolled around hoping for some sign to show they were the chosen one. There had been countless times over the years where she listened to her cousins nervously talk about a dream or some other small occurrence that made them wonder if this was the start of it. More often than not, it wasn't the case. The disappointment could be heard in their voices every time they realized it wasn't them. Not this time.

Unfortunately, throughout her family's history many of the ones not chosen would eventually grow apart from the magically inclined relatives. She had been warned of this from a very young age, but didn't understand why it would happen. Magic was not the center of their daily life generally. The exception would be her grandma's household as she harvested herbs and charged waters and oils for magical use not only for herself, but for her coven and friends as well. Everyone who received the calling was taught to never use their gifts as parlor tricks, or at any time really when it wasn't absolutely necessary.

Still, the others would slowly fade out of the lives of the witches. Not completely of course. They didn't abandon their siblings to never be heard from again. It just changed the relationships from the close knit family they had their entire childhood to one where they only saw each other a couple times a year. Everleigh had always been thankful she had no siblings. Not because it meant she would definitely receive the calling, but because she didn't have the risk of drifting away from someone who had once been so close to her. She didn't expect it to affect her as hard as it was being an only child.

There were some cousins who were already pulling back. As soon as Dorian and Isaac received the calling, their sisters drastically cut back their contact with Everleigh. She figured they feared she would ramble on about their brothers' training which would be like pouring salt in an open wound. Everleigh knew better than that. On the few occasions when they'd talk, she would keep the conversation completely magic free by asking about what they were up to instead. It didn't make a difference. They still continually slowed how often they communicated with her.

Grandma Eloise had three children. Each of those children would produce a witch. Everleigh was the first of this generation to be called. Her mama was the oldest of Grandma's children and had given birth very young. She died from complications in childbirth, so Everleigh never knew her.

Now, two of her cousins had been called. Each of her uncles' sons were ready to learn the craft. None of the female cousins had received the gift. She had been close with them while they were growing up, and she had always thought of them as younger sisters. It was hard on her now that they barely spoke to her. They knew without a doubt they weren't going to be called, and their disappointment kept them away.

The calling came to each person differently. For some, it was vivid psychic dreams or even visions while they were still awake. Others start to notice strange manifestations happening when they're around. Dorian noticed a line of foxes outside his bedroom window every morning, greeting him when he awoke. It had been happening for months before he finally told anyone. Even then, the only reason he said anything is because he started noticing foxes all over the place as time went on. They would be at the school, at his friend's house, everywhere he went. No one told him that weird animal behavior could be a hint to a calling, and no one could explain why the fox was so significant to him. Grandma had explained it would be revealed in time.

For Everleigh, it had begun with fire. One night in the winter when she was twelve, she woke and felt like she was about to freeze. She had long wished for a fireplace in her bedroom. It was something she saw once in a magazine, and she longed for a room like that ever since. She sat up in bed thinking about how cold it was and how nice it would be to have a fire in her room. Then her curtains went up in flames, and she ran screaming to her grandma. No one had to remind her to be careful of what she wished for after that.

Grandma, on the other hand, had been a little concerned with why fire had been the signal of Everleigh's coming into the craft. There was no such thing as a coincidence as far as Grandma Eloise was concerned. While her grandma didn't necessarily hold any ill will toward the other Elementals, she did like to keep her distance from them. She was from a different generation trained in the craft by witches who had heard the tales of the last well known witch persecution throughout their entire life by descendants of those who had lived it.

Long before Salem made a name for itself, the Elemental factions had faced many perilous times where small minded people tried to rid the world of them. People fear what they don't know, and none ever took the time to learn more about them to see they were harmless. Mostly.

There was a period when many from the Fire faction cured their boredom by toying with humans. Just because that period passed doesn't mean it was ever completely forgotten. Libraries could be filled with stories of their blood lust. Fiction always contains an element of truth.

There's always a risk with Water. They could take every precaution available, but still accidently hurt someone or worse. Once they transform, they are no longer captained by their human side. They are pure beast who could only be tamed by their alpha. The problem is not all of them have an alpha. There are far too many orphaned and rogue wolves who have no one to keep them in line.

Each time a group was in trouble, other groups would come to their aide. It served only to put a target on everyone's back. More and more would be caught up in the hunt and slaughtered. Too many times coming to the aid of another faction left them vulnerable and targeted. All involved who survived would have to move what little was left of their people somewhere new and start over only to do it all over again the next time a faction was being rounded up.

The Elementals decided centuries before Salem that their best bet for survival was to distance themselves from each other. It had turned into every Elemental group for themselves. This was how her grandma was raised. It was a way of thinking she had been around her entire childhood. There were very few people from groups other than Earth that she tolerated. Some more than others. Becoming too friendly with them could be a weakness because when it came down to it, a choice would have to be made between your people or the ones you cared about the most.

It was why she was whole heartily against intermixing the Elemental groups. Everleigh had always known that her grandma barely tolerated Aunt Meredith, but for a long time, she had no idea why. When she learned the truth, everything clicked. There was still one lingering question that had never been answered. If her grandma was so upset that Meredith became immortal for the vampire she loved, it would make more sense if she had cut ties completely. Yet, she never did. Aunt Meredith would come around from time to time much to Grandma Eloise's obvious disdain, but even so, she was still welcome.

The fire that illustrated her calling to the craft worried her grandma that Everleigh would somehow be tied to Fire in the future. It wasn't something her grandma need worry about. Being immortal had never appealed to Everleigh. She always embraced the natural view on life that stemmed from her own Earth heritage. We are not meant to live forever, nor should we long to.

Throughout high school as Everleigh started dating, her grandma's worries began to cease. None of the few vampires she knew caught her attention for anything more than friendship if she was even interested in that. It continued through college where the only men who caught Everleigh's eye were typical, average, young men who went about their day to day without the slightest clue of the type of bump in the night creatures that actually exist.

Now, she sat at the table with Dorian and Isaac trying to help them with the basics. This was her grandma's work, but she had asked Everleigh to help out. Beltane had passed before the boys came to stay with them for about a month, but Grandma hoped they would be ready to help with the Summer Solstice celebrations. They would soon be out of time to work with either of them. Both young men had been accepted to colleges out west. They needed as much training as they could fit in before they left in early July to begin football practice for the freshman year at their schools.

Their calling came late which Grandma chalked up to boys maturing later than girls. She said this was typical with male witches, but Everleigh had never met one till now. There were male witches of course. She had been aware of that, but they lived far off and weren't a part of her familial coven.

"So this is our first lesson? Lighting a candle?" Dorian asked Grandma Eloise.

Hearing Dorian speak snapped Everleigh free from her thoughts. It would be wise to pay attention and be helpful before her grandma got after her for daydreaming.

"It's your first magical lesson," she emphasized.

Dorian looked at Everleigh who mouthed the words, "I don't know."

"The first lesson for both of you is to stop calling yourself wizards," Grandma groaned.

"What? Well that's what we are? A male witch is a wizard." Isaac stated as if it were a well-known fact.

"A witch is a witch. It doesn't matter what you have in your pants," she scoffed.

"Nah." Isaac looked at his cousins. "Is that true?"

"They aren't called wizards." Everleigh agreed with her grandma, but it wasn't a full truth. There was one wizard her grandma talked about a lot.

"Warlocks then?" Dorian asked.

Grandma Eloise looked up to the ceiling and said, "Oh, I need patience to get through today with these two."

Everleigh chuckled which she knew wouldn't be appreciated by her grandma, but she couldn't help it. It was usually she who was the one driving her grandma to ask for patience.

"Who are you praying to, Grandma? God?"

Grandma Eloise lowered her head until she locked eyes with Dorian, "Did your father teach you nothing yet?"

There was no time to answer. The blank books in front of them flew open on their own to the first page, and as Grandma began to talk, the words she spoke would scrawl out on the paper in her own hand. Everleigh loved this feat and wanted to learn it herself someday.

"There were four Elements behind the veil that separates the spiritual world from the physical. They were the rulers of Air, Earth, Fire and Water. They controlled and maintained all the land. Balance was their sole purpose. Where one area experienced famine, another area would be fertile. Their existence was almost as old as time itself. They dared to cross the veil in human form to experience the physical world, so that they may better learn and understand. Rules were set forth for them to follow, but only one obeyed. He was Marcus, Air Element. Punishments were inflicted on all by the Divine Spirit because their fates are forever bound to each other as Elements."

The writing stopped when their grandma stopped speaking.

"So you prayed to the Divine Spirit?"

Everleigh covered her mouth to stifle a laugh when her grandma reached out with a kitchen towel and lightly smacked Dorian on the top of the head with it. "What am I supposed to do with you?" she asked him, then shot him a look to shut him up when he opened his mouth to answer.

"A witch is a witch," she told them when she was sure they would stay quiet. "Wizards and warlocks do not exist naturally in the Earth bloodline. When they do, a witch bestowed the title of Warlock would be one who went rogue and broke oaths. A Wizard would be an elder of his coven who had proven he was deserving of the distinguished title."

The boys never mentioned it again, and resigned themselves to being known simply as witches.

"Focus on the candles in front of you. Visualize the flame in your mind, and make it appear."

They stared at the candles for several moments without success. Everleigh walked to the window by the sink and looked at the bright blue sky while listening to her cousins' protest to their grandma they were concentrating. The wicks on both candles ignited, and she turned with a devilish grin.

"How can you do that so easily?" Dorian slumped back in frustration.

"Once you are able to do it, it's easy."

"That no make no sense," Isaac said in a mimicked voice and rolled his eyes.

"It will. Keep trying."

"Yes," Grandma Eloise continued, walking behind the two young men. "Keep trying. This is nothing compared to what you still have left to learn."

Isaac opened his mouth, but didn't get a chance to ask.

"And what you have left to learn is limitless," Grandma Eloise responded, knowing the question before it was asked.

Everleigh tried to hide her smile. This was the grandma she had always known. It was almost like she could read everyone's mind at any time she chose. There were no such things as secrets in this house. Trying to keep anything from that woman was impossible. Part of it had to be her skills as a witch, and no one could ever compare to her there. Mostly it was her lifelong experience Everleigh had always believed. Grandma Eloise had spent the better part of her years with at least one child in her care.

Dorian and Isaac stared at the candles until their eyes started to cross. Then they stared at them some more. While they worked at their simple spell, Eloise brought Everleigh aside to discuss something with her in private.

"Schooling is done isn't it?"

"Yeah, I graduate next week, remember?"

Grandma nodded like she recalled it was coming up, but she wasn't thinking about the graduation ceremony. "What are your plans?"

"None. Find a job I guess." Everleigh wanted to laugh, but the look on her grandma's face was too worrisome.

"So then there isn't anything lined up for you yet?"

"No. Well, I'm working at the theater again this summer. I already talked to them. I hope to find something better than that before summer is over." It worried her that maybe her grandma was asking about if she planned to move. The only reason she was still in this big house in this little town was because she had to raise Everleigh herself. Ever since Pops died five years ago, Grandma made it no secret she wanted to go somewhere warmer. To do that, this house would have to be sold.

Grandma covered the rubino pendant that always hung from a black cord around her neck with her hand. "Would I be able to talk you in to staying a little longer?"

"Stay?" Everleigh blurted out, then looked to see if the boys had taken notice. This was the last thing she expected her grandma to ask.

"I know it's a lot to put on you when you're preparing to start your way in life."

"No, Grandma. It's not that. You just surprised me is all. I... I thought you were going to tell me you were ready to sell the house and move to Florida or something."

With the gleam she always gets while passing on some tidbit of useful information, her grandma looked her in the eye, and said, "I'm afraid Florida may have to come here. That is one dream of mine I can't fulfill yet."

*'What does that even mean?'* Everleigh wondered. *'Florida come here?'* It must mean she

will have to turn this place into her dream retirement home. We couldn't exactly get away with making the weather warmer year round in this part of the country. "I don't have any plans to move far away, Grandma. I was going to look for a job in Trinity since there aren't many here."

"Good. I'm afraid I may need your help soon."

"Of course, Grandma," Everleigh smiled. The whole conversation had been cryptic, but at least it wasn't as important or devastating as she originally thought it may turn out to be. "What do you need my help with?"

"I believe a storm is coming, child."

"A storm?" Everleigh glanced back toward the kitchen even though she couldn't see the window from where they stood in the hallway. The sky had been clear only a few minutes ago. There had been no sign of a storm moving in.

"The biggest storm I've ever witnessed," her grandma continued, removing her hand from the pendant and looking down.

Everleigh followed her gaze and sucked in her breath when she saw it. Inside the pendant was a swirl of clouds moving fast with lightning striking throughout. The center looked clear like the eye of a hurricane. She could almost feel the wind blowing out on her face and a spray of rain coming from the necklace. She could also see the poor unfortunate souls who got caught in its path circling around helplessly.

"Hey! I did it!" Isaac yelled from the kitchen and drummed the table.

Dorian groaned loudly over being beat to accomplish their task.

The pendant went back to its solid red color right on cue like the commotion startled it back to secrecy. Everleigh's breath came out in short raspy gasps as she met her grandma's eyes. The look on Grandma's face was enough to frighten her even more. Whatever it meant, the storm in the pendant, it had her grandma filled with fear.

"Did you hear me?" Isaac came into the hallway and saw the two women deadlocked in a look that told him he interrupted something serious. "Oh, sorry. I'll... I'll just go."

There were so many questions flooding her mind. So many Everleigh couldn't think of where to begin, but now wasn't the time to ask anyway what with the two novices in the other room struggling with the simplest spell work. "Whatever you need, Grandma, I'll do it."

A small smile broke on Grandma's face, and she wrapped her arms around Everleigh. "I knew I could count on you to be by my side."

They went back to the kitchen where Grandma had Isaac repeat his feat which he did several times. "You're right," he said, holding his head high. "It's easy once you figure it out," he beamed.

Everleigh had a hard time focusing on anything happening around her. It would probably be impossible for her to light a candle with her mind now no matter how hard she might try. Everywhere she looked, she saw the storm and the dark clouds illuminated by flashes of light. A storm with an eye that had been filled with bodies twisting in the clouds and writhing in pain. It was the grimaced faces that shook her the most.

It wasn't an earthly storm headed for them at all. It was an end of time's catastrophe for the Elementals. The faces of all of them had been showcased. The fangy glares of Fire. The sneering muzzles of Water. The glowing minds of Air. And the illumination of Earth. None of them were safe. The biggest questions on her mind was what could possibly be coming for them all? And why?

# Chapter Three

Summer Solstice came and went almost uncelebrated. Everleigh knew her grandma would never miss a Sabbat Day, but the chaos that erupted so close to Litha was enough to make her worry this might be the first year she would skip one. It began when Uncle Roan called in the middle of the night mid-June in a panic. Something had woken him, and he felt a strong unease that made him check the house. Everything was fine. All the doors and windows were closed and locked. No sign of an intruder. No scent of fire. Still, he couldn't shake the feeling.

As he headed back to bed hoping it had been a bad dream that he couldn't remember, he checked on his daughters' rooms for a second time. Kiara and Jasmin were fine. They were sound asleep in their beds. Uncle Roan opened the door of Amber's room to find her floating in the air above her bed. He cried out, and she fell immediately waking up with no memory of anything that happened. It couldn't be possible he kept telling his mother. Dorian had already received the calling. There couldn't be two from his line. Eloise tried to calm him, but it was useless. Amber was put on the earliest flight to Trinity, and Everleigh picked her up from the airport.

It was like dominoes after that. Grace was next only two days later. She exploded the window in her bedroom after her boyfriend dumped her in a text message. Uncle Danny was already up to speed with the news of Amber's calling. Grace's flight had already taken off before he bothered to call to let anyone know she was coming.

Kiara found out her best friend slept with her

boyfriend when she wanted to borrow a dress from her to wear on a date. It was the same dress her friend wore the night she slept with him. As soon as she touched the garment, she saw what happened in her mind, and promptly laid her former friend out with just one punch. Uncle Roan had to wait to see if charges would be pressed before she joined the others.

Only Jasmin took a while to display anything. It didn't matter. When Kiara boarded the plane, so did Jasmin. Uncle Roan sent them both because he felt like it was only a matter of time. Grandma agreed with him, so Jasmin began her training by watching the others hoping she would be called too. While Kiara was trying to lift a leaf with her mind, Jasmin walked over and showed her up. She did it effortlessly on her first try without ever receiving a sign she would join the ranks of witches in the family.

In a matter of days, there were a total of six newly called witches at her grandma's house. Everleigh spent her whole life wishing she'd had a large family. She had always wondered what it would be like having siblings. Not anymore. It wasn't long before she couldn't wait for the quiet peace to return to her home. She was exhausted between working at the theater and helping them train.

The Solstice celebration was busier than any Everleigh had ever experienced. The number of newly called witches was almost enough for them to form a coven when they were ready. For this year, they would be present and would participate in smaller matters. Mostly, it would be another day of lessons for them as they learned by observing.

"What is next after the cleansing?" Amber was always full of questions. For someone who had only recently been upset that her brother had been called instead of her, she was always quick to try to get out of the work that had to be put in to the craft. Some of their magical nature was gifted, but there was a lot to be learned. Witches weren't exactly born with an encyclopedia of spells stored in their mind for later reference. Spells and potions had to be done just right. One small mishap, and the result would not be what had been desired. Not to mention, it could result in a horrible accident or much worse.

"We cleanse the house and our bodies then we work the garden. It is how it is done." Grandma Eloise wouldn't let anything, not even a chatterbox trying to get out of doing the groundwork dent her joy today.

"Why do we take a bath before we work in the garden? It doesn't make sense. We're just going to get filthy again messing around in the dirt."

"Come." Everleigh directed her outside and away from her grandma. "The cleansing was more for purification then for bathing. Weren't you instructed on how to clear your mind and let go of any ill will you were harboring?"

Amber nodded, but then her eyes widened like she was expecting there to be more.

"That's why we do it. We clear the negative energy to let the light and positivity flow freely."

"Hmm," Amber scrunched up her nose. "It sounds a little hippie-dippie if I'm being honest."

Everleigh rocked her head from side to side. It would be hard to disagree. "Just don't let Grandma hear you say that."

"And I'm still going to need to take a shower after this. It's a waste of time if you ask me."

Everleigh furrowed her brows. "We're not going to be rolling around in the ground. You know that, right?"

"Yeah. It's still dirty."

"You have gloves to wear."

Amber stopped midstride and glared at her cousin. "Still. Dirty."

"You are an Earth. It's natural for us to connect with it."

The look on Amber's face turned to one of sheer terror. "You mean I'm supposed to just walk around looking like I live in the woods all the time?" Her voice cracked near the end of the question.

Everleigh couldn't control herself. The laughter had escaped her lips before Amber was even done speaking. The expression on her cousin's face alone was enough to bring on hysterics. That was nowhere close to what she meant, but a little dirt and dust never hurt anyone. Washing their hands when they were through should be enough. Taking another full shower was a tad over the top.

Amber looked irate. She wasn't appreciative that her cousin found her desire to appear clean so humorous. Staring at her, she crossed her arms and drummed her fingers on her skin.

"I'm sorry," Everleigh gasped, shaking from laughing so hard and wiping tears from the corners of her eyes. "I was just picturing you dressed as one of those mountain people from that movie we watched last night." The sentence was interrupted several times as her laughter grew over the words she was trying to say.

Shaking her head, Amber cut her eyes at her cousin. She snickered as well. Soon the two of them were both collecting strange looks from the rest of the family as they enjoyed their private joke.

They laughed and walked through the garden gate in the backyard where Kiara was already clearing weeds. Soon Jasmin and the boys would join them in the work. The garden would be done in no time this year, thankfully, as it had always been her least favorite chore. There were those who found gardening to be relaxing and even therapeutic. Everleigh was not one of those people. To her, it was a dreadful chore. A dirty, mud filled, itchy, sneezy dreadful chore when there weren't enough hands to make light work of it.

Everleigh knelt down to start helping, but not without noticing the scowl had returned on Amber's face. "Gardening is part of the craft. It's work, yes, but therapeutic too," she said, repeating the words that had been told to her many times over the years even though she didn't fully believe them. "We need to tend the garden to honor the Oak King who departs us this evening."

"Yeah, yeah," Amber muttered. "And King Holly will arrive."

"The Holly King."

"Same difference."

Everleigh sighed in defeat. Deep down, she didn't doubt Amber knew the correct name. In fact, she was certain Amber was picking up on a lot more than she was willing to show. It would continue to baffle her all summer. This is what Amber had wanted all along. All of them had wanted it. The way she treated parts of the craft like it was something to scoff at, or make fun of made Everleigh feel less than thrilled about working alongside her. She didn't want someone on her team who did the work begrudgingly. It would be better surrounded by those who loved this life like Jasmin and Grace. Sadly, Amber had more natural gifts than the other two combined. It was a shame she didn't embrace and respect that.

The garden was finished before their grandma appeared outside and was able to lend a hand. Everleigh helped her charge crystals and stones while the others were assigned various tasks since they couldn't perform the spells yet. It felt good to have her grandma to herself again if only for a short while. Soon they would head out to meet the coven and begin their affirmations. The fledglings would not participate in this part during the ceremony, but they would possibly have a more active role later when the time for casting began.

"It's time," Grandma smiled at her with a nod, implying she was to lead the meditations this year.

Everleigh smiled back unsure because her grandma had to know how much she hated this part. Meditating was fine when it was done privately. When it was done with even one other person, it always felt awkward and forced. This many people would have to make that feeling intensify dramatically. That could be why her grandma wanted her to lead it. You couldn't push yourself to be more, better, greater if you never stepped out of your comfort zone.

"Let's do it outside this year. It may not be possible for all of us to spread out on the floor in the same room," Grandma said as she sat on the ground near the back porch.

"Alright everyone. Find a spot where you can sit comfortably with enough room between each other." Everleigh spoke loud enough for the stragglers still wandering over from the garden to hear her.

Amber raised her eyebrow and looked from Everleigh to the grass then back to Everleigh. "On the ground?"

"Yes," she answered, dreading Amber's reaction. Her cousin was the only Earth Elemental who seemed to hate the actual earth.

"No, thank you. I'll be using a chair from the porch," she scoffed. Amber took about two steps away before the glare from Grandma had her changing her mind. "You know what? On second thought, I think the ground is a nice idea. Connecting with nature is amazing. Am I right?" She crossed her ankles and dropped to a sitting position directly in front of Everleigh with wide eyes that showed she hoped nothing more would be directed at her from Grandma.

It was hard for Everleigh to not laugh at the whole scene, and she turned her back briefly using the need to stretch as an excuse to hide her grin. Grandma certainly had a way about getting people to do what was expected of them.

Once everyone had gathered, Everleigh sat facing them. It would be more effective if they were laying on their mats, but she knew her cousins didn't have a mat yet. Sitting cross legged would have to do.

"To begin, find as comfortable a position as possible."

Amber rolled her eyes and mouthed the words, "This is stupid."

Everleigh tried to ignore her. Not only would having any form of reaction ruin the meditation for the others, but it would bring the ire of their grandma upon her. No one wanted to have that happen to them.

"Close your eyes and surround yourself in a white light. You're becoming aware of how your body feels," she told them.

"Oh, I'm aware," Amber mouthed the words, while glancing down at her rather pronounced bosom.

*'Please don't do this, Amber,'* Everleigh tried to plead with her eyes.

"Deep breaths. Breathe in the white light that surrounds you. Exhale the negativity and stress."

Everleigh watched as everyone began following her instructions. "Again. Breathe in the light. Breathe out your tension. As you exhale, let your body begin to relax."

Amber opened one eye, and Everleigh tried to mimic her grandma's glare. "Relax my butt," Amber mouthed again.

This one was certainly a handful, and Everleigh wished she hadn't sat so close to her.

Maybe off to the side somewhere out of her main line of sight, but she continued with the meditation technique that her grandma had been using with her since she was little. "Breathe in relaxation. Breathe out worry."

She waited for everyone to take a couple more deep breaths. "Slow and gentle now. Take calm breaths while you focus on relaxing your body. Notice how each part of your body relaxes when I name it for you."

Amber was shooting her another unbelieving glance, but Everleigh ignored her this time.

"Feet... Relax... Ankles... Relax." Everleigh continued slowly until she made it to the top of the body instructing everyone to release any remaining tension as they exhaled. She began telling them to move a little more and to become more alert slowly before finally ending the meditation.

It surprised her that Amber had remained quiet as long as she had, but she was thankful. Everleigh glanced around at everyone sitting peacefully then she saw her grandma's warm smile telling her she'd done a great job leading the meditation for the first time. The calm and serenity that stretched out around everyone was brutally interrupted by a horrific noise.

"HngGGggh... Ppbhww... zZZzzzzZZ," Amber's snoring cut through the air startling everyone followed by snickering.

Everleigh looked to see Amber's head had fallen to the side, and she was completely out. She had to bite her lips together to stifle a laugh, but when she looked up, her grandma had even joined in the laughter of the others.

Amber snored again, "Pblhuu... zZZzz... BrGHfggh." Her eyes opened and her head righted as her snoring woke herself up which only made the laughter of the family increase. "Hmm... What'd I miss?" she yawned, looking around furrowing her brow because she didn't understand what was so funny.

"Feeling relaxed, Amber?" Grandma asked from behind her.

"Hmph," she snorted and stood up, realizing the joke was on her.

They made their way inside to finish loading the cars that would take them into the country where they'd meet the rest of the coven. There was a rather large clearing in a wooded grove near a farmhouse outside of town. The owner of the house never seemed to be home, but grandma claimed him to be an old friend of the family. It was someone who had known her grandma when he was little, Everleigh's great-great grandma.

The spot was perfect. It was large enough to do their work, and secluded from neighbors and out of sight of the road. Whether the owner happened to be gone when the coven met, or if it was planned was one of the many little mysteries Everleigh wondered if her grandma would ever explain to her.

It didn't take long to get everything set up this year with so many helping out. Usually, it was just the two of them. Grandma liked to keep the food away from the celebrations and rituals, so the tables were set up near the barn and the grills ready to be fired up, waiting for the rest of the coven to arrive. There were three parts to the annual tradition. It would begin with the Solstice celebration. They'd have a feast to celebrate. Then they'd go back to the clearing to end the night with spell work.

Members began to arrive, so everyone headed down into the trees. Grandma pulled Everleigh aside and asked a favor. "Get ahold of Meredith. Give her a message."

*'This is an interesting turn of events. Grandma can't stand Aunt Meredith. It must be something*

*important.'* Everleigh waited to hear what she had to say.

"Tell her this word for word. Sometimes the only way to make sure your love life doesn't go down in flames is by locking your heart away." Grandma abruptly walked toward the trees not giving her the opportunity to ask any questions.

*'It's about Luke. Has to be. Love life. Heart. Flames. Everything pointed to Luke, but what does she mean?'*

Everleigh sighed and called her aunt hoping if she answered, she could shed some light on the riddle for her. No luck. It went to voice mail. "Hey, Aunt Meredith! I have a message from grandma. She said to tell you, and I quote..." Everleigh repeated her grandma's words. "Love you!"

Down in flames has to be a reference to Luke since he's a Fire Elemental. But love life and heart could also be pointing to him as well. The riddle made zero sense, and it aggravated Everleigh as she tried to figure it out. The phrase also meant to end or ruin something. It couldn't be that. Aunt Meredith and Luke always seemed so happy together. She hadn't been around them much because of her grandma's strong opinions about them, but they always acted like newlyweds when she saw them. No one would ever guess they'd been together over three centuries. Heck, most couples can't make it three years.

*'Ugh! Why can't I figure it out? It's going to make perfect sense once someone tells me what's going on.'* Everleigh tried to push the message from her mind to concentrate on the Solstice celebration for now. There'd be time to ask her aunt to fill her in later.

She made her way through the trees to join the others. Everleigh was now the last to arrive, and she quickly made her way to her spot in the circle. The Solstice affirmations began, and Everleigh could hear the novices behind them join along. "We open our hearts, minds and souls to Divine Light. We honor the sacred energy of the Midsummer. We invoke the presence of the spirits...healing...and protection."

It was time for each of them to mind their turn around the fire. It began with her grandma as the Priestess of the coven and would end with her. Everleigh was the newest member, and her turn would be near the end before her grandma finished. Each affirmation was silently spoken in her head as each member spoke out loud as all would be doing with her.

The time had come for her to step forward. "I trust my intuition to lead me where I am meant to go."

"We are Divine Children beloved by Earth and the Universe," her grandma recited when Everleigh stepped back into place.

"Blessed be," they said in unison.

Summer Solstice was her favorite magical celebration. Everleigh enjoyed all of them, but the beautiful weather on the longest day of the year was an added bonus that put this one ahead of the rest. It was time to eat and visit well into the night. There would be spell work to do later on. Almost every member brought something with them for the coven to help them accomplish.

Once back at the farmhouse, she checked her phone. There was a text from her aunt. Everleigh expected her to ask what is that supposed to mean or something along those lines. She opened it to read, "Tell her I'm on it."

It didn't take long to find her grandma relaxing at one of the tables while the younger members fired up the grills. The table was the one closest to the spread where her grandma would still be able to run the show while resting her weary bones as she would put it. Everleigh walked over and relayed the message she had received from her aunt.

Grandma Eloise didn't offer a response right away, and Everleigh wasn't sure if she was supposed to stick around for one. She decided to wait on the off chance her grandma might mention something that would help her give context to the riddle, but she knew better than to hold her breath. Grandma Eloise had always been a private person.

Her attention was on everyone who was setting up for the feast. When she was satisfied everything was under control for a few minutes at least, she turned to Everleigh and smiled. "Good. I had hoped she would be, but one can never be too careful."

That was it. Grandma turned her attention back to her other grandchildren giving them instructions on what to do next. Maybe one day, she'd be able to sit at the adult table and be allowed to know more than what was shared with her now. All she could do was hope.

# Chapter Four

Anya awoke early in the morning and began preparing breakfast. Daniel was already in the barn working when she came to life and stumbled out of bed. This had been their routine for the better part of two months. She stuck primarily to the cooking and some mending that he had taught her how to do. She only went out into the cold to assist him when he needed the extra help and asked her to join in the work.

During this time, something had changed within her. There had been many opportunities when she could have left and tried to carry on with what she was supposed to be doing. She couldn't. Rather, she wouldn't. It seemed impossible for her to leave Daniel. That was the ever increasing truth.

The spring was her deadline. It was when she could move on more safely. That had been what she told herself while finding excuses to stay. It would be harder to leave the longer she waited, so she wanted to make the most of the time they still had together. Anxiously watching for the first signs that winter was fading even as it bore down around the cabin in full force, she feared the day would arrive too fast.

She had tried to understand what was making her defy the Divine Spirit so boldly. It was human emotion. It had to be. Humans are altogether different creatures with internal driving forces so powerful that they often do what they know they shouldn't. This was the reason for the Elements to venture here in the first place. Being an outsider who can only watch from afar makes it difficult to fully understand why things unfold the way they do. From the Spirit Realm, the Elements watched humans intentionally make a vast array of mistakes daily. None of them had ever been able to fully understand the reasons behind their actions. It's one thing to know humans are controlled by emotions, but it's entirely different to experience it firsthand. That is the type of true understanding that can only be divulged through experience.

Anya couldn't leave Daniel's home because she had developed feelings for him. She was in love, which while it warmed her and overjoyed her to experience the deep bond she had with him, it tore at her as well. There was no indication that Daniel felt the same way toward her which caused her unlimited pain, and it preoccupied her mind trying to understand why her love wasn't returned. While she longed for him to return her feelings, she knew that would only make matters worse as she was not supposed to have interfered with anyone or anything during her time in this physical realm. She couldn't undo any of her actions that had already come to pass. It was wrong to hope for more to strengthen the effect she left behind.

It would be easy to find out for herself exactly where she stood with him. All she had to do was touch him, and she would be able to read him easily. The temptation tugged at her every waking second they were together. Whether or not the Divine Spirit would frown on her using her powers for something so trivial didn't play a part in her decision not to do it. If she knew Daniel returned her feelings, it would be downright impossible for her to leave him. There wasn't a doubt in her mind. More so, she was afraid she'd learn that he didn't feel the same about her as she did for him.

Daniel returned from the barn carrying another load of wood. This was the fourth he had brought inside since waking. Anya could see the winter storm bearing down outside when the door opened. A strong bitter wind blew in with him, and

Anya shivered violently at the unexpected blast.

"It's upon us," he told her. "It's only going to get worse. I'm going to bring in more wood."

"More? You've enough wood here for days."

Daniel shook his head. "I'd rather have too much then run low and have to go back out in this monstrous weather."

Anya couldn't help but to agree.

"Stand near the fire, so the wind won't bite at you so much when the door opens," he instructed.

She did as she had been told grabbing a fur to wrap around her as she went. He made a couple more trips in with wood before he was happy with the stockpile. He joined her by the fire warming up his near frostbit hands and feet.

She stayed where she was longer than it took for her to get warm. These little moments brought her so much joy. She found herself trying to maneuver ways to be near him, breathing him in, whenever she could without making it look to obvious. On occasion, he would comment about it. His words would fluster her, and she'd try to keep a safe distance for days afterward. It confused and frightened her trying to understand all the feelings and sensations he stirred up. It excited her as well.

The storm raged on all day and into the night. The wind beat at the cabin without mercy. Drafts blew in all over, and they tried their best to stop it with what rags they had. The fire helped what it could, but a breezy chill could still be felt.

That night before bed, Daniel was uneasy. She could tell something was bothering him, but he would simply say it was just the storm that was on his mind whenever she pressed him about it. Finally as she started to arrange the blankets on her bed, he told her he had an idea to help them stay warm, but he had not mentioned it as he was worried Anya would react badly

Anya listened to him pitch the idea of pushing

the pallets together and sharing all the blankets for extra warmth. She stared at the floor while he spoke willing herself not to smile. Her body reacted to his words awakening parts of her that responded with an aching throb. It filled her mind with thoughts about his strong arms being close enough to touch her. She knew it was wrong. She knew she shouldn't enjoy these sensations, but she couldn't help the way it affected her. She didn't want it to stop.

She was so lost in her fantasies about being next to him, she wasn't even aware he had finished explaining his plan until she heard him say, "I didn't mean to upset you. We can keep everything as it's been."

"No," she quickly told him. The word escaped Anya's lips before she knew what she was saying. It rushed out so free and easily that it worried her how it may look. Daniel would be able to detect she wanted to be as near to him as possible.

He looked at her with surprise at first then a small smile formed at the corner of his mouth. The smile sent shockwaves through her.

*'Could he want to be closer to her as well?'* she hoped. It would be easy to learn for herself what was on his mind. She need only reach out to him, but that small gesture of touching him regardless of how innocently it may seem would only add to the risk of his discovering how she felt. It couldn't be chanced. "Your idea makes sense. We will need the extra warmth."

Daniel appeared to be disappointed by her comments, but he soon smiled and carried on as though nothing had changed. They rearranged the pallets and laid down with Anya closest to the fire. This had been his spot since the first night. He could rise and tend the fire without disturbing her sleep. While they shared the same bed, he thought he would like having to move over her to get to the fire. Somewhere inside was the lingering fear that she already belonged to somebody and was not available to any man, but the longer she stayed with him, the more he saw her remaining with him permanently.

They laid down inches apart and draped the blankets over their bodies. Anya laid on her side facing him. She wanted to lie that way all night long where she could hear his heartbeat, but she could feel her body's growing response to being so near him. Soon he would be able to notice how shallow and ragged her breath was becoming. Anya rolled over turning her back to him.

Daniel was frustrated when she turned away. He had been peeking out beneath closed eyes to see the outline of her face lit by the fire behind her. She moved again to get comfortable and bumped into him. His arm fell forward onto her side. When she didn't move away, he draped it down over her midsection. He held his breath waiting to see what she would do. She leaned back relaxing into his chest. They fell asleep comforted by one another's touch.

---

It had been a month since they first shared a bed. Even though the winter storm had long since passed, and many nights were nowhere near as freezing, they continued to sleep side by side. Anya would curl up into Daniel's chest, and he would wrap his arms around her. During the day, not much had changed between them save for a few stolen caresses or lingering glances. Not on the surface at least.

Underneath, a passion was growing between them. They spent the better part of their days longing for each other, craving for more. Anya was always torn between her Element orders and her human emotions. Daniel fought off his own desires by reminding himself that regardless of what people thought when they looked at him, he had been raised to act like a gentleman. He didn't want to take advantage of the woman he once believed to be a tree sprite.

One night in late January, it was unseasonably warm. The snow had been melting outside for days and was almost gone except for small patches that spent their time resting in the shade. It was warmer in the cabin, and Anya had taken to wearing her robes inside instead of the clothing Daniel had given her. They lied down much the same as they had been with Anya's back pressed against Daniel's bare chest, and his legs bent beneath hers.

Anya lay awake feeling Daniel's eyes upon her as she did every night. She enjoyed this time of the day the most. It used to make her feel dizzy with physical excitement, but it had grown stale. She wanted more. Needed more. Tonight as his eyes took her in, she tugged gently on her robes exposing her breast. Her anticipation grew waiting to see how he would react.

He was admiring her as he always did by the light of the fire. His gaze drifted from her face to her neck and shoulders then down to where the robes covered her breasts except the material had shifted. One breast was almost completely uncovered. Daniel reached his hand up and grazed it softly without thinking, almost by impulse. He yanked his hand back immediately.

She felt it. She sensed every bit of his reaction. Anya could feel him looking at the supple curve of her breast. She could hear the quick intake of his breath. Mostly, she could feel his manhood hardening against the small of her back. Then he did something she wasn't expecting. He reached for her. He barely touched her before removing his hand.

That brief touch sent tremors through her body. Her physical response was intense almost to the point of overwhelming her. She didn't want it to end, and she wasn't sure she'd have the nerve to manipulate this chance again if it wasn't optimized tonight.

Anya reached down and grabbed his hand. She slowly ran it up her side and placed it on her breast letting it go. It worked. Daniel began caressing her. Anya moaned, and that was the last push that he needed.

He propped up on one elbow and leaned his body down over hers. His hand began to roam her body, and his lips pressed down on her mouth. Anya let him have full reign over her. She was giving herself to him tonight freely. She didn't want to think about tomorrow. She certainly didn't want to think about the Return and the punishment that awaited. She only wanted to think about how good it felt to be his and for him to be hers.

Anya awoke the next morning, and the cabin was empty. She knew Daniel would be in the barn doing chores, so she arose to fix breakfast. There was an achy soreness in her legs and her groin that reminded her of the bliss she experienced the night before. She sat up and tried several times to stand before succeeding. Walking wasn't much easier. It was worth it. However long this recovery took, it was definitely worth it.

She went to the table to discover that the pan was already on the hearth. Daniel had started breakfast while she slept. Anya looked around wondering if he had already ate. *'Did I sleep too long that he couldn't wait?'* she thought. She sat down and began getting dressed. She would go help Daniel with his work since she overslept and put him behind. It was the least she could do.

Daniel happily walked in the door carrying a bouquet of braided evergreen. He handed it to her and kissed her cheek. "I searched everywhere, but I couldn't find anything close to flowers to bring you."

Anya inhaled their scent. She loved the earthly fragrances. "Thank you," she beamed.

"Have you eaten?"

"No, I was going to come help you with chores."

He took her hand and kissed the back of it. "No need. I've finished."

Daniel knelt down in front of her and put his arms around her waist. He looked up into her eyes and told her, "I am so sorry. I did not know last night would be your first time. I would have never..."

She interrupted him. "Don't you dare apologize. Last night was the most happiness I've ever experienced. Please don't tell me you regret it."

"How could I possibly regret loving you?"

Anya's mouth fell open, and she didn't know how to respond. Tears filled her eyes. She knew he was attracted to her. She had always known that, but she had been afraid to find out for herself how he truly felt. She didn't want to learn he didn't return her feelings.

"My beautiful Anya," he told her, taking her hands into his, "my love for you grows stronger every day. I've no idea how you magically appeared in the woods near my home one cold autumn evening, but I am ever so thankful you did. If I had been aware that you had never known the love of a man before, I would have been more thoughtful last night."

She shook her head. She couldn't speak without losing control of the tears that were trying to break free. "Last night was amazing. I wouldn't change anything."

"Let me show you." He arose and lifted her effortlessly. Daniel kissed her forehead and carried her to the bed. He spent all day slowly kissing and caressing her entire body. He brought her to new heights over and over again until way into the night when they collapsed in each other's arms utterly exhausted.

---

Spring was breaking in the countryside where Daniel lived. They were beginning preparations to make their way south. They had planned since the beginning that this would be when they would part ways. Both of them were aware that wouldn't happen now, but neither of them mentioned it. Daniel still had to make the trip to sell his wares and buy supplies for the coming year, and Anya would accompany him. Even though neither of them had spoken about Anya staying with him, they both suspected it was what the other wanted.

Daniel had the cart loaded to head to the shore where they would boat over to the main country. They would leave in the morning. Anya was excited to see new places and meet new people, but she was also filled with a constant dread that hung overhead. The more she did that went against orders, the worse her punishment would become.

He checked and tightened the straps again as he had numerous times already. He looked up, his eyes wide filled with a new thought, "I bet you prefer living where it's warm to this weather, don't you?"

Anya was devastated. He was going to leave her behind. "What do you mean?" she asked, preparing herself for the answer that would break her heart.

"I mean we don't have to come back here. If you are unhappy with the harsh winters, we could do my business then head farther south to the land where I come from."

Her face slowly filled with delight. He wasn't leaving her after all. He did want her with him still. She took a step toward him intending on wrapping her arms around his neck and smothering him with a kiss. Instead, she turned her head and vomited, nearly missing his feet.

Anya sunk to the ground wiping her mouth with the back of her hand. She hadn't been feeling ill until that moment. It wasn't over yet. She could feel her stomach churning like a boat being rocked by a storm at sea.

"Well, if you hate sunshine that much, we can come back here. It makes no difference to me." Daniel tried to make her feel better with a joke.

He reached down to help her up, but she batted his arm away. Round two was close at hand. He stood back and waited till she felt like it was safe to get up and enter their home. He walked alongside her. His arm that was wrapped tightly around her waist practically carried her inside. She felt so weak.

Anya sat at the table, and he brought her water and a rag to clean her face and hands. She cleaned herself up then sat perfectly still being cautious that any movement might make her sick again.

"Feeling better?" he asked.

"I'm not sure."

"You should have told me you weren't feeling well. You could've stayed inside to rest instead of helping me all morning."

"I was feeling fine," she insisted. "This was a surprise."

Daniel drummed the table with his fingers and stroked his beard with his other hand. He appeared to be deep in thought, and Anya worried he was contemplating the problems associated with taking a sick woman along on his journey. A smile slowly broke out on his face. He let out a chuckle which made her look up at him.

"This is funny to you?" She immediately felt hurt again and wanted to cry. Tears were becoming as natural to her as breathing, and she felt helpless to stop the emotions overtaking her at every turn.

"I'm not laughing in jest, my beautiful tree sprite. It's from happiness."

"Happiness?" Anya was confused.

"I do believe you will soon make me a father."

Anya gasped in shock. "You know?"

Daniel's eyes widened at her accidental confession. "You mean you knew?"

She had known since the baby was conceived the first night they became one. She could feel the presence of life inside her getting stronger with each passing day, but how could Daniel have known she wondered.

"Yes, I knew."

"Why didn't you tell me, darling?"

"I didn't know how."

"How about by simply saying you're pregnant?"

"I'm pregnant."

Daniel's laughter turned into a roar. He walked over and kissed the top of her head and rubbed her shoulders. "A little late now."

"How did you figure it out?"

"You're sick for no reason. It's a common sign. Plus you have been trying not to cry over everything the last few days. Also a sign."

"I have not," she felt belittled. Even so, that simple truth was enough for the tears to well up again. Everything made her want to cry nowadays, both bad and good.

"Yes, you have, dear. I know when you're upset even if I don't mention it every time," he said, giving her shoulder a gentle squeeze.

Anya's shoulders slumped, and she rested her head on the table. Until this moment, there had always been that one last chance no matter how miniscule, that she would be able to part ways from him and finish her mission. Now that he knew about their baby there was no way she could force herself to leave the very man she couldn't bear the thought of being apart from.

"Now what?" she asked softly.

Daniel grinned loudly. "Now, we have a baby," he told her.

# Chapter Five

Everleigh sat on the rail of Jackson's front porch watching him throw a football in the air. They were waiting for his dad to get home with his pickup truck before they could leave. His dad had used it to haul off something that morning, but had been gone most of the day. They would have been halfway to Trinity by now if Jackson had been able to leave when she arrived.

"Just talk already," he told her, still tossing the ball.

"What do you want to talk about?"

"How about whatever it is that's bothering you."

He knew her far too well. "I'm only wondering what's keeping your dad."

Jackson caught the ball and stood up to walk over to where she sat on the railing. "Have you met my dad?"

Everleigh laughed and took the football from him. She hopped off the rail and walked backwards away from him throwing the ball in the air as she went, taunting him.

Judd Montgomery was known for his uncanny ability to never be on time. "If I had known your dad was using your truck today, I wouldn't have let my aunt borrow my car."

He tried to snatch the football, but she was too fast. He threw his hands up. "Fine. Keep it."

She shot him a challenging look then tossed the ball in the front yard. It was becoming annoying listening to the constant whack of the ball hitting his hands every two seconds. "What do you suppose is taking him so long?"

"Hard to say. He probably had other errands to

run while he was gone and forgot to mention it," he said, leaning on the rail. "He's had a lot on his mind lately."

Everleigh bit her lower lip. It was no surprise to learn something was bothering his dad. The approaching storm she saw in her grandma's pendant was what she needed to talk to Jackson about, and she had hoped his dad might have mentioned something to him that would help her make heads or tails of what was coming. Jackson was like a big kid who was easily distracted. Trying to have a serious conversation with him was almost impossible unless he was already focused on something important like driving.

"I wish you'd just come out and say it."

"Say what?"

"I've been home for all of what? Two minutes? You called as soon as you knew I was here to plan a trip to Trinity that couldn't wait. I can tell something's up. You've been weird for weeks."

"Have not!"

Jackson raised his hands as if to say he was done, "If you say so."

She sat on the top step wishing Judd would just show up already, so they could leave. She needed Jackson's undivided attention which was hard to do. That's why she needed him stuck behind a steering wheel.

"Lee-Lee," he said, sitting down next to her.

Everleigh rolled her eyes and groaned. "Don't call me that."

"What? It's your name," he joked, nudging her side with his elbow which made her smile. "Lee-Lee, I know something is bothering you. Is it the family that took over your house this summer?"

There was the sound of a vehicle approaching on the side street, and she waited hoping it would be Jackson's truck. No such luck. "Alright," she said, pulling her knee up onto the step to face him.

"I will tell you, but boy, you need to focus."

"Did you just call me a boy?"

"Did you just call me Lee-Lee?"

"That's fair. What's going on?"

Everleigh had been debating how to go about this since he told her he was coming home. After graduation from college in the spring, he had decided to stay in Trinity instead of returning to Fairview. Many times she wanted to confide in him about what she knew, but it would be unfair to do so with him out of town. All it would accomplish is putting her best friend in a position where he felt useless and unable to help her out. It was like her prayers had been answered when he called saying he'd be back at the end of July.

"Has your dad said anything to you?" she asked.

"About what?"

She shrugged. "Anything."

"You mean other than when he asked me to come home because the world as we know it is ending? No. Nothing."

"He told you that?" she gasped.

"No, I was kidding," he laughed, but it was cut short. It was written on her face that what he had said hit close to home. "What's going on, Everleigh?" his tone filled with alarm.

"I'm not exactly sure what it is yet. I had hoped your dad said something to you that might help me figure it out."

Jackson leaned against the rail of the porch steps. "All he told me when he called was that he needed me home."

"That's why you're back? Because of your dad?"

"Yeah, he said there was a problem with the Elements, and he would feel better knowing I was safe."

Everleigh thought it over. "A problem with the

Elements," she repeated out loud.

"I asked him about it, and he said it was probably nothing. That he was being overly protective of me like always. I hadn't found a decent job yet anyway, so here I am."

She didn't understand how he could be so indifferent. Jackson was a great many things, and most of them good. Being a thinker was not one of his attributes. Unless it concerned food, she wondered if the boy ever really thought about anything. "And it never made you wonder about what the problem was?"

"Nah, not really. I mean it couldn't be too big of a deal if he wasn't talking to me about it."

Maybe she was talking to the wrong Montgomery she thought. Judd had a presence that had intimidated her since she was a little girl, but it was worth a shot to ask him point blank. The worst he could do was not answer, right? No, he could do a lot worse and with very little effort.

"Hey," he said, leaning down. He moved his head to the side until it tapped her shoulder. He pulled back then did it again. And again.

"Would you stop?" She pushed him away trying not to smile. There was too much running through her mind, demanding to be analyzed for her to get distracted by an oversized oaf right now even if he was her adorable best friend.

"Remember when we were kids? I don't know. I think it was fifth grade."

"We were in third grade," Everleigh corrected, knowing exactly where he was going with this.

"You don't even know what I'm going to say!"

"Actually, I do. It was third grade. That book series became all the rage. Fire and Water descendants all over the world went into a panic afraid of backlash."

"Okay, so yeah. That's what I was going to say," he straightened up, and stretched his neck from side to side. "I figured it was something like that. You know, something our people were being overly cautious about, but it would pass."

It made sense which was a surprise coming from such a simpleton. The only thing Jackson ever seemed to have on his mind was when he would get his next meal. The boy could eat enough in one meal to feed a family of four for a day if not longer.

"I don't think it's going to be that easy this time," she confessed.

"What do you know about it?"

Everleigh shook her head slowly while staring at the front walk. The only thing she could see was the image of the storm in her grandma's pendant. "I barely know anything."

"You obviously know more than you're letting on. Did your aunt say something to you?"

"No, my grandma did."

Jackson's eyes widened, and his mouth dropped. "Your grandma?"

"Yeah."

"Eloise?"

Everleigh glared at him. There had been many times while she was growing up that she would vent to Jackson about her grandma, and the way she was going about teaching her the craft. Grandma had never been one to be very open with anybody, choosing only to tell you what you needed to know, when she felt you needed to know it. Even after receiving the calling, Everleigh's lessons were slow and boring because her grandma needed to make sure each one was completely committed to memory, and each spell or potion was perfected before moving on. It made being gifted a grimoire on the first day almost pointless if there was never an option to reference it during her witch studies. There was never a game plan explained to her or a broad idea of what they would be doing. It was task oriented only. It was her way. This was probably the manner by which she had been taught, so it was how she was now passing the knowledge on to the next generation.

"Well, you know how I told you my cousins came to stay this summer?"

"Yeah, because Isaac and Dorian came out to your house after they were called. They wanted to visit too as much as it annoyed you."

"I didn't tell you everything." She looked at him then glanced away not realizing how hard it would be to say it. It was like it wasn't completely real until she told somebody. "They weren't just visiting. They were called too."

Jackson leapt to his feet and ran down the steps. He put both hands on his head and walked halfway to the sidewalk before coming back. "How the hell, Lee-Lee?"

"Exactly. It means-"

"I know what it means! How the hell could you not mention this to me before now?"

Everleigh stood up and brushed off her jeans then fidgeted with the loose knob on the top of the rail. The pressing concern she had before saying anything was how to keep him focused during the conversation which wound up not being difficult at all. This was a much larger issue, and one she hadn't predicted. She expected he might get upset because she hadn't told him sooner, but she was surprised at just how angry it made him.

They would have to bottle the rest of what she had to tell him until after his dad returned. As much as Judd Montgomery terrified her simply by being in his presence, she would have to involve him in this now. There was no one else better equipped to prevent Jackson from losing control. On the plus side, Judd had to know something, and he'd be more apt to share his knowledge with them than her grandma. Everleigh wouldn't get a chance to learn anything if Jackson's anger wasn't curbed. She had to find a way to cool him off now, or there would be no discussions with his dad later or ever again.

"You've known for what? Two months?"

"More like six weeks."

Jackson threw his hands down to his sides and balled them into fists. The bright blue of his eyes started to glow a hazy orange.

*'Oh no,'* she looked around, worried that she didn't have a clean way to run without going right past him. Not that it would matter. There was no chance of out running him.

"I'm sorry. You have every right to be mad at me, but Jackson, please," she begged. "Please just breathe and try to calm down."

He continued to stare at her, and she watched his eyes turn a bright orange. It wouldn't be much longer now if he didn't reel it in. The veins in his neck bulged and she could already see the muscles pressing against the sleeves of his shirt until the fabric was ready to rip.

"Please," her voice cracking, as she fought back tears. "Jackson…" There were only moments left before she would have to try to run from him knowing that he wouldn't be able to control himself once he caught her.

The skin around his cheekbones undulated and started to swell.

Everleigh screamed and ran to the side of the porch jumping over the rail. The distance between them wouldn't keep for long. He was coming fast behind her. As soon as she landed on the ground, she sprinted to the garage throwing the four by four beam of wood across it to latch the door behind her. The ladder to the loft was to her left, and she started to climb. The door splintered as Jackson punched through it sending pieces of her. "I'm just glad you're alright."

Everleigh closed her eyes again and waited as the nurse went over care instructions with Judd. It barely registered with her that the injuries they were discussing were more than just her head. The doctor was telling Judd she was lucky her ankle wasn't broke, but it was badly sprained. She would need to stay off of it as much as she could.

Tears stung her eyelids, and she didn't bother with trying to stop them. Anyone seeing her cry would assume it was from the pain of the gash on the side of her head. The sound of Jackson's whimper echoed through her mind. The whimper had been a painful cry, and Everleigh envisioned his lifeless body still lying in a heap outside the side door of the garage while she was alive and would recover.

"Did you hear me, Everleigh?" Judd asked.

She opened her eyes, and tried to say, "No." It came out as a hoarse whisper.

"I said it's time. I'm going to lift you into the wheelchair. The nurse insisted I not carry you all the way out."

"Okay," she nodded. "Go ahead."

Judd leaned over and carefully lifted, then carried her to the wheel chair that was waiting by the door. He did it so effortlessly one might think he was some kind of health nut who was a regular at the gym if they didn't know better. He removed the brakes from the wheels and started pushing her down the hall. "You really did give me a scare," he whispered to her as they headed toward the exit.

That couldn't be right she thought. She was the one who had feared for her life. If she was alive, it didn't bode well for what might have happened to Jackson. In the state he was in, there would be very few options to tame him. The most logical was also the most permanent.

The automatic doors opened, and Judd stopped, putting the brakes back on the wheelchair before coming around to lift her again. Everleigh lay draped over his arms while he walked her through the parking lot as easily as a person might carry a folded umbrella.

"Where's Jackson?" She mumbled, but there was no answer.

Judd walked to the side of Jackson's pickup truck, and still holding Everleigh easily with one arm, he opened the passenger door with his other hand then glided her onto the seat. Making sure she was completely inside before he closed the door, he told her to sit tight, and she'd feel better in a minute.

He opened the driver's door and climbed up in the cab. "Ready?" he asked her.

Everleigh thought he meant was she ready to leave, so she nodded then fastened her seatbelt. When she looked up, Judd was extending his right arm exposing a freshly bit wrist dripping with blood in front of her face. She clamped her mouth shut and squirmed against the back of her seat trying hard to get away from it, but he only inched closer. Tears fell down her cheeks. This was the last thing she wanted.

"Look," he told her sternly. "The only reason we came here instead of doing this from the start is because the neighbors heard you scream and called the police. I had barely hid Jackson's body before they showed up. There you still were on the floor of the garage, unconscious. Hell! They gave me an escort to the hospital!"

He had dropped his arm away from her, and she could see the wound was almost healed. "I don't want to, but thank you for offering," she told him politely.

"For offering?" he cried out. Putting both hands on the steering wheel, he took several deep breaths. "I know, Everleigh. I know why you don't want to drink." He sighed and looked at her. "But I am not sending you home in your condition. I am not facing the wrath of your grandmother."

He bit into his wrist again, and held it out to her. "Please."

Still, she hesitated.

"Please don't make me do this the hard way," he told her firmly.

Everleigh nervously leaned her head forward to his wrist.

"That's it. You only need a few drops. It doesn't have to be much."

She parted her lips, and he brought his wrist to her mouth. The bitter taste of iron covered her tongue immediately, and she started to gag.

Judd pulled his arm away. "That's enough. You'll be healed before we get home."

The last thoughts she had before the hallucinations set in was she might be physically healed that quickly, but the effect of the blood in her system would take most of the night to fade. As her eyes closed, she saw a larger than life beast charging toward the pickup in the side mirror following them home. The effect of the blood was just beginning its jolt to her system, so she was aware the beast wasn't really there. The fear it caused her, however, was very much real, and it played mostly from memory.

# Chapter Six

Everleigh sat on the sofa in the Montgomery living room staring at the painting on the wall of beautiful appaloosa horses. The horses were running through the rugged western open land and had been running for some time. They never did anything else, but she was fascinated and had been watching them for hours.

"How's my patient doing?" an oddly distorted, echoing voice asked.

Her mouth fell open in disbelief that the horses could talk.

"Everleigh! Over here," the horses spoke again.

The liquid air around her began to ripple out from her like the way a stone thrown into a lake would disturb the surface. The circular waves floated past her face taking her focus off the horses in the painting.

"Everleigh," the echo continued to bounce around the walls of the room.

The horses were trying to get her attention, but the floating waves were so close to her. She lifted her hand to touch one as it passed by.

"Lee-Lee!"

She snapped to attention quickly and looked up just in time to see the horses run off the painting across the wall and jump through the window to the ground outside. The sideways lake that had filled the room was gone, but it still gurgled near her like the draining of a tub. Her head spun, but the room almost looked like it normally did again. That's when she saw the figure in the doorway. She held her breath expecting to see Jackson's ghost come to haunt her for what she did. Only it wasn't Jackson. It was his dad.

"I thought that might get your attention," he said.

Everleigh saw him and understood his words, but she really didn't know what he was talking about. The room started to spin, and she put her hands to her head to still herself. The stitches scratched under her fingers, and she touched them gently several times.

Judd knelt down in front of her and moved her hand away. "Completely healed. I'll be removing those for you shortly." He looked around the area where the wound had been holding her hair to the side.

Bits of memories were starting to flash through her mind. When she saw his arm near her face inspecting where she had been cut, she jumped back in fear.

"It's okay," he reassured her. "You're fine now. You should be back to your normal self before much longer."

She wasn't sure what to think. Nothing made sense. There was a doctor laughing over Jackson's dead body as Judd tried to drink from her neck. Her breathing became quick and hard, and the fight or flight instincts rooted in the core of everyone started to kick in as she frantically wondered how she would get out. *'Why did that feel like déjà vu?'* she wondered.

"Hey, look at me," he told her gently. "Coming down can be hard. It's different for everyone. You're safe. No harm will come to you. Trust me."

Everleigh looked at the man who had always intimidated her just by being present, only now she saw a side of him she had never seen before. There was a softness in his eyes, and she could sense that he meant every word he said.

"Where's Jackson?" she asked, realizing she hadn't seen him for a long time.

"What do you remember?"

"I'm not sure."

"Try."

"I am, but nothing is making sense."

"Hmm," he looked disappointed. "It must not be done running its course yet. I'll be right back."

"Running its course?" she asked to his disappearing back, as he ran swiftly up the stairs. The spinning had stopped, but her head throbbed like it was the worst hangover she had ever experienced.

Judd was back in a flash with his arms full. "Here," he handed her a bottle of water before opening a bottle of aspirin. "These are for your head," he said, dumping a couple into her hands.

Everleigh wondered how he knew her head was killing her, but thought she must have said something that she couldn't remember now.

He sat down on the sofa with a small black case and unzipped it. Inside were several medical tools, and he pulled out a pair of surgical scissors.

A brief image of a nurse bending over a tray of surgical implements passed in front of her eyes. "Was I at the hospital?"

"Good. You're remembering." Judd turned to her, and tilted her head into position.

HIs arm sparked another flash. There was so much blood. "Did I...?"

He paused and waited for her to finish.

Everleigh looked from him to his wrist then felt the side of her head again. "I drank..." She couldn't finish saying the thought out loud.

"I healed you," he emphasized.

"But why was I... How did this happen?"

"Think," he coaxed. "You were in the garage."

"Yeah, I was." It was coming back to her now.

He tilted her head again. "I'm going to need you to sit perfectly still while I do this. No sudden movements."

"Yeah, yeah," she nodded, knowing not to

move around during something like this. "Where's Jackson?" she asked, as he began to cut through the sutures.

"In the garage," he replied calmly, concentrating on her head.

Everleigh didn't give it a second thought. Jackson spent a lot of time out there tinkering with one project or another. Of course that's where he'd be, but she felt like she knew that already somehow.

"Halfway done," Judd announced, pulling another suture through the skin. "I should've taken these out sooner, but it looks like the marks are fading." He turned to look at her face. "It's just slow going."

Judd went back to work removing her stitches leaving her to wonder how she fell like she did and just what she was doing in the loft anyway. She never went up there anymore not after Judd cleared out everything years ago. It came back to her like a flash of light, "Jackson!" she screamed, and jumped up.

With his hands in the air like he was caught up in an armed robbery, Judd sat terrified staring at her. His normally pale skin had turned almost fluorescent white as what little color he had drained from his face. The surgical scissors had been torn from his hand when she moved, and they bounced on the floor several times before finally coming to a rest.

"What are you doing?" he practically screamed at her. "I nearly gouged your eye out! Or worse!"

"Jackson. He's... Dead." The words were hard for her to spit out.

"What are you talking about, Everleigh?" He picked the scissors up off the floor and took them into the kitchen to sterilize them again. When he returned, he ordered her to sit back down.

"There is only one remaining. Let us try to get

this done."

Everleigh listened and sat still while he finished. It was becoming harder not to unleash the tears that wanted to break free. Jackson was dead. She had heard his dad say it himself. *'What was it he said? He had to hide the body?'* she tried to remember. It was difficult and made her head pound harder, and she was finding it challenging to grasp on to more than flashing images.

"There," Judd said, as he pulled the last stitch through. "We're done."

She didn't move a muscle. She was terrified of what Judd might do to her. The kindness he had showed her by caring for her would surely disappear when he learned she was the reason Jackson had been triggered. She was the reason he was dead even though she didn't yet know how he had died. It had to be her fault.

"Now what's this business about my son?" Judd asked, as he picked up the black case and stitches taking them to the kitchen to dispose of them.

Everleigh didn't know how to answer him. There was no way around telling him the truth. He would find out for himself eventually. Knowing she needed to come clean about what had happened, and actually telling Judd the truth were two different things. It was proving quite difficult for her to speak to him.

He walked into the room and motioned for her to follow him. "Let's go to him."

She followed him out the door to the garage. Even in the darkness, she could see where the side door was busted from when Jackson tried to maul her earlier. They went inside, and Judd walked to the old Firebird Jackson had been fixing up for ages. He grabbed one corner of the drop cloth partially covering it and yanked it off in one movement. He opened the passenger door of the car and stepped back allowing Everleigh to see inside.

"There he is," Judd pointed out. "Sleeping like a baby."

Jackson lay in the seat covered by an old blanket. Even several feet away, Everleigh could see the rise and fall of his chest with each breath he took. "But I thought he was dead."

"What would make you think that?"

"You. You said you had to hide the body before the police came."

Judd cocked his head to the side in thought, then grinned. "Yeah, I guess I did say that, didn't I?"

He slammed the door of the car shut loudly, and Jackson's eyes shot open. He looked as confused as Everleigh felt not long ago. "What happened?" he asked sitting up and looking around. "Why am I in the Firebird?"

"Get in the house, son. We'll talk there." Judd walked to the door then looked to see if Everleigh was following. "Dear, I didn't mean his dead body. I meant his unconscious body."

"What happened to him?"

"Tranquillizer gun," Judd laughed. "Never leave home without it."

They went to the kitchen where they waited for Jackson to join them. "I'm going to whip up some breakfast. You hungry?"

"What time is it?" Everleigh craned her neck to see the clock on the microwave near where Judd stood.

"It's not even nine o'clock. The night isn't over yet. You know my boy will walk through that door half asleep and feeling starved. Breakfast will be the fastest meal I can whip up for him. I might as well get a start on it since I know what's coming."

Everleigh laughed at how true it was, but it was quickly stifled when she saw the look he shot

71

her. The front door opened, and Jackson wandered inside looking half asleep, saving her from what was sure to be an awkward exchange with his dad.

Jackson saw the pancake mix on the counter near his dad. "Oh, good. Breakfast. I feel like I could eat a buffet out of business. How long was I out?"

This time it was Judd who laughed, flashing Everleigh an 'I told you so look.' "You slept pretty hard. You've been out about eight hours or so."

"I don't even remember going into the garage," he confessed, sitting down near Everleigh.

The next few minutes passed in silence. Everleigh wasn't sure what to say. It wasn't unheard of for Jackson to experience blackouts, but she wondered if she should tell him what happened. She was also deathly afraid of Judd finding out the reason for Jackson's behavior.

Soon the pancakes were done, and Judd set a plate in front of his son that was piled high. "Coffee?" he offered Everleigh.

"Yeah, that would be nice. Thanks," she said nervously. The intimidation she always felt when she was near him was back in full force.

Judd set three mugs on the table then filled them all before setting the carafe down. He pulled out a chair and flipped it around straddling the seat and resting his arms on the back. "Alright," he looked at each of them. "Everyone good?"

"Yeah," Jackson mumbled with a mouthful of food.

Everleigh barely smiled in response.

"Good!" Judd said with a little too much enthusiasm.

Even Jackson gave his dad a questioning look after it.

"Now, would one of you two dear kids kindly tell me why the hell my son tried to kill his best friend this afternoon?" he demanded, striking his fist on the chair back so hard the top brace splintered in two.

Everleigh jumped and cried out. She was afraid to move away, but she was just as scared to stay in her seat.

Jackson stopped eating and even pushed his plate away. He never turned away food. "That's why I don't remember going into the garage."

"You don't remember because I had to carry you in there after pumping you full of enough tranquilizers to kill a horse. Hell, if I'd been two minutes later coming home, your girl here?" he pointed to Everleigh. "She'd be dead. I have no doubt." His anger cut through the room, and almost every word he said made Everleigh feel physically ill.

Judd took a long look at Everleigh and noticed the way she squirmed. He hung his head a moment and calmly said, "I'm sorry, honey. I wasn't thinking about my blood still being in your system. That's why it's hurting you right now hearing me so mad."

"Your blood?" Jackson jumped from his seat, and his dad quickly rose to meet him.

"Sit," he ordered his son.

"Why the hell, dad?" Jackson's eyes were wide, and he started to pace the kitchen.

"Jackson! You need to sit and calm down before you work yourself up again. Don't make me use that tranq gun again tonight."

It didn't look like he was going to at first, but then Jackson sat down and worked on his breathing.

Everleigh stared at the table with her arms folded across her chest tightly hugging herself and rocking back and forth. Tears were flowing down her face, and she was too frightened to do anything else.

Judd sat between them again and turned to

her. "Calm down, Everleigh. You're safe. You're at peace. You have nothing to be scared of," he told her softly.

She took a couple more ragged breaths then it was over. Everything about her composure changed. She looked and felt more relaxed, and the tears stopped. Her eyes closed as she rolled her head from side to side stretching her neck. When she opened them, she saw the two men watching her, and she smiled.

"Dad," Jackson looked down. "Don't do that. She's my friend," he said, sounding forlorn.

"That's exactly why I did it, son. There's no need for her to tremble so hard she shakes the table when there's no reason for her to be afraid. I can take that fear from her right now. It's a gift."

"But why, dad? Why did she...?" Jackson couldn't say the words.

Judd reached over and turned Everleigh's head to the side. "See those faint marks there?"

"Barely," Jackson squinted to see.

"That's where her stitches were," his dad pointed out.

"What happened?" Jackson understood now why his dad fed Everleigh his blood, but not what caused the injuries in the first place.

"That's what I want to know. Something happened between the two of you. When I came home, you were moments away from finishing her off."

"I did that?" The look on Jackson's face broke Everleigh's heart.

"No," she told him. "It happened during it, but it wasn't you directly." She could tell it really didn't do anything to make him feel better.

"Well," Judd turned the chair to face her. "My son is having one of his infamous blackouts, so it's up to you to fill me in...to fill us both in...on what caused him to lose control this afternoon."

Everleigh was too nervous to speak. She knew if she didn't start talking soon Judd would order her to, and she would have no control over what came out of her mouth. It would be better to talk now while she could decide what to say and what to leave out if she needed to omit anything. Their eyes were on her. She wasn't looking at them, but she could feel their stares penetrating her skin.

"I wanted to see if you had told Jackson anything," she began.

"Told me about what?" Jackson asked.

Judd held up his hand to silence his son. "Go on," he encouraged.

"I don't know much. I only know a storm is coming," she glanced up at Judd, then quickly darted her eyes away again. "So to speak."

"You are not wrong," Judd told her, nodding and encouraging her to continue.

"I told him about my cousins receiving the calling, all six of them." She looked at Jackson to see if there was any spark of memory when she said this, but he looked just as surprised now as he had earlier.

Everleigh waited before saying anything more. This news had sent Jackson off the edge earlier, and she didn't want a repeat of that seeing as how it was like he was hearing it again for the first time because of his black out. So far, he seemed okay.

Judd noticed her hesitation. "He'll be fine. There's still enough drugs in him to keep him calm even if he is awake and moving around."

"I knew he would be upset with me that I hadn't told him sooner, but I didn't think it would trigger... It would trigger..." she didn't want to say the words.

"Why didn't you tell me? We talked all the time, and all you ever said about them was that they were visiting." Jackson was hurt.

"I wanted to wait until I knew more. You

weren't here, and I was afraid it would make you come home thinking I might need help. I wanted you to live your life for a change instead of always having to look after me."

Jackson picked up his fork and spun it through the syrup on his plate. "Looking after you isn't something I despised doing. I'm your friend, Lee-Lee. I will always have your back," he flashed a sheepish look, as though he realized he didn't have her back this afternoon while he was saying the words.

Everleigh wanted to say more, but Judd lifted a finger to his lips looking at each of them to ask for quiet. Judd gripped the back of the chair with both hands and started bouncing his leg while he thought it over. "That would be my fault."

"You weren't even here, dad," Jackson leaned back, frustrated. "Or is that what you mean? It's your fault because you weren't here."

Those words set Judd off. "Your friend is alive because I got home when I did, Jackson. Think about that," he said, tapping the side of Jackson's temple hard. "You were going to kill her."

He looked to Everleigh. "Jackson told me not to be late because the two of you had to run to Trinity. Were you planning on telling him then?"

Everleigh winced because it was true. It had crossed her mind already that if the day had gone as planned, her body would be found in a field somewhere. Her death recorded as an animal attack.

Judd sprung to his feet and paced the room. "I know you're both young. This life isn't exactly new to you as you grew up in this world, but neither of you have much experience with it yet. There's enough for me to worry about without having to wonder if either of you are out doing something stupid."

"You're right, dad," Jackson told him.

"And you..." Judd swung around to eyeball his son. "You're going back on your medication."

"Dad!" Jackson objected.

"End of discussion, son. Look at her!" Judd grabbed his son's head, and turned him to face Everleigh. "How would you have lived with yourself?"

Everleigh saw Jackson's eyes fill with tears, and she tried to comfort him. "It's alright, Jackson. Everything worked out. We're fine. I still love you."

"It's not fine!" Judd bellowed. "Do you know what Eloise would've done to him? He'd be dead right alongside you."

The distraction was enough for Jackson to pull loose from his dad, and he jumped to his feet. "Did you ever think about how this is partly your fault?"

Judd looked like he had been punched. "My fault? Because I was late? Looked to me like I got here right on time."

"No, dad. It's because you still baby me all the damn time! Just because of what happened..." Jackson looked away. It was still a hard subject to talk about.

"Because of your mom, right?" Judd finished for him.

Jackson didn't say anything, and Everleigh could tell he regretted bringing it up.

"I've kept you safe. That's what I've done. I moved you here, and I begged Eloise to help me protect you which she graciously has done since you could barely walk." Judd rubbed his temples. Talk of his late wife always hit him hard.

Everleigh wasn't sure if she should interfere or not. She knew Jackson had been feeling this way for quite a while. They needed to talk it out, but not like this. The tempers on the two of them could level the town if they didn't keep control of their emotions. It was going to be difficult for him to hear this, but she knew what she had to do. "Jackson, maybe going back on the medication for now isn't such a bad thing."

As soon as the words were out, she wished she hadn't said them. The hurt in his eyes could be felt in her chest. They had always been so close. The last thing she'd ever want to do is cause him pain, and she could tell he thought she agreed because of what happened this afternoon.

"Well, at least one of you is starting to make some damn sense," Judd announced sitting back down.

"Jackson, please," Everleigh begged, pointing to his chair and pleading with her eyes.

Reluctantly, he sat down, but pulled the chair as far from the table as he could first. He crossed his arms and outstretched his legs staring at his feet.

"Go on, Everleigh." Judd nodded toward Jackson while looking at her. "Tell him."

She hated being the bad guy. "All I'm saying is the worst isn't over yet. There's going to be other blows coming at us. The medication might be a good idea until we're on the other side of this thing."

"Spoken like someone from a long line of wise witches," Judd followed.

Everleigh couldn't tell if it was a joke or a compliment. "That's not all."

Judd looked at her curiously. "What is it?"

"I think Jackson is right too. There's too much being withheld from him. He's a part of this and deserves to know."

Jackson's head was still looking down, but Everleigh could see the corners of his mouth turn up however briefly.

It angered his dad like she knew it would, so she continued quickly. "If he knew some of what was happening, he might not have reacted as badly. Or he may have said something to me over the summer which would've given me the opportunity to tell him what was going on with the witches."

"So you're saying it's my fault he almost killed you this afternoon?" Judd raised his eyebrow at her.

"No, I think we're all a little to blame."

"I think there's only one person to blame," Judd insisted, walking across the room to a cabinet looking for something which he must have found. He walked back and slammed a pill bottle on the table, "And I think these would've prevented everything whether I had told him or not."

Jackson partially stood and pulled his chair to the table. He picked up the bottle of pills and looked at them with disgust. "Dad, if I promise to start taking these again, will you tell me what's going on? Tell us?"

"Oh, we're striking deals now, is that it?" Judd retorted. "Boy, I just want to know you're safe. That's all that matters to me," he said softly. "I will do whatever you want if it means you will start taking those again."

Everleigh could tell this wasn't easy for him by the look on his face, but she didn't have to see that to know how hard it was. These pills had long been a source of grief for Jackson. He had hated them since the first day his father gave him one. They worked perfectly for what they were supposed to do. The pills kept him subdued, so he never had to worry about losing control like he did earlier. The side effects weren't always worth the benefit of them.

They made him sick to his stomach which is not good given the amount of calories he has to consume a day with his high metabolism. Food is by and large Jackson's main thrill in life. It had been since around junior high. All he does is eat, talk about food, buy food, and dream about food.

Everleigh used to tease that the only time a woman turned his head was if she were eating or cooking. With the pills, he still needed to eat vast quantities, but it made him sick. Took the joy out of it.

It dulled all of his emotions too not just the ones that needed to be tamed. His personality definitely suffered from the effects of the medication. Jackson was not the same happy, prank pulling, jokester he usually was when he was on them. When he first started taking them, Everleigh loved it. Made her life a little easier not always putting up with his shenanigans. It didn't take long before she wanted her old friend back, and she has always felt guilty about her initial response.

It wasn't until he was in college before his dad let him start weaning off them slowly. Jackson had to learn to meditate, had to practice breathing exercises, and he even joined a gym to release the energy in a healthy way. Eventually, his dad caved, and Jackson had been medication free for over a year. He was back to his usual self as far as his personality was concerned, and Everleigh couldn't be happier dealing with everything that boy tried to pull constantly.

The only reason he was even considering them now is because of what he did earlier. It didn't matter that he didn't remember it, and Everleigh thought it was better that he didn't. Just knowing what he almost did was enough for Jackson to go back on the medication. If his dad hadn't brought it up, he probably would've done it on his own. Everleigh was sure of it.

"Do I start now?" he asked.

There was a softness that came over Judd's face. Everleigh saw it plain as day. As hard as he was, he truly loved his son.

"You always took them before bed, didn't you? They made you sleepy."

"Yeah," he looked at his dad. "I just wasn't sure if I should with, you know, the tranquilizers."

Judd chuckled and said, "You know as well as I do your body has probably already flushed most of that from your system."

Jackson slowly nodded then opened the bottle and popped a pill in his mouth swallowing it immediately. He looked off and sadness filled his eyes.

"It's just temporary, Jackson," Everleigh tried to help.

"Yeah, boy. Just until you get your wits about you again."

"Whatever," Jackson scoffed. "I did my part. It's time for you to do yours."

Judd nodded slowly and inhaled deep. "Yeah, I suppose I can't keep it from you much longer. What has Eloise told you?" he asked Everleigh.

"Not much," she answered, leaning in eager to learn herself.

"That tells me nothing," Judd sounded annoyed.

"I saw into her pendant one day," Everleigh began.

"She showed you that?" Judd's surprise was immense. "Really?"

"You know?"

"Of course I know. I've been around awhile," he looked offended. "There's not a whole lot I don't know."

"What are the two of you talking about?" Jackson looked lost.

Everleigh had planned on telling them both about the necklace at once. When Judd let it out that he knew about it, she had forgotten about Jackson. "You know that necklace my grandma always wears?"

"Think of it like a crystal ball," Judd cut her off again then looked her in the eye. "Continue. What did you see?"

Everleigh shuddered remembering the image that had been reflected inside of it. "It looked like a hurricane. Well, like the images you see on the news. The eye surrounded by the swirl of clouds."

They both nodded to acknowledge they knew what she meant.

"It was like that, only..."

"Only what," Jackson asked.

"It was filled with Elementals. I could see all four of them represented."

"Hmm," Judd gripped the broken back of the chair again and leaned forward. "How did you recognize Air?"

Everleigh realized he had a point and didn't have an answer to give him.

"I get what you're saying. There are ways to represent most of the Elemental groups, but Air? That's a different story. I'm just curious how you knew it was them."

"I... I guess I didn't," she stammered. "I clearly saw Earth, Fire and Water, but the rest were just...I don't know...normal looking? Their heads did appear to glow when I saw them which made me think it was a third eye reference, but looking back... I'm not sure it was a glow. It could've been the distorted picture coming through the pendant. I just assumed-"

"So you don't know it was Air? It could've been humans?"

"Yeah, I guess. I don't know."

Judd looked deep in thought, and he seemed to be processing this information carefully.

"Why, dad?" Jackson asked. "What's going on?"

"Before I tell you, I don't know who or what is behind it. If Air was represented, it would make me think about ruling them out. Right now, I'm thinking it could be Air against the world."

82

Everleigh laughed. As soon as the sound escaped her lips, she wished she could've taken it back. It was too late. The wrath of Jackson's dad was upon her.

"You think this is funny!" he bellowed.

"No! No, I really don't. It's just that it's Air. There's only like twenty-five of them? What could they do?"

"It's closer to fifty."

"What is?" Jackson was growing more frustrated.

"The number of Air. It's around fifty."

"Even with fifty," Everleigh questioned, "what would they be able to accomplish against the rest of us? Our numbers...each of our numbers...are much greater. It's got to be what a hundred to one?"

"It's not only a numbers game," Judd explained. "You are underestimating their power. Like Earth, their power is increased when they work together, but their power individually is considerably greater than any of us. The element of surprise. Their ability to change form. There's so much you're not factoring here." It was obvious he had given this a lot of thought.

"Would you please back up?" Jackson sounded irate. "Someone tell me what is going on?"

Judd took a deep breath, "I'm sorry I didn't tell you sooner, but I think something is hunting us."

"Us? What would someone want with us? We don't do anything to anyone."

"Not us, you and me, boy. Us, as in Fire. Us, as in the Elementals."

"I know I saw Earth and Water too even if I'm not sure about Air," Everleigh reminded him.

"It worries me that other Elementals will be in danger too."

"Why?" Jackson asked.

"Why not?" Judd blurted out. "The Elements

have gone through this before. Any of us would be stupid to think we'd never be hunted again."

"Okay, so then who?"

"If not Air, I don't know. Not for certain at least."

"So you have an idea?" Everleigh asked.

Judd cracked his neck to the side and stood up. He walked to the window and looked out at the busted door on the garage. "Yeah, but it almost seems impossible."

"Who is it?" Everleigh turned in her chair to watch him walk away.

"I don't want to say anything until I know for sure."

"Dad, you promised," Jackson spat out.

"And I'm talking, aren't I?" A flicker went across Judd's face. It could have been missed if you didn't know what to look for. He almost lost control of his anger The Fire in him almost broke free. Judd had much better control of his alter ego than Jackson had ever learned how to do. A change in his dad wouldn't have been near as terrifying for Everleigh to witness as she'd seen it many times before.

The tempers between the two of them often made Everleigh wonder how the house ever remained standing. Tonight further reinforced that surprise. "Let's back up," she told him, wanting to diffuse the fight before it began. "Why do you feel the vampires are being hunted?"

It didn't look like he'd been listening. He continued to stare off at the garage almost as if he was looking for something. Slowly he turned around to face them and leaned against the counter. He crossed his arms and took his time before answering. "The numbers are dropping."

"Dropping? As in dying?" Jackson sounded alarmed.

"That's exactly what I mean."

"You're sure?" Everleigh asked.

"I'm positive. There's no rhyme or reason to it either. I can't get ahead of it no matter what I do."

"What do you mean get ahead of it? You're not getting involved in this, are you?" Jackson was angry, but Everleigh could hear the worry in his tone.

"Of course I am!" Judd acted like it was the dumbest thing he ever heard.

"Wouldn't that make you a target?" Jackson countered.

"Boy, if someone is after Fire, I'm already a target."

"Why would Air want to come after the vampires?" Everleigh asked.

"They wouldn't," Judd said simply.

"But you just said..."

"I know what I said," he told her, turning back to the garage. "I'm just exploring all possibilities."

That would be smart Everleigh thought, but it didn't give much of an answer to who it could be.

"I've told you all I know," he said in a tone that implied the conversation was over.

"Hardly," Jackson scoffed.

"All I have are the same questions as you do, boy," he walked away from the window toward the doorway.

"Dad, wait!" Jackson insisted.

Judd stopped and glared at his son.

"Who do you think is behind it?" he pleaded to know.

His dad cracked his neck again and said, "I don't like pointing fingers unless I know for sure."

"Fine. So we know it's just a suspicion. You've made that clear. Tell us who you think it is."

Judd continued walking. "We'll talk more tomorrow. It's time to head to bed, kids. Everleigh, you're welcome to stay," he said from the bottom of the stairs. "Jackson, we've got a garage to repair tomorrow, so get some rest."

Jackson bounced his knee and shook his head repeatedly. They were so much alike Everleigh thought. There was so much of his mother in him, but his mannerisms were all Judd.

"I hate it when he does that," he said.

"Does what?"

"Keeps me in the dark," Jackson whined.

Everleigh laughed. "I'm sorry. I am. But that's all your dad does."

"And I'm tired of it," he insisted.

"I know you are, but he said he'd talk more tomorrow."

Jackson huffed and crossed his arms. "Yeah, but not about anything I want to talk about."

She knew how frustrated Jackson was. This had been Judd's way as long as she knew them. It's why Jackson wasn't going to come back after college. He just got home and already found out his dad was keeping things from him again. It would surprise her if he stuck around, but she wanted him to stay. She needed her friend. "Well, think about what we do know. The answer is there if you look for it."

He rolled his head back and looked through the floor like he could send daggers to his dad with his eyes. "Vampires are dying."

"Yes, and I can tell you with certainty it's not the witches doing it."

"That leaves Air and Water," Jackson said like he had already figured out that much.

"It has to be the wolves," Everleigh stated.

That got his attention. He sat straight and looked at her dead on, "It has to be Air," he countered.

"Think about what your dad said a few minutes ago when I asked why Air would do this. He said they wouldn't," she explained.

"Yeah, but you said-"

"And your dad said that he had a suspicion of who it was, but didn't want to say unless he was sure," she cut him off.

"I know that. Still-"

"So it's not Air. His tone of voice was confident when he said they wouldn't attack the others."

"Everleigh!" Jackson said loudly, irritated she wasn't letting him speak. "You said you saw wolves in your grandma's pendant. The wolves are at risk too."

"I also saw Air," she reminded him.

"Or you simply saw humans."

Everleigh knew he had a point, but she knew she was right. She could feel it. "The wolves could be there because they caused the storm," the words came to her easily and even she was impressed with herself.

Jackson's head cocked from side to side as he thought about it. "Maybe," he said.

"Maybe? I know I'm right," she said defiantly.

"I hope not."

"Why is that?"

"I know what my dad said, but it just seems to me like Air would be an easier fight."

"I don't know," Everleigh shrugged. "I'm going to head out." She stood up and walked over to give him a hug goodbye.

"Wait," he shot up. "You aren't staying?"

"No," she took a deep breath. "I'm going to try to get ahold of my Aunt Meredith. I think she may be able to help us figure it out."

"Don't you think she'd tell you if she knew?"

"My Aunt? Meredith?" Everleigh laughed. "Maybe. If she thought she could get away with it without my grandma finding out, she would. But, she does know a few wolves. It doesn't hurt to ask."

Jackson looked upset, and Everleigh felt bad about leaving him after everything that happened. "Alright," he said, without looking at her. "But if you hear anything, you let me know immediately."

"I will," she agreed, then hugged him before she left.

# Chapter Seven

Anya's belly had grown considerably over the summer. Easy tasks were now much harder for her to accomplish. Bending was all but impossible. It was becoming a small fear of hers to drop anything when Daniel wasn't in the home near her. She would have to pull a chair close to use as she slowly squatted to retrieve the item and pull herself back up. It was a task all of its own.

Standing for too long would result in ankles the size of tree trunks. Most of her chores had to be refigured to allow for her to do them while sitting down. Preferably with her feet up whenever possible. Even sitting didn't always save her poor ankles from the swelling and pain.

Sleeping wasn't any easier. It was hard to become comfortable no matter which way she lay down. Poor Daniel's rest was being interrupted as well. Not only was there far less room in their bed than he was used to having for himself, but her inner body temperature was that of the hearth on the hottest day of summer. She was sweating him awake.

It would do no good for him to make even the most helpful suggestion to her whether it be to help make light work of her chores or to ease their sleeping arrangements. Even the best spirited suggestion was met with her tears of failure at not being able to do anything correctly.

This pregnancy was turning out to be quite more than she had ever expected to handle. Anya had seen women who were with child many times while in the Spirit Realm, but she had never paid close attention to them. The human connection and draw to pregnant women she felt now was like an overbearing magnetic pull that she couldn't escape. While she was interested in every woman's pregnancy stories now, it wasn't the case on the other side of the veil. Anya entered this journey of motherhood not having any idea of what to expect along the way.

Daniel, on the other hand, was much more versed in it. His mother had several children after he was born, and he had been old enough to remember the pregnancies of most of his siblings. He would chuckle softly at Anya and shake his head wondering how she had never learned about everything pregnancy entailed. It irritated her how he made light of what she deemed to be massive issues she had to face, but that was no surprise to either of them. Everything irritated her now.

On the bright side of all of this, their new home was substantially larger than where they lived after they first met. They had been in the Mediterranean since late spring. Once they arrived in Europe, Daniel arranged a quick wedding. They did business, trading with people down the coast and finally settled near the area where he had grown up.

Anya had grown to love this child she was carrying more than she had ever realized was possible. It would be a difficult task explaining this to the other Elementals when they reunited. Not only because she have to face the judgement of the Divine Spirit, but she would have to face the others knowing she hadn't followed orders. It would be hard because she could barely understand it herself. There was a tiny person inside of her. One that she had never met. Of course, she knew it was a boy, but she couldn't let on that she knew without being able to explain how she was certain. Still, this tiny person was someone she had never met, yet his life was far more important to her than anything else, even her own life.

With every passing day, Anya had found it harder to conceal her sadness from Daniel. She knew she would have to leave her baby and Daniel behind to attend the Return. The thought that haunted her the most was what would happen if she didn't bear her child before she had to leave. It was a fear that gripped her thoughts endlessly whenever her mind ventured to the looming date ahead. She did her best to distract herself with busy work to keep her mind occupied on other matters, so she wouldn't have to think about the possibility of being pregnant when the day came.

It was hard enough to leave them behind, but to go to the Return while she was still with child would mean her baby would cease to exist when she crossed over. She had a deadline in mind for when she must make the trip back to the north to be able to find the woods where she first appeared. The trip would have to be planned to allow for any delays or setbacks she might experience. It couldn't wait until the last minute. She would have to make it in time to Return, or all of the Elements would be stuck here.

Anya didn't know what would happen if she didn't show up for it. She worried the Divine Spirit would take her anyway and increase her punishment to include not being present with the others. As the date for her to make her trek north approached, she found that she couldn't do it. She couldn't leave Daniel and just runaway without a word. The only way she would make it is if Daniel came with her, but she couldn't think of any reason that would convince him why they had to go back. They were so happy in the life they were creating for themselves here. No one in their right mind would want to leave it behind. It was decided that she would stay and miss the Return regardless of the consequence instead of breaking his heart by trying to go by herself. Besides who would care for her baby once the Return occurred if she went alone?

Daniel sensed her worry and unease. He assumed it was due to the impending childbirth. Many first time mothers were often filled with worries and doubts about becoming a mother. It is a new journey, and nothing can prepare you. He was always there with a reassuring word or a small gift telling her over and over again that she was going to be a terrific mother.

It would be impossible for her to tell him the true cause for her concern. The fears she had would have to be hers to face alone. There was nothing anyone would be able to do to calm her.

---

Anya sat slowly massaging her rather round belly. It wouldn't be long now before their son was born. She had never given much thought to whether she would prefer a boy or a girl since she knew the child was a boy when he was conceived. It pleased her knowing how much Daniel longed for a son. She wanted to name their little boy after his father.

The Return was tomorrow. The time had long past for her to do anything to be able to attend. She just hoped that whatever punishment the Divine Spirit rained down upon her wouldn't affect Daniel or her unborn child. Fully expecting to be yanked back to the Spirit Realm regardless of where she might be, she intended to shy away from her husband as much as she could. The knowledge that his new wife left him suddenly, whether it be before or after giving birth to his son, would be enough for him to bear. All she could try to do would be to save him from seeing her disappear into thin air. Or worse. There were no limitations to what the Divine Spirit was capable of manifesting.

Daniel was working outside, and she heard him call for her. Standing to go to him, a gush of water surged forth from between her legs, soaking her and spreading across the floor. He called her name again. This time she yelled out for him to help her. The panic in her voice was so strong it would be nearly impossible to not pick up on the urgency.

Daniel rushed inside at once and recognized in an instant what was happening. The terror in her face told him she had never learned about this stage of childbirth. "It's quite alright, my love," he soothed her, taking her hands. "Our child will be here soon. Your labors have begun."

At that moment, a pain ripped through Anya's abdomen, and she bent over from the force of it. She felt his strong arms encompassing her, keeping her on her feet and was thankful to have him near.

"Breathe," he guided her. "You need to breathe."

"I am breathing!" Anya spat at him. Breathing was a natural body action that didn't require thought. It wasn't something she could just turn off without knowing she did it.

"Anya," he said, a little more direct this time. "Breathe."

She opened her mouth to fire off a retort when she became aware she had been holding her breath. Inhaling long and slow, she leaned into Daniel for support. Another deep breath, and the pain was subsiding. "It's working," she told him, smiling at him ever appreciative that he knew how to take away her pain.

"It's decreasing, yes, but it's not over. We need to get you comfortable before the next one hits you."

"Next one?" Anya's eyes widened.

Daniel shook his head and chuckled. "Oh, my tree sprite, what shall I do with you?" he asked, leaning forward to kiss her forehead. He helped Anya to their bed then ran out to fetch the midwife. His smile seemed as though it would never fade from his face. He had the most beautiful and mysterious wife of any land he had ever traveled, and they were about to become a family.

The midwife appeared a short time later and checked Anya over. It was still very early in her labor, and Daniel should have waited before bringing her to the house. "Up," she ordered Anya, pulling her arms to raise her to a sitting position. "On your feet," she instructed.

Anya's eyes darted to the midwife, and she started to object.

"How many babes have you helped come into this world?" the midwife asked patronizingly.

Daniel was not to be found to support her desire to stay in the bed. With the midwife's help, Anya rose to her feet and walked out of the bedroom. That's where she spied her husband sitting at the table nervously fidgeting with a piece of fruit. He looked just as surprised to see her as she had been to learn she had to leave the comfort of their bed.

"There's still time before the child makes his appearance," the midwife informed him. "Keep her active." The midwife walked to the door of their home.

"Active?" Daniel asked perplexed.

"Yes," the midwife answered tonelessly. "There is no reason for her to waste the day in bed. You can have her finish her work if you'd like, but make sure she moves around. Walking is good."

"Walking?" Daniel's voice sounded lost as he looked at the woman wide-eyed and unsure.

The midwife scoffed and shook her head at both of them. "It will help the labor. I shall return later to check on her progress. There's too much time left for me to stay here throughout."

With that, she was out the door. Anya turned her frightened eyes to Daniel just as another pain ripped through her. He quickly came to her side to aide her.

Not sure how to help his wife, he merely spoke gently to her and rubbed her back while making sure she didn't hold her breath again like she had at the onset. He tried to help her while she bent over gripping the table for support. There was little else he could do for her, and it made him feel useless.

When the pain passed, Anya straightened again and found a mug to get a drink. Her doting husband quickly took the mug from her hands and filled it for her. After wetting her dry throat, she smiled at him. There couldn't be a more perfect man she was certain of it.

"Better?" he asked her.

"For now," she raised an eyebrow and flashed a smile in jest. "I liked what you did. With my back... It felt nice. I think it helped."

Daniel beamed knowing he was somehow being beneficial. Most men would leave at this time returning much later in the day if not the next to meet their new child. It was almost as much tradition as it was a deep seeded disinterest to be present during the hard bit that women suffered. The man's place was anywhere but the home when a baby was welcomed into being. It would take an act not of this earth to keep him away from his tree sprite when she was most in need of him.

"Should we walk then?" he asked.

Anya's eyes told the answer. It was a devastating thought to endure this hurt away from her small comforts of home.

He smiled gently at her and caressed the back of her hand. "We don't have to go far. Around the house should be enough."

"That's it?"

"To see how you like it, yes."

Anya was about to decline the invitation. Climbing back into bed seemed like the best plan for her current situation.

Daniel continued his plea to get her outside, "The midwife would know what is helpful and what is not."

She followed him outside begrudgingly, but found herself enjoying the fresh autumn air until the next pain ripped into her abdomen. Daniel held onto her, giving her support and talking to her throughout. It passed, and they continued to walk around their property side by side. For hours Anya and Daniel walked trying to work through the pains that came faster and faster for her.

When the midwife returned, she was happy to see they had followed her instructions. She was also more than a little bemused to see Daniel so close and attentive to his wife where most men would have long since fled leaving her to suffer alone. Night was already upon them, and the air was becoming chilly. She ushered them both inside where she could check the baby's progress with more comfort and in private. It wouldn't be much longer now. There would still be a short wait before the baby made his debut, but not enough time to make it worth it to return to her home first.

Daniel proved to be an eager and willing assistant if not a little too much underfoot. The midwife delighted in sending him out on small errands just to rid him from her hair for a spell.

He'd also return as quickly as he was able bringing whatever unnecessary items she had requested. The hard part was finding a reason for the need behind what she asked him to find, so he would not discover it was mere trickery to keep him occupied.

When the time neared for the baby to be born, she gave up giving him tasks to complete unless they were important to her work. Daniel sat behind his wife holding her while agonizing screams ripped from her throat. Impressed as she was, the midwife knew it was a matter of time before he made a permanent exit or passed out from shock. It was long suspected that men skipped out being present during their wife's labor because they could not handle the shear vulgarity of it. Men couldn't see past the intensity of the pain, the blood, and the rest of the discharges to embrace the act that women found to be beautiful. A fact she found quite comical since there was never a qualm in them regarding the birthing of their livestock.

Little Daniel was born in the early morning of the day of the Return. The miraculous bundle was placed into Anya's arms, and the memory of everything she had endured during labor and childbirth began to dissipate from her mind. All that occupied her thoughts was this tiny creature who was a product of the love she had for Daniel. It filled her with awe how she was equipped with the capacity to grow a person inside her until he would be ready to survive outside the womb. Survive with assistance, of course. Little Daniel would be at the mercy of his parents for quite some time yet. Well, at the mercy of his father as Anya was sure to depart soon. It was one less thing to control her already over stressed mind. Her child had been born first, and this was the best possibility Anya could have possibly hoped to play out.

He was handsome like his father with his mother's eyes. This tiny little being who was the embodiment of the love his parents shared brought her tears of joy as she examined him carefully in awe of how perfect he looked. This child would grow up to be a magnificent young man, and she tried not to dwell on all of the years she would miss.

The midwife tidied up a bit around her while the new parents were awestruck by their son. She encouraged the new mother to let the boy suckle soon. It was better for both of them. With a little assistance to show her how, she put Little Daniel to her breast for his first meal. Anya nursed him then rested for the better part of the morning with Daniel keeping close watch in case they needed anything.

When she awoke around noon, it was the first thing she noticed. There was a pulsating energy nearby. It hummed low and constant. She couldn't see it, but she knew it was there. Anya knew it was for her. She didn't have to go anywhere to complete the Return like she had thought all along. It had found her. She tried her best to ignore it and to push it from her mind. It only grew louder and shriller as the day wore on. It wanted her to leave.

Late that evening after Daniel had fallen fast asleep, she nursed Little Daniel. She sang a song to him she had learned from the women in the village. Once her newborn baby was resting comfortably near his father, Anya walked outside and disappeared into the air alongside her hut. The energy was everywhere. All she had to do was accept it to be transported back to the rock.

She saw Air had already arrived. He grabbed her by the arms welcoming her back with a smile so warm and genuine. As hard as she tried to greet him in kind, she couldn't keep her pain from surfacing. They only had a brief few seconds together before she found herself back alongside the home she shared with Daniel. Fire and Water had not made it. Anya knelt in the soft, familiar ground and let the tears flow. She had thought she would never see the two men who owned her heart again, but she was back.

In the darkness, she heard a voice speak to her. "Anya, the Elements left together; they must return together. You will have one chance to attempt the Return on this day each year for as long as it takes to complete. Make the most of your time with your family."

She held her breath and waited for more. There would be consequences for disobeying orders the first year even if she was given permission to be with her loved ones now. She was absolutely certain of it, but nothing happened. Despite the punishment she would face, she smiled knowing she would have the year to spend with her family at least.

Her happiness thinking about the time she had been granted was short lived as pain suddenly overtook her. It was a struggle to stand upright, but she finally managed to make it to the door. She walked inside willing herself to make it to the bed where she could rest.

Daniel lifted his head and asked, "Anya? Where did you go?"

"I went for Air," she replied smugly, realizing how slyly true those words were.

"Don't overdo it, my love. You need to rest."

Anya walked to the bed and looked down at both of them. The full moon was shining enough light through the window for her to see their faces well. She was truly in love with Daniel, and her heart felt more love for her son than she had believed a person could be capable of feeling. She was unimaginably happy in her simple life. She didn't know how long she would have with them, but she vowed she would make every moment of their time together count.

Anya carefully got into bed. Little Daniel lay between them. She kissed her husband's forehead and stroked her son's headful of black hair. She was exhausted and soon drifted off to sleep. The rest would be short lived of course as her newborn son was sure to awaken before long and often. None of that would bother her. She was too thankful to have the chance to be there to experience it to mind the disruptions.

# Chapter Eight

Grandma Eloise came into the hall as soon as Everleigh walked in the front door giving her a long look over from head to toe. *'This isn't a good sign,'* Everleigh thought, but forced a smile to pretend she had no reason to think her grandma should be alarmed.

"How was your visit?" her grandma asked, stepping closer and eyeing the side of Everleigh's head.

It was no use ever trying to keep anything from her. It wouldn't surprise her to find out her grandma knew about it as soon as it occurred, and that had been biding her time waiting to see if someone would give her the courtesy of a call to let her know what happened. "Good," she lied, trying to keep the smile on her face.

"Hmm," her grandma frowned. "You wouldn't believe the horrible thoughts that crossed my mind while you were gone."

"Thoughts? About me?" Everleigh tried to act coy.

"Yes, and your friend," her grandma was studying her now, looking for anything to use as evidence. "I suppose I shouldn't press for details. It might make things... difficult for us where your friendship is concerned if my fears proved to be true."

"You are a wise woman," Everleigh stole Judd's line.

Her grandma scoffed and walked to the kitchen. "How is the old devil doing?"

Everleigh smiled and shook her head. It shouldn't come as a shock either that her grandma knew who she was copying. This woman always knew everything. "He seems well. Same old Judd," the corners of her mouth curved up. It was amusing how her grandma would call him anything except his name.

Grandma Eloise opened her mouth then thought better of it.

"What?" Everleigh encouraged. "What's on your mind?"

"Nothing, dear. I was going to make another remark about him, but I believe it wouldn't be prudent seeing as how I have fallen into his debt on this day."

*'She does know.'* Everleigh felt herself begin to worry. *'Why did I ever think I could keep something from her?'*

"I'd like to know that answer myself," her grandma told her sternly.

"Grandma, it was my fault-"

"Shush, child. I have no desire to learn the details more than I am already aware. I know that boy would never mean you harm, but you need to learn your limits with him."

"Yes, ma'am." Everleigh knew her grandma was not open to a discussion about it.

"You know the dangers. He isn't bound by the same natural rules as others of his kind who have no choice but to obey."

This had been drilled into Everleigh since she was a young child. Each Elemental group had their own nuances. Earth typically skipped a generation. Fire and Water did not. All of their children would inherit the traits. In rare cases where hybrids occurred, it changed their natural attributes. One Elemental side would always be dominant with a few residual traces of the other shining through at times. Jackson was unique, and no one really knew why. If they did, they weren't sharing the information, not even with

Jackson. He was almost an entirely different being than the others save for a few details that held fast.

She knew the risks of her friendship with Jackson, but rarely had there ever been an incident. None had ever been as close as today. Seldom had she ever seen his eyes change color and glow. When he first began to experience his nature, his temper would flare instigating the change. The medication had helped to keep him tame, but pieces of the Hyde to his Jekyll would shine through. It wasn't lost on her that she had become a little too comfortable around him, but after the events of the afternoon, her guard would definitely not be down again for quite a while. That is if she ever lowered it again.

"Is there anything else I should know?" her grandma asked, slowly climbing onto a stool without breaking eye contact.

Everleigh knew the odds were good that her grandma had the answer before she asked the question, so coming clean was her only option. "Judd spoke to us about what's happening to Fire. Something has targeted them."

Grandma Eloise sighed and looked at her hands. She drew one finger down the back of her hand smoothing out the wrinkles then removed the pressure letting the skin return to its original form.

Everleigh watched her grandma play around with her hand for a few moments wondering what she was thinking. Grandma Eloise was not one for vanity and felt sorry for those trying to hide their years beneath products meant to turn back the clock on their appearance. She believed wrinkles and graying hair were badges of honor showcasing a long life that many aren't fortunate enough to experience.

Her grandma sighed, and turned her to face her. "Death has so many meanings and fears attached to it. Everyone approaches it differently."

"The vampires are being hunted then?" Everleigh sat on the stool next to her.

Grandma Eloise looked away. Her eyes were distant like her mind was traveling to some time and place from long ago. "Earth and Water are a lot like humans in our regard of death. We are aware from youth that our days are limited. The smarter among us know to appreciate every day because not everyone is afforded a long life."

It was a treat to hear her grandma speak like this. Judd had been right about at least one thing. This woman had a lot of wisdom to pass on. The answer to her question would come, but her grandma would get to it in her own way and time.

"Others have the comfort of knowing that their life will continue on while ours must come to an end. It makes them smug. Not so much with Air, but Fire...," Grandma Eloise chuckled. "Fire can become quite cocky. It has always been this way which is why the rules were set in place for them centuries ago."

"Still, as the years roll by, the boredom sets in. With boredom, you become complacent. You start to relax far too much. You start to think about what you can do to make this immortal life more bearable instead of remembering you need to stay safe. Do you understand?"

Everleigh thought about the choice of the words her grandma had used. It was no coincidence that she spoke similar words to the ones that had been on Everleigh's mind moments before when thinking about her friendship with Jackson. She thought she knew what her Grandma meant. "Fire has brought attention to themselves again."

Grandma Eloise shook her head. "No, not so much that, but they've grown too comfortable. It's been centuries since any of us experienced a hunt of our kind. They began to think those days were behind them. They wrongly accepted they would never die."

"They weren't ready for an attack which made it easier," Everleigh said, understanding now what her grandma was saying.

"Ah, exactly," her grandma patted her hand. "They let their guard down."

"Do you know who it is?"

Grandma Eloise nodded slowly and chewed the inside of her lip, but she didn't answer.

"Who... Who is it?" Everleigh was almost afraid to ask only because she wasn't sure if her grandma would be willing to divulge the answer.

"I have a pretty good idea who is doing it, but what I don't understand yet is why. There has to be more to it than what I've managed to discover so far. Some crucial piece of missing information that would tie everything together to make sense."

Everleigh waited, but that seemed to be all her grandma was going to tell her. She knew not to ask the same question again. If she was going to say who it was she suspected, she would have done so by now.

"It would appear you've figured it out yourself," her grandma continued.

"Me?"

"Yes, I believe you know who is behind it."

Everleigh opened her mouth then closed it, but her grandma widened her eyes and looked at her intently wanting her to voice it. "The wolves," she softly uttered.

Grandma Eloise nodded. "Indeed. It has to be Water."

"How can they be stopped?"

Her grandma leaned back in shock. "Do you think this is where our focus should be? Meddling in the affairs of Fire when we have our own people to protect?"

"Yes," Everleigh challenged. "I think if we help

Fire, they will help us, or we could stop it before it reaches us at the very least."

A grin spread over her grandma's face. "I believe that's the right answer this time, child."

Everleigh felt relieved. In a way, the only real option was for everyone to work together. The image of the storm her grandma had shown her last spring represented all of them. It was only logical to increase their numbers by combining forces. On the other hand, her grandma was very set in her ways and did not approve of consorting with other Elementals too much. "You do?" she asked. "I thought…"

"You thought I'd risk the lives of our people over foolish pride."

"No," Everleigh insisted. "Nothing like that."

"Exactly like that if we don't work together, dear. I have very strong opinions, and I have always been very vocal about them. Of course you would think I would be hard to convince on this matter."

Everleigh smiled weakly. This was the first time her grandma had even come close to admitting she was wrong. Even so, she wasn't wrong. Her grandma was making the right choice as always.

"Off to bed now. We have work to do in the morning."

"Work? I thought my cousins would be gone for a couple weeks?"

"They will be, but you and I need to figure out a way to prevent Water from extinguishing Fire."

Everleigh smiled and hugged her grandma. On her way out of the room, she stopped to ask, "How did you know about what happened tonight?"

Grandma Eloise looked across the room as if she hadn't heard.

Everleigh was just about to leave when she pulled the necklace from inside her shirt holding the pendant in her hand. "Divination. When I felt that you were in trouble, I looked to find out why."

As she walked up the stairs, she heard her grandma call out again. "You were right about something else too. I spoke with your aunt. She is making arrangements to stay with us soon."

She ran up the rest of the stairs smiling and squealed into her pillow after she jumped on her bed. Aunt Meredith was always a riot to hang out with, but they didn't see each other as much as she'd like. Grandma and Meredith did not see eye to eye on pretty much everything.

Everleigh took out her phone and sent Jackson a message to see if he was awake. He answered immediately, and she knew he had probably been waiting on her since the moment she left his house.

"Meet tomorrow?" she sent.

The dots showed up instantly. "When?"

"Don't know. Grandma needs me for something first."

"Let me know."

"I will."

A few minutes later, he messaged her again. "Anything to update tonight?

"Meredith is coming. Grandma confirmed it's the wolves."

She laid down, but was too excited to sleep. It was getting late, but she knew her aunt never cared when she called. Propping up on her elbows, she dialed the number.

"I wondered how long it would take you. I was beginning to think your grandma decided not to tell you."

"Hello to you too," Everleigh joked, relaxing like the weight of the world was lifted off her shoulders just by hearing her aunt's voice.

Meredith's smile could be heard through the line. "How have you been?"

"Busy!"

"I heard Eloise has been having you help train the called ones. How's that going?"

"Was I that bad?"

Meredith laughed hard.

"Be honest. I don't remember being so slow to pick up on anything."

"You were a star pupil," her aunt told her. "You were the only child your mama had. Eloise knew you'd be called, so she started immersing you in her world from a very young age."

Everleigh could remember all of the herbs she helped to plant and harvest. There were numerous rituals and celebrations she at least got to attend if not take part in. She had never thought of it as training because she enjoyed it so much, but looking back, that's exactly what it was.

"I heard you had a run in at Jackson's house today."

"Grandma told you?" Everleigh sat straight up. It was hard enough to digest that her grandma had reached out to Meredith, but for the two of them to chat and catch up was unbelievable.

"Of course not. Are we talking about the same grandma?"

Everleigh laughed, "Then how do you know?"

"Luke told me."

"How did he find out?"

"Jackson's dad called him while you were unconscious. He was worried to death about what almost happened to you."

"I'm fine," Everleigh insisted.

"Make no mistake. You're fine because Judd got to you in time."

"I know," she said quietly. Her aunt wasn't wrong. If not for Judd, she would surely be dead or worse. Everleigh tried not to dwell too long on what could have happened.

"Did he agree to take the pills?"

"You knew about that?"

"It was my idea," Meredith stressed. "I need to know you're safe. Now, let's discuss something else before we get too upset."

"Like what?"

"How about what is really going on between you and that boy."

Everleigh rolled her eyes and groaned. They'd been hearing this their whole life, but there would never be anything more between them. "Nothing, Aunt Meredith. We're just friends."

"Then let me ask you something else."

"Sure, anything."

"Why the hell not? That boy is as gorgeous as they come."

"Aunt Meredith!"

"Don't Aunt Meredith me. I might not be a spring chicken anymore, but I know handsome when I see it."

Everleigh clamped her hand over her mouth. She couldn't believe this was her aunt talking. Her aunt who had fallen in love with Luke the moment she met him and had been cast out by many in her family because she defied them when they forbid her to continue to see him. This aunt thought Jackson was good looking? A giggle broke through even though her mouth was still covered.

"Laugh if you want. You know I'm telling the truth."

"Yes," she mumbled. "He's good looking."

"So why not flirt it up, and try him on for size?"

Everleigh shook her head. There were many reasons why she had never allowed herself to think of him in that way. Reasons her grandma clearly laid out many years ago. Now they'd been friends so long that it was hard to see him as anything else, and that's what she told her aunt.

Meredith sighed. "I suppose I can see that. A good friendship can be as hard to find as a good man."

"Exactly."

"We need to find one for you."

"A good man?" Everleigh scoffed. "Good luck with that."

"You are much too young to sound so bitter."

Everleigh was glad her aunt couldn't see the look on her face. Her mom had been head over heels in love with someone everyone thought was a good man. Late into her pregnancy, he came home drunk and accused her of cheating. Claimed the baby probably wasn't his. They argued, and he left. Her mom ran out the door after him and fell down the steps. He didn't stop. He didn't care. If he had, she might've got to the hospital in time. She might not have bled out so much before help arrived. She might still be here. There was nothing anyone could say to convince Everleigh she needed to find a good man.

"You still there?"

"Yeah," she yawned.

"Hmm... Maybe we should wait and talk more when I get there."

"Wait. Do you have any news about the wolves?"

It was her aunt's turn to go quiet for a spell. "No, sweetie. I wish I did. I've got in touch with a few people who are going to see what they can find out and get back to me. Hopefully, I'll know more when I get there."

"When are you coming?"

"Soon. I just have something valuable I need to put into safe keeping first."

If that doesn't sound cryptic, she thought. "Okay, but hurry. I need an ally."

Meredith cackled. "An ally against who? Eloise or that boy of Judd's?"

"I think you know," she said before getting off the phone. It got under her skin the way everyone always pushed her toward Jackson. Even if she did like him in that way, which she did not, she knew her grandma's feelings about pairing up with someone like him. It would never be allowed.

Everleigh lay back and closed her eyes. She drifted off to sleep worried about what the future held. That worry was surely what influenced her dreams that night.

She was running through an old empty building. It looked bleak and drab. Something like what the basement of an old hospital might look like. She was being chased by something, and even though she never saw it, she could hear it snarling behind her. Just before the wolf reached her, someone knocked her out of the way and saved her by killing it. In the dream, she knew this man who saved her life, and she loved him.

In the morning when she opened her eyes, she was certain of only one thing. There was no chance it had been a psychic dream. There was no way she would ever fall for a guy like the one she saw behind her closed eyes.

# Chapter Nine

"Aunt Meredith!" Everleigh ran outside to greet her. It had been far too long since their last visit.

"Where's your grandma?" Meredith asked.

Everleigh smirked, and her eyes shone. "She had some unexpected errands to run today."

"Imagine that," Meredith said, linking her arm through her niece's before they both exploded in fits of laughter. They walked into the house side by side where the cousins were busy working on magical exercises to commit spells to memory.

"I was hoping we could have some time to ourselves before Eloise returned," Meredith told her quietly, frowning at the number of people gathered downstairs.

Everleigh glanced at their work and knew it would be unwise to pull them away. When grandma put you to task, she expected you to deliver on it. "We could go outside to the garden, perhaps," she suggested more like a question.

"Brilliant," Meredith's eyes lit up. "I am in need of some more bloodroot. Has your grandma any?"

"You already know the answer to that," Everleigh told her, leading her aunt through the house to the backdoor. Once outside and out of earshot from her cousins, she added, "And you know not to let me see you slip any of it in your pocket in case grandma asks later."

Meredith grinned from ear to ear and turned in circles with her arms outstretched. "Some things never change," she laughed. "I do miss this place though," she said, opening the garden gate.

"What do you mean?" Everleigh narrowed her eyes. Aunt Meredith had never been entirely welcome. Grandma merely tolerated her when necessary. Her aunt had already found the bloodroot, so Everleigh moved away where she couldn't watch what she was about to do. Grandma Eloise could sniff out a lie before it was told, and she wanted plausible deniability if asked about whether Meredith helped herself to anything in the garden.

In a few minutes, Meredith walked up behind her brushing the dirt off her hands. "Did I ever tell you I'm the one who sold this house to your grandma?"

"You're kidding?" Everleigh gasped in disbelief with her mouth hanging open.

"I didn't know who the buyer was until after it was done. Luke and I were long gone and hadn't been to this house for quite some time when it sold. The sale was handled by a third party."

"No. No, I never knew that." Everleigh stared at her aunt.

"I don't think she likes to let that secret be known."

"What secret is that, Meredith?" Eloise's voice boomed from behind them both.

Meredith's eyes widened, and she stifled a laugh before turning to greet the old woman. "Eloise, always a pleasure. I was just telling my niece how I was actually the one who started this garden, but you have certainly grown it into something even far greater."

Everleigh avoided looking at either of them fearing she may chuckle out loud if she did. Flattery like that was nothing more than showboating where her grandma was concerned. It didn't have an effect on her. If anything, it irritated her even more.

"Hmph," Eloise frowned. "Just because you planted the first seed doesn't mean you still get to harvest from it whenever you get the notion." Her eyes darted to Meredith's satchel. Eloise turned on her heel and marched into the house.

After she was gone, Everleigh whispered, "How does she do that?"

"She's stronger than you could possibly know." Meredith never tore her eyes away from the door Eloise disappeared through. "Never underestimate her."

"You don't have to tell me that. I live with her," Everleigh joked.

Meredith's eyes danced devilishly. "That doesn't mean you are privy to all her secrets."

"What's that supposed to mean?" Everleigh asked her aunt's back as she walked toward the house.

"It means you still have much to learn about her, and from her as well."

Everleigh stopped just a few steps from the porch thinking about the volumes of information she still didn't know. There had been many unanswered questions over the years. Enough for her to fill entire journals, hoping one day to learn the answers. It wasn't hard at all to recall one of them now. The tricky part was trying to decide which ones she was curious to know the most.

Meredith continued walking until she reached the back door before realizing Everleigh was no longer following close behind. She saw her niece hanging back lost in her thoughts about something. "What's on your mind?"

"How did you meet Grandma Eloise?"

The question caught her aunt off guard. "What do you mean how?"

Everleigh shrugged. "I know how she feels about... Well, you know... About your immortality. How did you come to be involved with the family?"

"She never told you?"

"No," Everleigh shook her head, knowing she had never asked before either. All questions that concerned her aunt in even the smallest way were kept quiet unless she could ask Aunt Meredith herself. It was discovered a long time ago that she was one topic her grandma tried to avoid at all costs.

Meredith sighed and looked off at the garden trying to think of how to answer the question carefully. "Your grandma is related to my ancestors."

"That much I did know," Everleigh told her.

"Well, ever since the choice I made to be with Luke, my family have passed my secret along to each new generation of witches. They have always included me to some degree. Some have been more accepting of the blood that flows through me than others."

"Like Grandma Eloise."

"Exactly like your grandma. For her generation, she was the only witch. She was stuck with me whether she liked it or not," Meredith smiled. "And I'm willing to bet it was not."

Everleigh slowly nodded. Honestly, her aunt hadn't completely answered her question nor had she told her anything she didn't already know. Still hearing it all at once like this seemed to make a little more sense than figuring out the bits and pieces she'd been able to pick up on over the years. The part she really wanted to hear was how she was even introduced to her grandma and when. Was her aunt always a part of her grandma's life and eventually she was told the truth?

That's how it had been for Everleigh. When she was old enough to question how her aunt's looks never changed no matter how long it had been between visits, her grandma told her about the choice Aunt Meredith made to become immortal. Grandma Eloise had said everything she could to change Everleigh's opinion of her, but all it did was make her more fascinated with her aunt. She was thinking of how to word her next question to get the most information when her aunt reminded her there were other matters to tend to.

"Come. We have much to discuss with your grandma."

Everleigh threw her head back and sighed. Nothing was ever revealed at once. It always had to dance out of reach in a shroud of mystery before showing itself a little at a time.

The two went inside where Eloise was checking in on the progress of her other granddaughters in the kitchen. There would be no time for them to catch up until Eloise was through discussing whatever was concerning her with Meredith. Everleigh sat at the island in the kitchen preparing to once again take over on lessons while the two older women met in private.

To her surprise, her grandma gave the girls the afternoon off and sent them on their way to explore the town and enjoy their free time. Amber hung back hanging out in the kitchen with the rest of them which was not a shock. She had always been more interested in trying to learn by snooping then the actual spell work their grandma wanted her to practice.

"Did you understand what I said?" Grandma Eloise asked her sternly.

"Yeah," Amber replied. "We got the day off."

"To explore the town," their grandma repeated.

"I'm good," Amber said, opening the refrigerator to find something to snack on.

"When I give you time off telling you to explore the town, it's my subtle way of saying I need you out of my house," Grandma Eloise spat. "Now get your butt out of my sight as fast as your legs can manage."

Amber's head whipped toward her, and her eyes widened in disbelief. There was a moment of hesitation while she processed what she had just been told.

Eloise took one step in her direction, and that was enough.

"I'm already gone," Amber called out, as she quickly trotted down the hall to the front door to catch up with the other cousins who had already left.

Everleigh couldn't help but smile watching the whole scene unfold. Once it was only the three of them in the house, a heavy tension fell in the room. She looked up to see her aunt and her grandma staring at her. It was her turn to hightail it out of the house. She jumped from the stool and started toward the hall.

"Where are you going?" her grandma asked.

"To help my cousins explore the town," she said, looking back to face them.

"Nonsense," her grandma said, making a cup of tea. "Come and sit. It won't be long before they realize there's nothing much to this town and head back home."

Everleigh walked back to the stool she had just been sitting at surprised she was included in the conversation too. It hadn't been that long since she had last been sent on some fool's errand just to give the adults the privacy they needed to talk while she was gone. The calling of her cousins had changed everything for her and brought her into her own as an established witch in her family and coven.

"Meredith," Eloise began, "I need your assistance with something."

Both Meredith and Everleigh were surprised. It was unlike her to admit she needed help at any time, but to ask Meredith to help her was completely out of character.

"Anything you need," Meredith told her.

Eloise stared at her cup of tea for several moments before carrying it over to join the other two ladies. "What do you know?"

It sounded like an undefined question to Everleigh. Her grandma could have been asking about anything even though she was fairly certain it either involved the coming storm or what had happened with Jackson. Maybe even both.

However, Meredith knew exactly what was meant by the question. "I know that the Fire Elementals are afraid. Many have gone into hiding. The ones who haven't are trying to discover who is behind the attacks. It doesn't matter what they choose because they are still being hunted. Even some of the ones who've gone into hiding have been found and murdered."

Everleigh listened with growing interest. There had been some talk about mysterious circumstances around the deaths of a few vampires, but she hadn't heard anything as alarming as this. Most of what she had heard was picked up from other people's conversations, and it wasn't much. Jackson hadn't been around to keep her updated, but even if he had been home, his dad likely would've kept most of the details from him. It definitely pointed to the wolves. If an Elemental wanted to go off grid, they could usually do so without incident. It would take intense tracking skills to find a vampire who didn't want to be discovered.

"Everything okay?" her aunt asked.

She snapped back to attention concerned neither of them wouldn't be happy she wasn't following along. Grandma Eloise wouldn't tolerate someone spending all their time lost in space as she referred to it. Your mind should always be focused on Earth, not lost in the clouds. "Yeah, why?" Everleigh asked, worrying she missed part of the conversation.

Aunt Meredith shook her head and gave a weak smile. "It's nothing. You looked upset."

Slowly she began to nod her head. Of course she looked upset. It was disturbing news. "They're found even in hiding?"

Her grandma sighed slowly. "Yes, dear. It saddens me as well. To take every precaution for your loved ones and leave the life you know behind in effort to keep everyone safe, only to be found anyway, but without the strength of the numbers you would've had if you had stayed? It's heart breaking. Many of them are killed while they sleep. Cowardly if you ask me."

"Killed?" Aunt Meredith scoffed. "They're being slaughtered. It's worse than a slasher flick from what Luke tells me."

Everleigh gasped. This hadn't been divulged to her until now. Immediately she worried about Jackson and his dad. Judd might be intimidating without effort, but he had never done anything to warrant meeting an end like her aunt was describing.

As if she knew her thoughts, her grandma told her, "Don't worry about your friend, child. There is no one who could protect him better than his father."

Those were the kindest words her grandma had ever said about Judd Montgomery. Everleigh almost asked how her grandma knew what she was thinking then realized it would be for naught. Grandma Eloise would probably only ask her why she was surprised about it. A wry smile formed on her grandma's lips while she had the thought, and if she didn't know better, she'd have sworn her grandma was hearing her thoughts word for word. No one could do that. Not except for Air.

"Have there been any leads on who is behind it?" Grandma Eloise asked.

Meredith closed her eyes and took a deep breath. "Near as we can tell, it's the wolves. They're carrying out the orders. That much we know for fact. We don't know who the mastermind behind everything is yet."

Eloise nodded. It was something she had already determined as well. "No one suspects Water is behind this, then?"

"Honestly, no one is really certain about anything when it comes to Water. Every lead we've ever had has been a dead end. It appears no one knows Water's identity."

"Yes," Eloise agreed, sipping her tea. "Water has always successfully remained elusive."

"If it's the wolves, wouldn't it be Water behind what's going on?" Everleigh asked, thinking it seemed obvious.

"Not necessarily," Meredith told her. "We've exhausted a lot of leads including whether it was a member of Air posing as the Water Element. Air is not a part of what is happening."

That was one scenario Everleigh wasn't sure she would have ever considered, but if it was already checked into, there was no need for her to contemplate it now. "How else would anyone be able to control the wolves?" Everleigh's eyebrows lifted. It wouldn't make sense for the wolves to go against their leader.

"There is always a way to persuade someone," her grandma told her. "You just have to be able to give them what they want in return."

"And what do the wolves want?"

Her grandma shook her head slowly. "It could be anything, but the most likely choice is an end to their curse."

"But that isn't possible." Everleigh let the words slip out as soon as they popped into her head. Everyone knew there was no way to stop Water from transforming during a full moon.

"That's not entirely true. There is a spell," Meredith said quietly.

That caught Everleigh's attention. It was the opposite of what she had understood as truth her entire life. None of the Elementals were supposed to be able to affect factions other than their own. "What spell? How does that work?"

"For starters, there's a coven in the south that has been able to remove the pain from the transformation," Grandma Eloise revealed.

"But I thought..."

"It's not that cut and dry," Grandma Eloise went on. "There has been blood shared between Earth and Water in that area for centuries."

Meredith cut her eyes away without Eloise seeing it. "What she means is there has been some interbreeding between the Elemental groups in that region."

Everleigh thought it over, and it would seem to reason that their spells would work if they were related. "Okay, so they can help with the pain. They can't take away the transformation completely."

"You're right," Grandma Eloise agreed. "Only the Divine Spirit could stop it."

"Although it has always been rumored Anya could spell it to stop successfully if she were so inclined," Meredith added. "Maybe for only one cycle at a time."

Eloise scoffed at the remark. "Even if she was capable of something so profound, I doubt she could ever be moved to do it though."

"I don't understand. How could they be promised something that can't be done?"

Meredith furrowed her brow. "People make false promises all the time."

"And why would the wolves believe it can be done?"

As soon as the question was out of her mouth, Everleigh realized the answer and sucked in her breath quickly. "It's because of the success the witches had in the south, isn't it?"

"That's the theory I'm behind," her grandma answered.

Everleigh looked down and slowly drummed her fingers on the counter top. "That makes it sound like witches are involved."

Eloise stood up and placed her cup in the sink. She turned back to face the ladies and rubbed her temples. "This brings me back to what I said at the beginning. Meredith, I need you to help me with something."

"What do you need me to do?"

"Do you have any contacts in the south?"

Meredith shook her head. "I know only a couple of them, and I barely know them at all. There is one woman. Her name is Rita. I can try to get ahold of her."

"See what you can find out. Also, that friend of yours. I believe his name is Todd?"

"What about him?"

Eloise walked closer. "He knows people from every faction. Try to bring him in on this. We need to find out who is behind this to put an end to it before it reaches us."

The atmosphere around them turned urgent with those final words, and it couldn't have come at a better time. As soon as Eloise was done speaking, the cousins bounded in the front door and quickly made their way to the kitchen ignoring the tone of the room. They were talking over each other about the lack of anything to do in town besides go out to eat. When they finally took notice of the seriousness of the three women gathered around the island in the middle of the kitchen, it was too late to ask questions. Meredith made her exit claiming she had errands to run, and Eloise quickly set the newly called witches back to practice on their spell work.

# Chapter Ten

Anya shuffled crates around setting up their spot in the marketplace. They were here every morning selling what they could to the townsfolk. She hoped there would be a need for chickens and eggs today as that was most of their haul.

A kind woman about twice the age of Anya was their first customer. She was a servant who shopped for the house she worked for and regularly bought from them. Anya always looked forward to seeing her not only because she was a consistent sale, but because she enjoyed their chats.

"How are you this morning?" Anya asked her.

"The pains let me know I'm alive," she responded, rubbing her lower back. "It's a blessing."

Anya arched an eyebrow. "Pain is a blessing?"

"Growing old is a blessing. Not everyone is afforded that luxury."

"That is very true," Anya agreed, admiring the wisdom this woman had. She always saw life in a different light than any of the others Anya had met.

"You, my dear, are blessed more than most. You don't look a day older than when we met. When was that anyhow?" She thought it over for a minute, but was distracted when the children ran up behind the table.

"Mother! Mother!" Little Daniel was yelling excitedly. He wasn't quite so little anymore. At ten years old, he was already almost as tall as his mother. She knew she would have to stop thinking of him as Little Daniel, but she couldn't bring herself to do it.

"What is it, Daniel?" she asked, in one of the

rare moments where she left out the word little.

"Nicholas found a baby rabbit! Can we bring him home?'

"Ask your father," she told him, knowing quite well that there would be a new animal joining them at their home today. Daniel never could tell the boys no.

Anya turned her attention to the woman who was watching the boys run off. "That's right. Little Daniel. He was just a babe you were wearing on your chest the first time I met you at the market. How old is he now?"

"He'll be eleven this autumn."

The woman shook her head and commented, "And you look young enough to be his older sister. Blessed indeed."

The old woman's words plagued Anya the rest of the day. She would never age. She was immortal. She wondered how many other people had taken notice of her youthful looks who hadn't mentioned it to her. How long would it be before someone looked at it as more than just a blessing? She'd often spent many a night thinking about what she would do when her ageless appearance began to be noticed. She wasn't ready to leave her family, and it wasn't really an option in her mind. They could move. They could always start over somewhere new where she might pretend to be a sister or an aunt, but what explanation would she give to Daniel or their children? There was no easy choice.

Even the good day they had at the market couldn't clear her troubled mind. Solving this dilemma was her priority. She would need to figure out what to do soon. She let it take over her thoughts well into the night after her children were fast asleep.

"Are you going to share with me your burden?" Daniel asked her shortly before they turned in themselves.

Anya wasn't sure how to respond. She didn't want to lie to her husband, but she wasn't sure she could tell him the truth either.

"Is it the rabbit?" he asked. "Shall we set it free?"

"No, I rather like him," she smiled at him, wanting to ease his mind that it wasn't his decision to bring home yet another creature that had been bothering her.

"Then tell me what is wrong. I don't like seeing your mind so heavy with worry."

"Do you think I look young?"

His eyes widened, and he sunk into a full belly laugh. It irritated her that he would insist she talk to him only to make fun of her worries. She rose from the table and headed to their room.

"Stop," he said, still laughing. "Come back."

Anya walked back to her chair and sat dutifully.

"Yes, you look young, but that is because you are not old, my love," he told her, and reached for her hand.

She sighed. "The woman at the market said I looked no older than I did when Little Daniel was a baby."

"You don't," he agreed, without giving it a thought. "You are a tree sprite! I wouldn't expect age to affect you in the same manner it attacks everyone else."

Anya took her hand back from him, and his eyes lit up playfully. He had been calling her a tree sprite since the night he found her in the woods. Sometimes she enjoyed it, but at times like this when his words hit too close to the truth, she did not. It was hard to have a serious discussion with him about the matters on her mind when all he did was make light of them.

"Listen to me now. I have known since the moment we met you were unlike any woman I had ever known," he tilted his head. "You don't show your age as fast as others do. This is a good thing."

"It is?" she asked.

"Yes! My wife will always be the envy of other men who have wives showing their years."

She waved her hand at him and went to bed. He joined her soon after and laid behind her, holding her in his arms. He kissed the back of her neck and told her, "If it bothers you so much, put some chalk in your hair. Let people believe it is your age turning it white."

Anya rolled her eyes then realized that is exactly what she must do. Not chalk of course, but she must cast the changes herself. She lay awake concocting the spell in her mind before allowing her eyes to close. In the morning, she would gather the ingredients while doing chores and would cast it before they headed to market. With any luck, a wrinkle or gray hair would start to appear in no time at all. She had to cover her mouth at the thought. She didn't want Daniel to waken and ask her if she was mad, laughing in the darkness at nothing. She knew she had to be the first to ever look forward to signs of old age.

In the morning while everyone was busy with chores and loading up the wagon to head to the marketplace, Anya busied herself in the kitchen preparing breakfast. She nervously went about gathering what she needed. It would be too risky to cast a circle now, and she had considered waiting for a better opportunity. It was too pressing for her to put it off any longer, so a potion would suffice. Stirring the pot on the side of the hearth, she hoped it would be ready before her family bounded back inside, wondering what she was making. This potion would work, but it was missing something.

"Molasses!" She let the word come out in her excitement without meaning for it. Glancing around, she listened to her family working nearby outside of the window, trying to determine if anyone paid attention to her outburst. Certainly no one outside heard her. She added some molasses to the pot to make the effects take hold slowly.

Anya walked to the windows to check her family's progress. She didn't want anyone walking in on her. It looked like she still had time. She stood before the hearth stirring the pot and recited her chant.

*'That's it,'* she thought. She removed the small pot carefully and poured it into a mug. It would need to cool before she could drink it. She got the table ready for the meal, and brought the food from the hearth. She scowled at the set up. She was thankful for the chickens as they provided well for her children, but there were only so many ways to prepare eggs.

The voices outside were getting closer which told her they would be at the door any moment. She hurried to the counter and drank down her potion as fast as she could. It was disgusting. *'As it should be,'* she thought. For most, the thought of growing old disgusts them. She finished it off just in time. She set the mug down as Daniel burst through the door. Her face was scrunched up and her eyes tightly closed in reaction to the horrid taste slowly sliding down her throat. *'Ah, yes, there's the molasses,'* she joked to herself.

When she opened her eyes, there was Daniel and her children staring at her. "I experimented something new with the mead," she told them.

"I take it you won't make it that way again then," Daniel joked. He took a piece of bread from the table. "Here. This should help."

Anya took it and ate it greedily. It did help move everything down, but the flavor was still there. Her family didn't take their eyes off of her.

"Better, thank you. Let's eat," she said, wanting to move to the table where she hoped she could get the taste out of her mouth.

Mealtime was always a joyous occasion for them. They were truly blessed. Their three sons were healthy and able, witty and strong. There was always enough food on the table for all to be full and content. Today was no different as she listened to her sons chat happily about their new rabbit. They had wasted no time last night constructing a cage for it, but Geoffrey decided that the rabbit needed freedom. The boys woke in a panic and spent several minutes searching for their new friend when they awoke. Its luck that the rabbit didn't find his way outside where his real freedom would await.

She became aware that Daniel was watching her without looking at him. His gaze was penetrating as though he were looking through her. He often did this. He would watch her at the most random moments, and when she caught his stare, he would tell her it can't be helped because she's so beautiful. Sometimes it made her uneasy when she was set upon a task. She would not want a witness to any mistakes she might make. Here and now in this moment, she didn't mind. She could feel the love he felt for her shine through his eyes and saturate her skin.

"Would you look at that?"

Anya turned to her husband who was still watching her intently. She crinkled her brows together and asked, "Look at what?"

"As I live and breathe, I just watched a white streak appear in your hair."

Fear filled her eyes and she reached both hands to her head. It wasn't supposed to work like this she worried frantically. It was supposed to age her slowly. She rushed to their room for a little trinket box that had shiny sides. It was the only mirrored like surface they had. It was too dark to see anything in the house. She took it outside to look in the morning light.

Daniel remained calm, watching her as she hurried through the home with the box to the door. She thought she had found a solution, but now what would she do. It would be difficult to fix this now when they would be leaving soon. She had no reason to skip the market this morning. They all knew she was well. She bit the corner of her lip and fought to keep the tears at bay as she panicked thinking the only option might be to flee from them. That was what she had been trying to avoid with this potion.

Once safely outside and away from the windows where spying eyes might see her, she took a deep breath and held the box up to look at herself on its side. She saw nothing. She moved the box from side to side and over her head. All she saw was her long shiny black hair.

She marched back into the house irritated at the joke that she did not find funny. She walked to Daniel and demanded, "There is no streak. Why would you play those games?"

"It is right there," he said, pointing to the side of her face.

"Where?" she asked, bringing the box to the window hoping there would be enough light to see.

Daniel walked over and stood behind her. He took the box and held it with one hand then tilted her head slightly with the other. "Right here," he said, holding out a small section of hair.

Anya still couldn't see anything. She took the section of hair from his hand and pulled it around in front of her face. There were only a few strands of gray, hardly anything she would call a streak. Relieved it wasn't anything like Daniel made it seem, her fear was replaced with anger. If Daniel had simply said a few white strands were noticeable instead of making it sound like she had a skunk stripe, they would all be finishing up their meal by now. She whipped around to face him so fast he had no warning to move away from her. She hit her head on the side of the trinket box, he was still holding high. The pain was immediate and severe. She brought her hand up to her temple.

He dropped the box and looked at her head. There was some blood, but it was only a small scratch. "It's not too bad," he told her. "Come. Let's get the wound cleaned."

Anya sat down and let him tend to her. Daniel soaked a rag with some fresh water and wiped the small cut. "It's nothing," he reassured her again.

She pointed to the box still lying on the floor, and he fetched it for her. She held it up studying the cut. He was right. It was barely more than a scratch, but it throbbed fiercely.

"Would you like for me to make a poultice for it?"

It didn't need any dressing. She was sure of it and told him so.

"I'm sorry, love."

There was guilt in his eyes, but Anya knew it was an accident. She had done it to herself. No matter how guilty he looked, she couldn't help herself from not being over what brought them into this mess. "It's only a few strands. You had me believe I had a whole streak of white in my hair! I thought I turned into a skunk."

He kissed her head near her wound then wrapped the hair where the gray strands were around his fingers. "But I watched them appear."

The trinket box was in her lap, and she looked at her reflection on the side even though she couldn't see the strands of white. Studying her looks, she thought about how her potion had worked. Soon her face and skin would show signs of aging as well. "The gray didn't just appear. My hair must have shifted as I moved, revealing them off to you."

"Look at that!" Daniel said with surprise.

She turned her head up to him. He was staring at the top of her head again. Not more gray hair she thought. She didn't expect the potion to work like this, but there was no way to guarantee the results until she tried it. In her haste to get the aging underway, no time had been planned to allow to fix anything if it went horribly wrong. In hind sight, she should have waited until after everyone had gone to bed that night. It would've been much safer.

He pointed near where her head throbbed, and remarked, "Now, you've got a red streak as well," he winked at her.

She playfully pushed him back. "Enough of you for today. We need to ready ourselves to leave. We're late."

They made quick work of clearing the table and cleaning up to head to the marketplace. Anya sat beside Daniel, and their children rode in the back of the wagon.

"It is odd, don't you think?" Daniel commented
"What?"

"It was only last night, you were worried about your youthful looks then this morning, your hair has begun to gray."

He looked at her in a way that made her feel uncomfortable. She knew an accusation, or at the very least a question, would surely follow. One that she was not prepared to answer.

"It can only mean one thing."

Anya braced herself for what he would say next. She had always known this day would come. Her vivid dreams that gave her insight of future events often had her crying out in her sleep which disturbed Daniel and brought on endless questions. The way she always seemed to have luck in choosing the best spot for the hunt was more than coincidence or intuition. It was winter four years ago when she had the foresight to know exactly what herbs to hoard for the illness her family would face. Nicholas certainly would not have made it through that year if it hadn't been for her preparations. It was time for her husband to piece things together to figure out the truth.

"You are a tree sprite!" Daniel said with a hearty laugh.

The relief poured over her like a downpour. She had grown tired of his old joke over the years always proclaiming her to be a sprite because of how they found each other in the woods. She was overjoyed to hear it once more at this moment.

She rested her head on his arm, and he kissed the top of her head. She had met him going on twelve years ago, and she spent almost every day of those years in fear. Fear of being discovered for what she really was. One day there would be an accusation that could be quite consequential for her and her family. Some people passed witches off with a wave of their hand as though it was not for anyone to have alarm. There were those however who treated anyone different as something that should be banished.

There was also fear of the Return. She often dreamed of returning to her true home, but it would mean leaving her family behind. They would endure, and once in the spiritual realm, her human emotions would disappear. There would be no pain or longing. She knew this with absolute certainty, but she was also just as certain that she wasn't fully ready to leave.

After this, the worst of all the scares experienced so far, she decided she would not let this fear rule her anymore. She would enjoy the time they had together for however long it lasted. While she may be able to alter her looks to appear to age, her family would grow old around her. Their days were finite where hers would continue until the Elements successfully completed the Return. It could be this year, or it could be in a hundred years. She would not let her worry stand in the way of anything anymore.

# Chapter Eleven

The bonfire was tonight, and Everleigh could sense something was coming. It had been floating on the air for days now, but it was getting stronger. Something told her it wasn't the storm that she had been preparing for, but it was connected somehow. Whenever her thoughts turned to the party, the sensation got stronger. There was always the option to not go just in case something was going to happen there, but she hadn't been able to talk Jackson out of it.

He had met some girl briefly, and now he acted like the moon rose and set in her eyes. It was sickening. All he had talked about since last night was the dark haired, sun kissed girl from the restaurant. At least the mystery woman now had a name, Lilah.

Everleigh was a smidge jealous. There had been other girlfriends, sure. Jackson was good looking by anyone's standards and had no problems finding a girl for his arm. There had never been one he had taken to as much as this one. Definitely not as fast as this one. She was used to being the only woman in his life. That's how it had been since as long as she could remember when her grandma began babysitting him. They were only friends and would only ever be friends, and she was happy with their friendship. She wasn't used to having to compete with another woman for his attention, and it was something she wasn't looking forward to getting used to. The worst part would be all the secret keeping and having to act a certain way around her until they knew she could be trusted. That's if that day ever came. It never had with any of the other girls who had caught his eye before this one.

Reluctantly, she had agreed to let Amber tag along. Most of the cousins were eagerly working on the craft in their free time from school, but not Amber. It was always a struggle getting her to focus on anything. Part of it was because everything was starting to come more natural to her than the others. That didn't mean it was time to scoff at the practice work thinking you didn't need it anymore. Yet that was exactly how Amber was treating it.

The main reason why their grandma heavily encouraged Everleigh to take her along was because she needed a break from trying to teach Amber as much as Amber needed a break from the work. Many times since their arrival, Everleigh had assisted with the lessons or took over completely. It went without explanation as far as she was concerned why her grandma needed the night off from time to time.

There were three other cousins who would be staying back while the two ladies went out. At first, there were many objections over being left out of the fun, but they were a couple years younger than Amber. Most of the people at the bonfire would be college age, so taking a high school senior along was the most Everleigh would want to push things anyway. They didn't like it, but they did understand why they were staying behind.

Everleigh grabbed a water to bring with her from the refrigerator on her way to the front of the house. While she stood there taking a swig from the bottle, she looked at the calendar on the freezer door which her grandma was using to track earthquakes. The number of disasters were increasing daily, and it was becoming more and more worrisome.

Humans didn't have a clue. Most of the ones who did notice an increase in anything chalked it up to natural patterns over Earth's history. It would make sense to them because they don't have the key knowledge that the current pattern of these events started to slowly build up after the Elements took human form. There isn't an accurate record of anything prior to their arrival for a scientist to make the connection that something drastically changed a millennium ago.

As she stood there, writing began to appear. Everleigh was startled until she turned to see her grandma standing in the doorway, not knowing she had popped out of the sunroom where the girls were working for a minute. Looking back at the words that were forming, she read out loud, "Liberty, Maine – 5.7 magnitude. Maine?" she asked, not turning away. "Have they ever had an earthquake before?"

"Yes," Grandma Eloise answered, walking into the room. "Not of this magnitude I don't think, but it's not unheard of for earthquakes to occur there."

"That's the fifth one today."

"In the states. That doesn't count all of the others around the world."

Everleigh gasped, and her eyes widened. She opened her mouth to ask her grandma more, but Grandma Eloise held up her hand.

"There will be plenty of time for that later. Are you on your way out?"

"I just have to put my boots on," Everleigh smiled.

"You have time," her grandma said in her knowing way.

Everleigh didn't know what she meant by that, but she learned long ago to trust it to be revealed soon enough. "What do you need, Grandma?"

Grandma Eloise smiled at her and leaned against the wall. "Maybe we could talk for a bit before you go. I'll probably long be in bed before you return home."

There was something her grandma wasn't telling her, but it would do no good to ask. Her grandma reveled in riddles. "What do you want to talk about?" Everleigh asked.

"How do you think the girls are coming along with their progress?"

That cemented her suspicion. Grandma Eloise didn't actually need her opinion on this matter. She was stalling, but why? "They're coming along. It's still early, Grandma, so I'd say they're on track."

"Exactly what I was thinking," her grandma agreed.

They continued to talk about how their progress compared to Dorian and Isaac who were still working on the craft while away at college. Grandma Eloise detailed some lessons she had lined up for the upcoming weeks as well, and she was never one to divulge her plans.

"What's this about, Grandma?" Everleigh asked softly. "What's really on your mind?" Worry was beginning to mount inside of her as she tried to figure out what it was that her grandma wasn't saying.

"It's nothing," she replied, looking off wistfully. "I just want to make sure you stay safe more than anything."

"I'm always safe," Everleigh narrowed her eyes, wanting to decipher exactly what her grandma meant.

Grandma Eloise smiled at her and placed her hands on Everleigh's shoulders. "I know you are. It's not you I'm worried will..." she cut her eyes to the side for a moment, "make a wrong turn," her grandma looked back at her and smiled.

"I'll be careful," Everleigh reassured her again.

"I know you will," Grandma Eloise started to walk away. "Oh, and one more thing," she said, stopping in the hall to speak back over her shoulder. "Let me know if you find out anything about our new friend."

"How did you...?" she stopped herself from finishing the thought. Her grandma had already disappeared into the sunroom leaving Everleigh shaking her head. It was a pointless question anyway. Grandma always knew everything, so it should be no surprise she knows about the new person in Jackson's life without Everleigh having mentioned it.

"You aren't ready yet?" Amber asked from the entryway.

Everleigh walked past her irritated gaze into the living room. "I just need to put on my boots."

"I thought you said we were leaving. I've been waiting."

Everleigh took a deep breath to stay calm. The entire night was going to be like this with her in tow. "Grandma needed me for a minute."

"More like fifteen," Amber snorted.

It didn't take more than a couple minutes to slip her boots on and zip up the sides. She had just finished when she heard the screeching metal on metal shrieks from somewhere close by. Jumping to her feet, Everleigh immediately felt panicked over whatever had happened outside.

"Holy..." Amber said slowly from the doorway.

There was nothing visible looking out the front window, so Everleigh joined her in the hallway.

Amber had the door wide open and was looking out the glass outer door. She stepped aside to let her cousin have a look. Turning her head to the left, she saw the crumpled mess of red metal wrapped around a light pole. Flames were already shooting out of the engine. She turned to face her cousin and saw a flash of grandma disappearing into the sunroom again from the corner of her eye.

This is what she had meant by keeping her safe. If Grandma Eloise hadn't stopped her to chat for a moment, her and Amber would probably have been at the stop sign on that corner waiting to turn out onto the highway when the driver lost control. They would have been smashed between that heap of fiery metal and the light pole.

Everleigh grabbed her phone and called it in, but several reports of the accident had already been made. Hanging up, she headed back to the front room to wait out the emergency crews. They could take a different route to the highway and would still get to the bonfire, but there was no hurry. They could wait until the chaos outside had calmed substantially.

---

The bonfire was as large as it had ever been when she arrived. Sometimes Everleigh thought Jackson's friend Sam was intentionally trying to get the cops called out to his dad's property. There had been many reasons why she was nervous about going tonight, but most of them melted away soon after arriving. Even with Amber's sometimes annoying presence, it was good to catch up with old friends.

Jackson and Lilah could be seen around the other side of the field, and she would have to make her way to them eventually. If not, Jackson would surely find her. Maybe it could wait a little longer. She secretly hoped that if she put it off, pretending not to notice them long enough, they'd leave before the introductions could be made. It was too much to ask, and she knew it would only serve to put her in the doghouse with her best friend.

Near the end of the night, she found them again only they were looking straight toward her and her friends. It was time to get it over with. As she started to walk in their direction, she heard the name that was worse than nails on a chalkboard to her, "Lee-Lee!" It was Jackson. The truth is she didn't mind the nickname. In fact, she rather delighted in it, but she hated when he used it around other people.

Not wanting to take her eyes off Lilah for a minute, she listened while Jackson made the introductions using her nickname again. She corrected it quickly for Lilah's benefit. There was nothing to be picked up from this girl. She would have to be an Elemental, but if that was the case, Jackson should have been able to pick up on that. The only other explanation would be a protection spell, but her family would know of any other witches in the area. It didn't make sense.

*'Of course!'* The thought hit her out of nowhere. Her aunt had been working on getting in touch with different Elementals for months now. That would definitely bring attention to the area. This was probably someone connected to one of her contacts.

Everleigh caught herself nodding at her own discovery and realized she would need to say something quick before Jackson tried to dive into her mind to find out what she was thinking. She attempted to cover it by talking up what a great catch Jackson was which she immediately regretted. The boy already had a big head and ate up compliments like his life depended on them.

They talked briefly, and Jackson confessed he thought Everleigh wasn't going to show tonight. He didn't say it in front of his girlfriend, but she knew it was because he thought Everleigh didn't approve of her even though they hadn't met. He wasn't wrong. Their kind, especially his, were in danger with very little information about who was responsible. No plan in place. Each day could be the one that brought an attack on Jackson or his dad. Soon it would be Earth's turn to encounter whatever faceless menace was hunting them. This wasn't necessarily the time to add a new flavor of the week to the mix even if the boy insisted this one was different.

It also wasn't the place to have this conversation with him again, so she filled him in about the car wreck not even a block from her house. Maybe it was her already substantial suspicion of the newcomer, but she thought she saw something come over Lilah's face when she talked about it. Something that indicated it wasn't news to her. Even when Jackson mentioned a reckless driver they encountered on their way out, Everleigh could tell Lilah knew they were talking about the same person. But how?

It wouldn't be wise to hang around with them for long. Soon Amber would find her way over, and it was hard to say what might come out of her mouth when she couldn't get a read on Lilah. Not to mention, Everleigh knew her directed questions and comments toward her might wind up showing her hand as well.

Using Amber as an excuse, she left the two lovebirds to enjoy their evening. *'Hopefully, Grandma will be able to fill me in more about her when I return home. It's obvious she knows more than she's told me. She always does.'*

# Chapter Twelve

It was the day after the bonfire, and Everleigh had dragged Amber to Jackson's to hang out with Lilah. There had been something about her that Everleigh couldn't quite put her finger on in addition to being unable to read her. It made her not want to give the new woman in Jackson's life a chance from the start. The unknown can be hard to embrace. The last thing she had wanted to do was spend the evening with this woman who had somehow managed to wrap him around her little finger from the moment they met.

Disappointing Jackson would have been worse, and that's exactly what she'd be doing if she hadn't agreed to go. He wanted his best friend and girlfriend to get along. Taking Amber had been her way of preparing for the worst. If the night was too unbearable, she could have her cousin be the excuse for why they had to leave.

Turns out an escape route wasn't needed after all. The night began horribly with Everleigh dreading her decision to go in the first place and wondering how soon was too soon to take their leave. Lilah's offer to give them a ride home left her regretting every life choice she had ever made bringing her to be in that situation at that point in time. Not accepting the ride and walking home in the cold would have seriously upset Jackson. Everleigh was sure of it.

That car ride wound up being exactly what she needed to put a spin on everything. Not only did she learn Lilah was an Air Elemental which answered more questions than Everleigh had the chance to think of yet, but she'd be able to let her grandma know that Air was definitely not behind the attacks on Fire. They were also willing to assist Earth. That could quite possibly be the biggest news of the night. Air had notoriously kept to themselves, and their involvement would be monumentally huge.

Even so, there were a few things left to figure out. Everleigh knew Lilah's identity, but she couldn't be absolutely certain whether Lilah knew all of Jackson's secrets. It didn't seem likely. If Lilah knew everything, there would be no cause for hesitation in telling him the truth about who she really was. The fact that she was keeping her background from him was enough to make Everleigh believe that Lilah was in for more of a shock than Jackson would ever be.

Everleigh walked away from Lilah's car when she dropped her and Amber off after their talk. She waved at her aunt who had just pulled in the drive. Meredith had been in town for a few days, but they'd hardly had any time to spend together. She was hoping maybe they'd have a chance now. She half skipped the last couple of steps over to her.

"Aunt Meredith!" she said excitedly.

"Heya, hun," Meredith said and leaned over to give her a hug. She hugged her and rocked back and forth. "I was hoping you'd be here when I got back. How you doing, Amber?" she asked, and turned to give her other niece a hug.

"Good," Amber answered.

"Handling everything alright?"

Amber shrugged.

"It has to be a lot to take in when you weren't expecting it."

"Yeah, but what are you going to do?"

"You're right, Amber. What can you do?"

Meredith put an arm around each of her nieces, and they headed toward the front walk. "Have you ladies been out causing trouble tonight?"

"We were out with Lilah," Everleigh told her nonchalantly.

Meredith looked at her with curious eyes.

"You know. Your friend Todd's niece." Everleigh cast Amber a sly glance.

"Oh?" It was obvious Meredith wasn't sure how to respond.

"She's an Air," Amber added, picking up on what her cousin was doing.

Meredith looked surprised for a moment then remembered, "Well, yeah, you would know that since you know about Todd."

"Yeah, that... And she told us she was," Everleigh said, walking away from her aunt to run up the porch steps. She reached the top and looked back. Her aunt hadn't moved, but was staring after her with wide eyes.

Amber turned away trying not to laugh and was making weird chortling noises instead.

Meredith looked between the girls and thought she figured it out, "Oh, I get it. You're messing with me?"

"No, Aunt Meredith, she really did tell us about her family," Everleigh insisted.

"What?" Meredith wasn't sure what to think. "Air never talks to anyone. It took Todd years to trust me. Her family won't be happy about this."

"Her family knew she was going to tell us, Auntie M," Amber said.

Meredith put both hands up in front of her and opened and closed her mouth several times. "Girls, let's get inside. I need a drink to process this. What is the world coming to?"

"That's why she told us," Everleigh told her. "Because of whatever is happening in our world."

Meredith's face turned solemn, and she nodded. "Yeah, I supposed that's right, baby girl. We all need to be reaching out to each other."

The three of them walked inside, and

Everleigh's grandma was waiting for them several feet from the door looking like she was about to let someone have it.

"Grandma, I'm sorry. I sent you a message from the coffee shop." Everleigh's thoughts swarmed, but she had no idea why she was in trouble.

"This has nothing to do with you. Get on up to your room, and take your cousin with you. Your aunt and I need to have a talk."

Everleigh looked at Meredith who only nodded toward the stairs. It was her way of saying do what your grandma told you. The cousins headed upstairs, but were barely halfway up when their grandma started yelling at Meredith.

"I don't know what games you're playing at, but you need to get that vampire out of my house now!"

Everleigh stopped mid stride and watched the conversation below her.

"Vampire?" Meredith tried to act like she didn't know what Eloise was talking about. "What do you mean?"

"Don't act like you don't know. You stashed him in the attic days ago."

"Grandma," Everleigh headed back down.

"Get upstairs. This don't concern you."

"I was in the attic earlier looking for those candle holders you wanted for tomorrow. There was nobody up there."

Her grandma ignored her, and brought her attention back to Meredith, "You spelled it so we can't see him, but you think I don't know what's going on in my own home? I don't want him here. You need to take him somewhere else."

"I'm trying to protect him!" Meredith shouted. "I'm out of options," she lowered her voice, with tears starting to stain her cheeks.

Everleigh couldn't believe what she was

hearing, and she looked up at the ceiling overhead. She wondered if there could really be someone hidden up there by a spell. There were spells that could hide objects, so they were unseen by anyone around them. She'd never heard of it being used on a person.

"And you'd put us at risk to do so?"

"We're already at risk, Eloise, and you know that."

"Exactly. We have a big enough target on our backs. I want him out."

"Where are we supposed to go?"

"Go to your friend's house in the country. Stash your boyfriend there."

Meredith was caught somewhere between hurt and surprise. Her family had never approved of her relationship, but she hadn't expected anyone to be this cold. Luke had never done a damn thing to hurt anyone in this family, or anyone period. Eloise didn't think much about Air either, but she did hold them in slightly higher esteem. That's why Meredith hadn't mentioned to her that they were using the old farmhouse outside of town. No one had to tell the old woman anything. Eloise has her ways of finding out. Todd would've been just as much of an outcast to Eloise as Luke except Todd wasn't the one who lured her away, tricking her into falling in love with him. That's how the family always saw it, like Luke concocted some evil plan to win her heart.

"That's right," Eloise continued, "I know about the psychics gathering too." She tapped her finger to her temple. "I'm smarter than you give me credit for, always have been."

"No one thinks you aren't smart," Meredith closed her eyes, and took a deep breath.

"Says the girl who thought she could play with Fire in the attic without me knowing."

Meredith sighed in defeat. "Okay, Eloise, we're

going."

She started running upstairs with Everleigh and Amber at her heels. Meredith went down the hall to the doorway to the narrow attic stairs. She stopped and looked at her nieces. "What do you think you're doing?'

"I want to meet him," Everleigh said point blank.

"Me too," said Amber.

Meredith rolled her eyes and shrugged. "Why not? Air are giving up their secrets. Elementals are turning on each other. It seems like everything has been flipped upside down overnight. C'mon, then."

She opened the door and headed up with the girls close behind. Once inside the attic, Everleigh looked around carefully. It looked just like it had earlier. Boxes and trunks were scattered around with a few pieces of old furniture thrown in for good measure. There was no evidence of anyone else having been there.

Her aunt walked toward the far side of the room. Everleigh saw nothing except a couple dusty boxes and an old mirror. Meredith held both arms straight down at her sides with the palms up and slowly lifted them while chanting a spell in Latin.

Everleigh couldn't make out everything her aunt was saying, but she picked up on a few words. She stared ahead waiting for some magical veil to drop, and a vampire to appear. Nothing.

She turned to her when she had finished, and said, "I don't see anything, Aunt Meredith."

The corners of her aunt's lips slowly turned up into a smile. "He's here."

Everleigh was about to ask where when she glanced back at the mirror and screamed. In the reflection standing behind her was a very tall and very handsome man. He looked young, younger than her aunt appeared to be. He could easily pass for mid-twenties. His hair was jet black, and his skin had a dark tan. They laughed when she screamed.

He put his arms around Meredith and kissed her. "I didn't realize it was show and tell tonight, dear," he teased.

"I'll explain soon," Meredith told him, furrowing her brows with worry.

Everleigh turned around to look at him directly.

Amber was standing several feet behind them with her eyes wide open. "He just appeared."

"It's a hiding spell," Meredith explained, "to protect something valuable, and Luke is most valuable to me."

He hugged her tighter then let his arms fall to get a good look at the other two girls in the room.

Amber was still staring. "He wasn't there. Then he was."

Luke smiled at her. "I was here all along. You just couldn't detect me."

"You saw us?" Everleigh asked.

"Yes, of course. I was the one who was hidden, not you."

"Luke, these are my nieces, Everleigh and Amber. Girls, this man is my one true love."

"It's a pleasure to meet you ladies," Luke said and did a slight bow. "I've waited far too long for your aunt to get around to introducing me to the family," he said, laughing at his own joke.

"Let's go downstairs," Meredith instructed. "We have to be on our way soon I'm afraid."

"Where are we headed?"

"I'm hoping my friend Todd will take us in," Meredith answered him, concern wavering in her voice.

They made their way down to the main floor of the house where Eloise was waiting. As Meredith put on her coat, she could feel the watchful eyes of the old woman on her at every moment.

This wasn't the first time Eloise had to sit back and watch as she forced Meredith and Luke away. It made her heart heavy thinking it probably wouldn't be the last time either. The Elemental factions had decided centuries ago not to mix the lines. It was a hard test of loyalty when one of the groups was being hunted. There would be a hefty choice to make. Do you help your own people? Or do you aide the person that holds your heart?

Too many times their kind had seen this play out. Bloodlines being betrayed in the name of love, or a family member sacrificed because the one they loved turned on them when they chose their family. The repercussions of the decisions, regardless of what they might be, affected the factions for generations to come every single time. That's when the elders decided it would be best to not intermix.

Meredith had been informed of this. Still she chose her heart over her family. That was her decision to make, and as far as Eloise was concerned, she made the wrong choice. There would be no way to know whose side she would take in a moment of battle. Best to keep her at arm's length.

They drove off to the farmhouse, and Meredith chuckled.

"Pray tell, what's so funny?" Luke asked.

"Oh, nothing, I was just picturing the look on Todd's face when we arrive."

Luke was puzzled. He and Todd had been acquainted since long before he met Meredith. "Why would he be surprised to see us?"

He checked the time. It was after midnight. "Is it because of the hour?"

"No. Air has been gathering here for days. Some of Todd's family have never met a witch or a vampire before, and now we're about to drop by unexpectedly."

Luke mulled it over. He could see the humor in it, but it left him uneasy. "Will he allow us to stay?"

Meredith shook her head, "I honestly don't know. I'm certain he will take us in for the night, but after that," her voice trailed off, and she shrugged.

"We'll worry about it in the morning if that's the case," Luke said, looking out the windshield. He brought her hand to his lips and glanced her way briefly. He tried to smile at her reassuringly, knowing she could see right through his façade. It was hard to stay positive when every time you had to move, you were placing an even larger target on yourself and helping your enemy track you down.

They turned down the lane toward the farmhouse and parked at the end of the drive. Luke looked out the window at the light pouring onto the porch from the downstairs windows. It didn't look like they would have to wake anyone at least.

"Are you coming?"

He looked over and saw Meredith was already out of the car, leaning in to get his attention. "Oh, sorry. There's a lot on my mind."

Luke quickly unbuckled and got out. They walked up the steps and could hear voices from inside. He quickly knocked on the door then stepped to the side.

A minute later, Todd opened the door. "Meredith!" he greeted her, happily as always.

"Can we come in?"

"We?" Todd asked.

Luke stepped out from where he had been standing and nodded at Todd.

"Hello, Luke," Todd said. "You are always welcome here. Please, come in."

The two of them walked inside where the family were gathered deeply concentrating on something. The only one who paid them much attention was Lilah who couldn't tear her eyes away.

"What brings you out so late?" Todd asked, indicating he knew it wasn't a friendly meeting.

"Eloise kicked us out," Meredith said, regretting coming here. Even if everyone staying there was accounted for in the living room, it was too many for one house. There could be even more scattered throughout the home. Todd's family opening their home to them was a long shot, and it looked like they were already overbooked.

"What?" Todd seemed amused.

"Well, to be fair, I didn't exactly ask permission to stash a vampire in her attic."

Meredith heard a gasp and looked behind Todd to find Lilah staring with her mouth open. She was amused. Lilah's face was identical to the expression Amber had in the attic not long ago.

Todd gave them a sly grin. "Luke, this is my niece Lilah. You have to forgive her. She didn't even know vampires were real until a few days ago."

Lilah couldn't stop staring. Meredith snapped her fingers in front of Lilah's face. "Aren't you going to say hi?"

"Hey," she said, turning her attention immediately back to the vampire standing before her. "Are you really going to be staying here?"

"That's up to your uncle," Meredith said, exchanging a quick look with Luke. They hadn't asked about staying yet. Neither had thought that far ahead to work out the best way to go about bringing it up. If Everleigh had given Lilah a head's up they were coming over, she wouldn't have been so dumbfounded over seeing a vampire in the flesh. Both of them were left wondering how exactly she knew that's why they were there.

'It had to be a lucky guess,' Meredith told herself. She had revealed Eloise had kicked them out. It might be a logical conclusion that they at least needed a place to crash for the night. *'No Elemental's gift can cross faction lines, so there's no way she could've picked up on it with her powers, right?'*

# Chapter Thirteen

"I'm worried about Isobel." Nicholas mentioned to his mother one afternoon during a visit.

"Is there something wrong?" Anya asked. She looked at Isobel playing on the floor with the other children. She looked healthy and well.

"Not wrong per se," he looked unsure of how to express his thoughts.

"Take your time. The words will come."

"She has these night terrors. They wake her up many times each night leaving her frightened and hard to return to sleep."

Anya kept her eyes on her granddaughter. She knew what was happening all too well. Isobel was almost a woman now. If she was experiencing the dreams, there were other signs as well even if they were not yet noticed.

"I have those dreams myself," she told her son.

"I remember. This is why I brought it up. Is there anything we can do? There are nights where we hardly get any sleep at all."

"Is she not in her room? How do you hear her?"

"She wakes us up."

Anya smiled, "Then simply tell her not to. She is of an age where she can sooth herself."

"It's not always like that. She rarely comes into our room, only when the night terrors have really frightened her. Her siblings hear her cry out sometimes and wake up. Regardless, she will be up for hours doing busy work because she's afraid to sleep. Soon others are disturbed then the whole home is awake."

There were many nights when Anya lay awake

in the dark frightened by a vision. She rarely got up because she dared not disturb Daniel, but there were times when her dreams effected everyone.

"What can we do, mother?"

She sighed. There was a lot she could teach Isobel, but nothing she could pass on to her son. "I have an idea. Why not allow her an extended visit with us?"

"How would that help?"

"Well, I can tell you what to do in the hopes you would do it well, or I could teach her myself. Your family will have a rest filled break while she's here to help us in addition to learning how to overcome the night terrors."

Nicholas thought it over. It wasn't what he'd had in mind, and he knew his other children would not receive the news of having to pick up the slack from Isobel's chores that well. Yet, the thought of sleeping through the night without ruckus or alarm rousing him was too tempting to pass.

"For how long do you think?" he asked.

"Hard to say. A few weeks at the most would surely be enough. Daniel and I will bring her to you when she learns how to handle herself well without disturbing others after one of these dreams."

He couldn't find good reason to turn down the offer. The next day Isobel came to the house with a small crate of belongings. Daniel and Anya happily welcomed her. It had been far too long since a child lived within their home. Isobel knew why she had been sent there, but was surprised no one had mentioned it all throughout the evening. Before turning in, Anya explained she wanted to see for herself how bad her night terrors were in order to better help her. Isobel laid down to sleep on a bed that used to be her father's with her grandmother next to her.

It was very early morning when Isobel awoke screaming and kicking at an unseen presence.

Anya reached out and took her shoulders. She exhaled slowly in front of her face nodding at her to follow. Isobel continued the long intentional exhales until she was calm.

"Tell me, child. What did you see?"

"I'm not sure. I couldn't see it, but it chased me."

"Chased you where?"

"Through the forest. I ran as fast as I could, but I could never shake it. I tripped, and it was upon me."

Anya knew exactly what it was that had chased her through the trees. She had dreams very similar to this herself many times over the years. "It can frighten you, but it can never harm you. Tomorrow, I will teach you how to tame it."

Isobel looked at her grandmother with a growing admiration. They had always been close. Her grandmother was close with all of her family, making each of them feel important and appreciated unlike how most adults treated children. No one had ever treated her nightmares with such kindness, and she was grateful to not suffer consequences this time for something she couldn't control.

She laid down again next to her grandmother. Somehow knowing she understood and was sympathetic toward her made it easier to fight her apprehension and try to sleep. She had long ago given up making any further attempts once she had been so cruelly jarred awake. Her terror was enough to keep her eyes peeled searching the shadows on the walls for anything that might be trying to attack her. In the middle of the night when the world is at its darkest, it's easy to see anything your mind can imagine even if you know it's not really there.

The next morning, the two women set off on a walk into the woods after breakfast had been cleared away. They walked a long while before Anya said anything. "I will not be able to make these dreams of yours go away completely. I can teach you how to resolve them when they occur to reduce the times you disturb others."

This was great news to Isobel, but she didn't understand how the woods would help with anything. Her grandfather knew why she was visiting. It didn't need to be a secret.

"The first thing we must do is decrease the number of times they occur."

"You can do that?"

"No, but you can once you know how."

"How do I do it?" Isobel was excited, thinking there might be a solution that would actually help her.

Anya continued to lead her through the woods, but she didn't answer. They came to a clearing where a tree stump sat in the middle. It seemed deliberate to Isobel that they found themselves in this spot, like her grandmother had previous knowledge of this location's existence. She wondered what it had to do with her night terrors.

"The beast that chases you is yourself."

Her grandmother made absolutely no sense. "How could I chase myself? It is not possible."

"It's a part of yourself that you aren't acknowledging. When you ignore it, it will come after you demanding attention. That is what is happening in your dreams. It wants you to accept all the parts of who you are."

Isobel had no idea what her grandmother was talking about. "I'm not sure what is meant by that."

"Have you noticed anything else?"

"Like what?"

Anya rubbed her shoulder trying to think of how to lead Isobel down this path gently. She couldn't blurt anything out for fear of her running back to Daniel. "Anything that is different about you from your family or others that you know?"

This was starting to worry her. She wanted to head back. She was suddenly uncomfortable with her grandmother out here alone, but she didn't know why it bothered her.

Her grandmother reached into the pocket of her apron and pulled out an item keeping it hidden in her fist. "Tell me. What is in my hand?"

This was absurd. Her uneasiness was building. "How would I know what... It's an acorn." Isobel would not be able to explain how she knew, but she was certain beyond any doubt.

Anya slowly opened her fist revealing a small intact acorn laying on her palm. She smiled at her granddaughter gently.

"But how? I must have seen you pick it up," she said more to herself than to her grandma, trying to explain the trick.

"I put it in my apron before you awakened this morning."

Isobel shifted uncomfortably. She knew actions like these were taboo. You could be run out of town, strung up, or worse, left to live as an outcast that people spread falsities about for generations.

"You needn't worry. What else have you done?"

The urge to run back to her grandfather was still there. She wanted to believe that she was safe here. Her grandmother would surely protect her, but she knew of others. They were turned out by their family over much lesser acts than knowing a secret item was an acorn.

As she stood there trying to decide what she should do or how much she should share, her grandmother dug in the dirt near the stump. She pulled out a burlap bundle from a shallow hole and set it down.

"Let's take turns, shall we? You knew I held an acorn, and now you know where I keep my most precious belongings."

Isobel thought it over. She was very curious to see what was inside. There had been much to occur recently, and she hadn't been able to tell anyone. She had longed to be able to discuss it. Running seemed like the only option she could afford. She could run now away from her grandmother who obviously knew something about her she had tried to keep to herself. Or she could run later after she had been exposed at any time there was an opportunity. The only real choice was did she play along with her grandmother's game. With a heavy sigh, she chose trust. She trusted her intuition that her grandmother wanted to protect her.

"Last winter, you and grandfather gifted me with a beautiful chest."

"You already knew didn't you?"

"I thought I had overheard a conversation, but when I saw it..." She looked to her grandmother lost for an explanation.

"You recognized it." Anya reached into the bag and pulled out a vial. She turned it over in her hands almost lovingly before offering it to her granddaughter for a closer view. "It's moon water."

She held the vial in front of her face by the bottom peering closely at the liquid inside trying to see how it looked any different than other water.

Anya laughed. "It's water that was charged during a full moon." She took the vial back and set it on the stump.

They went back and forth until all the items were laid out to view. There were vials of liquid, herbs, salt, candles, and a dagger among them. Isobel looked them over trying desperately to establish a different meaning than the one that had already taken hold in her mind.

"These are the most important or most needed of all my tools," Anya said, noticing the uneasy silence from her granddaughter had stretched out.

"Tools," Isobel repeated.

Anya gathered everything back into the bag and buried it again near the stump. "I think that's enough for today. Shall we head home?"

"Enough?" Her granddaughter was still dazed and trying to find logic behind the events of the morning.

"Enough for your first lesson."

"My first lesson of what?"

"You already know. I can feel it. It's okay to speak the words."

"You're a," Isobel looked off toward the woods. She couldn't look her grandmother in the eye any longer. "A witch," she finished, barely above a whisper.

"Goodness, no," Anya replied with a smirk.

Isobel felt dizzy. The trees were turning in wide circles around her. She thought she might become sick. She sat on the stump then jumped to her feet not sure if she should.

Her grandmother placed her hands on her shoulders and gently pressed down, guiding her to sit. "It's quite alright, child. You can sit here when it's not put to use."

Not a witch she thought. She had long suspected it of herself, so hearing those words brought relief. "What are you then?"

Anya sighed and sat next to her. "That may be difficult for you to comprehend, but I will do my best."

Isobel listened as she explained that witch was the word all would use to describe them if anyone found out their truth. Witches had been around long before Anya arrived here, so it would be highly inaccurate to label themselves as such. The world had not been exposed to what she truly was yet.

"Arrived here? You mean before you were born?"

"I wasn't born. I came to earth in this form only slightly younger in appearance."

Her head swirled again. "You came here?"

Anya explained everything. She told her granddaughter her true nature and how she came to be in this realm. She also divulged the Return and how one year would be the year she never came back to her earthly home. It was a lot to take in, and Anya tried to bear that in mind. Taking caution in not going too fast, she allowed her granddaughter to ask as many questions as she needed.

"You are an Earth Elemental. In simple terms, you are a witch, but what you truly are is so much more than that."

They sat side by side while Isobel digested everything her grandmother had shared with her. These were the answers she'd been hoping to find about herself for years, but a part of her wished she was still searching for an explanation. A different explanation. She had long wanted to be normal without her intuition or dreams, and now she had the evidence proving that could never happen.

"Come," Anya said, standing. "Daniel will want his supper on time. We need to head back."

"Does he know?" Isobel asked. "Grandfather. Does he know who you are?"

"Your grandfather believes me to be a tree sprite."

Isobel's eyes widened. "He does know then."

Anya's eyes lit up in amusement. "No, child. I think he has had his own questions about me at times, but he has had the good sense to never ask anything he didn't want to know the answer to."

They walked back to the cabin and began supper. Isobel was surprised that her grandfather never said a word about the time they were gone and what they could have been doing. She thought about what her grandmother had said about not wanting to know the answers. This must be what she meant.

She had a lot on her mind all evening, well until it was almost time to retire for the night. She was an Elemental. Something like a witch, but not. It wouldn't matter if the truth were known. They would still be treated accordingly. The punishment could even be worse if they tried to claim to be something else. Something that came from the heavens above, or the spirit realm as her grandmother had called it.

There was so much on her mind that she hadn't heard her name called until her grandfather tapped her arm to get her attention. She smiled weakly at him, "Yes, grandfather?"

"What troubles you?"

"It's not troubles," she lied, hating that she couldn't tell him the truth. "I was just thinking is all, about everything and nothing."

"Tell me, young one. What has distracted you tonight?"

Isobel glanced at her grandmother, but she was no help. She was sitting by the fire mending a shirt. "It isn't just one thing," she told him truthfully.

He nodded as though he understood how thoughts could get away from you sometimes. "How was your time with your grandmother?"

Isobel looked at her again. The conversation was beginning to make her nervous that she might say the wrong thing.

"Why do you keep casting looks her way? Is there something you aren't telling me?"

Still her grandmother did nothing. It seemed like she wasn't paying any attention to them whatsoever. Her grandfather was waiting for an answer, so she said the first thing that came to her mind. "You never asked what we did in the woods for so long."

"I don't have to," he said, glancing at his wife. "I already know."

"You do?"

Her grandfather leaned in closer and in a hushed tone said, "She's a tree sprite. Did she tell you?"

"I can hear you," her grandmother finally spoke.

"Of course you can," he said, sitting upright. "You're a sprite, and I would expect nothing less from you."

Without stopping her sewing, she shook her head and sighed. Isobel could see the smile on her grandmother's face and knew she secretly enjoyed grandfather's playful actions even if she pretended to be annoyed.

"Tree sprites," her grandfather continued, "need time in the woods to be amongst their friends. It's how they stay healthy and happy. I believe you might be a sprite too."

Isobel stood up from the floor and gave her grandparents a hug goodnight. When she put her arms around her grandfather, she told him softly, "I think you are right."

It was the first night in many months Isobel did not awaken from the beast chasing her in her sleep. She didn't rouse until the first light of the morning started to brighten the house. Her grandmother lie beside her still asleep. She tiptoed to the hearth to fetch a pot for water wanting to surprise them with breakfast.

In her mind, she had come to terms with what her grandmother had shared with her about her true nature. It had been a lot to take in and would take months, even years to fully comprehend it, but she was an Elemental. That much she accepted. In her heart, she knew she was safe and loved here. This place had always been a peaceful retreat, and that belief had even deeper meaning now. In her soul, she yearned to learn more and eagerly awaited the next lesson. She couldn't wait to embrace the remaining pieces of who she really was.

She stayed with her grandparents for several weeks. Many mornings she would walk to the clearing in the woods to learn how to channel her power within. There was so much to learn, and she tried to absorb every word her grandmother spoke. Other days, they would work on potions in the house while grandfather was busy tending to business in the barn. She learned the magical uses of countless herbs. Not once was she harshly jolted from sleep again after the first night.

The time came for her to return home. Her grandfather was going to take her while grandmother stayed behind. Before leaving, her grandmother pulled her aside and gifted her with a thin leather bound book. The pages inside were all blank save for the first one where her grandmother had drawn a beautiful oak tree.

"Fit for a tree sprite," her grandmother's eyes lit up, noticing how Isobel admired it.

"Thank you. It's beautiful."

"It's a grimoire. It's for you to record your spells, potions and other notions to look back on as needed, or to pass on to your own grandchild one day. Keep it hid well."

"I promise."

If she had known this would be the last time her grandmother would share her wisdom and teach her how to control her power, she would have asked more questions. She thought she had plenty of time to learn about the elements found in nature and how to use each one. Balance between them was of the upmost importance. There would certainly be no reason to think there wouldn't be more chances to walk in the woods together, sharing ideas and bonding in their talks at the stump. There would never be a next time. There would only be a hand bound book wrapped inside a piece of material. Her father would hand it to her while telling her that her grandmother had written her name on it. The pages were blank to the unknowing eye, but a revealing spell would show the words of her grandmother's grimoire to anyone who knew how to use it.

# Chapter Fourteen

"You invited that girl to our Samhain celebration?" Grandma Eloise sounded extraordinarily irate. "I only said I wanted to meet her, not that I wanted to include her in our ceremonies."

Aunt Meredith stepped back getting out of the direct path of grandma's anger. It made it evident she would be no help in Everleigh's defense.

"I didn't realize," Everleigh began, not sure what to say to explain her actions. "Lilah's not coming," she offered, hoping it would make a difference.

"And if she could make it?" Grandma Eloise fired back. "What then? How would you explain it to your friend when you revoked the invitation?"

Everleigh sighed. It had been too long since she'd been on the receiving end of her grandma's disapproval. This was not where she wanted to be, and she hadn't expected this reaction. "I thought it would be a good idea to invite her."

That wasn't what her grandma wanted to hear. It looked like it only upset her even more. "How? Everleigh, what were you thinking?" her grandma sounded confounded.

"We want them to help, don't we? Air? We want them to join with us to fight whatever or whoever it is that's after us. They've been isolated so long they don't know us. It seemed like the right thing to do to introduce her to us...the family...as well as the ways of our Element."

Grandma Eloise turned away from her and didn't say anything. The moon water she had been harvesting for their rituals the next night was ready, and she set to work distributing it into smaller vials to pass out to the coven.

Everleigh wanted to leave the room. The quiet solitude of her bedroom was calling to her to hide out in safety, but it wasn't time yet. More was coming. She knew her grandma well enough to know this wasn't over and not to leave until she had been dismissed. The longer her grandma's silence went on the more uncomfortable she became.

They were the only ones left in the room. Aunt Meredith had slipped out undetected. Perhaps it was better than sticking around to gloat. She was the one who was usually on the crossed side of grandma, but it provided some comfort while she was there just knowing an ally was nearby. Her aunt had warned her not to invite Lilah. Everleigh had been certain that with all the strides made recently to unite the two groups, this was the logical next step. Nothing her aunt tried could talk her out of it.

"Child, I understand your heart was in the right place, but remember, they are not the only ones who put themselves into isolation. We all did. All of the Elementals agreed to keep to themselves for their own protection. Now, yes, some smaller groups here and there have been more open to mixed company," Grandma Eloise flashed a look behind Everleigh.

The sound of Aunt Meredith's wince could be felt even if it was nonverbal. Everleigh might not have been able to see her from where she stood, but her aunt was still nearby. Grandma never missed an opportunity to take at jab at her aunt's love life.

"Even so, my coven and especially here in this house, we mind our own first and foremost. Do you understand me?"

"Yes," Everleigh replied softly.

"Working together is for the benefit of us all,

and it will take some adjusting on everybody's end. That does not qualify us as friends as such. You will discuss with me any future invites and inclusions before extending the welcome."

"Yes, ma'am," Everleigh told her. "I'm sorry."

"I know you are. You need not be sorry for trying to build a bridge, only for setting to work on construction before getting the blueprints."

Everleigh understood what she meant. Many times her grandma would talk in riddles using euphemisms and analogies. This one was fairly straight forward. There was a way to heal the distance between Air and Earth, but Everleigh should ask the Elders for advice on how to go about it.

Grandma looked off out the window overtaken by her thoughts. "You feel it too, Eloise," Aunt Meredith commented, slowly walking back into the room.

Not breaking the gaze she cast at nothing in particular, Grandma Eloise nodded. "I do. Japan."

Everleigh glanced between the two women waiting and hoping one of them would fill her in, but neither of them said anything more. "What's in Japan?"

When her grandma didn't answer, her aunt turned to her, and said one word, "Volcano."

"Another one? Wasn't there just an eruption in... Iceland? Right?"

Aunt Meredith nodded.

"Earthquakes are inbound too. The southeast of the US will be rocked overnight." Grandma Eloise looked down with a heavy breath. "Not time to linger. Not now. We have preparations for tonight to get underway."

Everleigh knew the relentless increase in natural disasters was a sign of the chaos caused by the Elements having been trapped here for so long. Balance wasn't in order any longer. The

Elements needed to get home. Today was the only day of the year they could do so. Their celebration tonight would begin with blessings for a successful Return. If the Return wasn't completed, they would begin rituals for a blessed New Year.

No one knew for sure how the night would end if the Return was completed. There was no way of knowing what would happen to those remaining. They could lose their powers immediately or worse. They could cease to exist. Everleigh tried not to dwell on it as did everyone else. Nothing could stop the outcome whatever it might be. The only way to prevent anything bad from possibly happening to them would be to prevent the Return, but with the ever growing list of disasters happening every day, the planet may not last much longer. It would be better to sacrifice your own for the good of the whole.

In years past, they would be at the farmhouse outside of town where they gathered for all of their celebrations. Something was preventing them from going there this year, but as usual, Grandma Eloise wasn't being forthcoming with an explanation. It plagued Everleigh's unending curiosity, but she knew the most logical choice was almost always the right answer. Grandma was probably staying close to home for safety.

No one had an accurate count on the remaining amount of vampires, and it would be next to impossible to know for sure with the vast number who went into hiding. Their numbers had dropped substantially enough that any day now Earth could find themselves under attack. It wasn't a matter of if, but when.

The celebration would have to be at home this year. They tried their best to set up outside near the garden. It should work for the Return blessings, but it would be too cold to stay out there all night without a fire. Town ordinances dictate that's out of the question. Tonight would be too important to risk one only to have a cop show up interrupting their work.

Everleigh had participated in this ritual every year as long as she could remember. They offered all the Elements a blessing hoping for a safe Return. Water had become more and more emphasized as the years wore on since that was the only Element to never make an attempt.

Halloween was her favorite day of the year. This was their New Year. It was Samhain. This was the biggest Sabbat of their wheel. The celebration would begin tonight and continue into the next day. It was a time to remember those you've lost and honor them. Granted, the idea of a fire festival usually implied a fire. This year's celebration would be entirely different than what she had been accustomed to experiencing.

It was also the scariest day of the year. The fear had nothing to do with goblins or clown costumes. It was fear of the unknown. As much as the Return needed to be completed for the good of everyone alive, it was worrisome for the Elementals. No one had any way to know their fate. The Divine Spirit had been asked countless times over the centuries, but no answer had ever been handed down.

The best case scenario would be nothing changed for the descendants left behind. Life would continue as it always had for them with their Elements on the other side of the veil doing what they had been created to do. Balance is necessary for survival. Most people expected all powers to be stripped. Those like Everleigh would live out a mortal life no longer capable of spell casting or any other magical gifts. It was not as easy to presume where that would leave Meredith or any of the Fire Elementals. Would they become mortal and live out their life? Or would they become mortal and instantly age their actual years? It would be certain death for almost all of the Fire line.

The topic wasn't discussed by many, but most had a gnawing fear the Return would result in their disappearance as well. None of them were supposed to be here. The races of Elementals had never been planned into existence by the Divine Spirit. If all of the Elements had obeyed orders the first year, there would be no witches or werewolves, and no approaching storm intent on wiping them out. There was a chance regardless of how small or how paranoid some may think it to be. The chance remained that they could simply be obliterated by some means whether they vanish, their histories erased, or they die on the spot leaving the humans to figure out the mass deaths across the globe.

Each passing year made it more difficult for Everleigh to clear her mind during the blessings. When she was younger, it seemed more like an old wives' tale that Elements walked in human form and were her ancestors. Now, she knew the stories to be true. The Return was real, and the lingering questions never got easier.

With the Return blessings completed, they decided to go ahead with the ritual spell casting outside before coming in for the celebrations. Grandma Eloise disappeared inside for a few moments and came out with her shawl. It was a family heirloom. A great-grandmother somewhere down the line had been the one to knit it. The only time Everleigh ever saw her grandma wear it was at Samhain.

The spells didn't take long, and soon they took turns making offerings to their dearly departed loved ones before going inside. Grandma Eloise always went last, spending ample time communicating with her late husband. It was both heart breaking and romantic knowing her love for him was still so strong.

Between the nightfall and the nearby houses and trees, it was nearly pitch black in the backyard without a fire. Everleigh peered out the window, but couldn't make out her grandma's silhouette amongst the darkness. It was probably for the best. Even as she gazed out over the backyard, she knew her grandma would rather have total privacy anyway.

When her grandma made her way in to join the others, she was clutching her rubino pendant in her hand. Words weren't necessary. Grandma Eloise's face gave the answer of whether the Return had been a success.

"Water again?" asked Aunt Meredith.

It was the obvious choice. Water had never shown for a Return in the last millennium. Water was the reason it had never been successful. There were many years, as many as half if not more, where Fire went rogue and skipped out. It didn't make a difference since Water never showed either.

Grandma Eloise solemnly lifted her face to meet Meredith's eyes than cast her eyes around the living room at everyone. "Fire."

That's it. One word was more than enough. Grandma gave no more explanation than that. It was all that needed to be said.

A collective gasp went through the group. There would be much to discuss as the night wore on. It was not unheard of for Fire to be absent, but three of the Elements had made a pack last year. They resolved to see to it that Water be located and brought to the Return regardless of whatever it might take to accomplish the feat.

There was an uneasy foreboding that cast a shadow over the mood in the room. It was known by all present that the vampires were being hunted with members of Earth soon to follow. Fire had vowed to help bring Water to the Return. The absence left the fear that something had befallen Fire. Fire's immortality was not limited, but detainment could be a possibility.

Grandma Eloise walked into the hall placing her pendant on the end table near the sofa as she went. An act that did not go unnoticed.

"Get ahold of Jackson. Now, Everleigh," Aunt Meredith ordered.

Everleigh already had her cell phone in hand sending a text to Lilah that the Return failed. That was all the information she was giving out until she was told otherwise. After the trouble she caused inviting Lilah over tonight, she wasn't taking any risks. It struck a guilty note promising to let Lilah know if she learned more when there was already information she was withholding from her.

Next she messaged Jackson telling him the same thing without divulging it was Fire who didn't show. He would be home alone, and it would be hard to say what would happen when he lost control from the news. They wouldn't be able to keep him from finding out for long, but it bought them some time to figure out what to do.

While she was looking at her phone, she didn't see what had happened until the screaming started. The shock made her jump so hard her phone almost went flying. Everleigh looked up just in time to see Grandma Eloise violently yanking her pendant out of Aunt Meredith's hands.

"Bold move considering how thin the ice is beneath your feet around me, Meredith!" Grandma Eloise bellowed.

"I'm sorry," Aunt Meredith began. "My curiosity got the better of me. No one knows anything about Water."

"Save it. Your words are meaningless. You know better than to touch this stone."

Something about what Eloise said to her

struck a nerve. "You know better than to forget some of us know more of your secrets than others," Meredith threatened.

"Get out!" Eloise screamed, pointing to the door.

Meredith stood motionless. Her mouth gaped open as though she honestly hadn't expected her actions to come to this result.

"Now!" Eloise cried out again.

Meredith began gathering her belongings to leave. "You know what to do," she said to Everleigh, before heading to the front door.

"I'll go to him," she promised her aunt, hoping her grandma would allow it.

"No. It has to be Lilah."

"Are you sure?" Everleigh had every reason to doubt it was a good idea. Lilah was still in the dark about too much.

Aunt Meredith paused with her hand on the front door and looked directly at her niece. "She's his anchor."

Everleigh nodded, and she began to understand what her aunt meant by it. She fervently began texting her friends. There was no way she would be allowed out of the house this evening. Not only was it supposed to be a time of celebration, but her grandma would surely try to prevent her from running after her aunt.

She let Lilah know it was Fire who didn't show to the Return then invited her out again. Figuring Lilah's family would be hard pressed to let her go to her boyfriend's on the night of a failed Return, Everleigh invited her over to her house. If Air thought she was coming here, they may allow it hoping for shared updates on the events. Her plan worked.

Next, she had to send Jackson to pick her up with specific instructions to follow. They needed a way to make sure her thoughts were blocked without letting on that Jackson knew anything about Lilah's abilities. This secret keeping was becoming exhausting. Lilah needed to tell him about her family soon. There were worlds of information that couldn't be discussed around her until she made the first move by opening up to him.

Once everything was arranged, she looked at the spot where her grandma had set the pendant down not long ago. Thinking her grandma had gone upstairs, she walked closer and pictured the pendant as grandma had placed it. It was too perfect. The pendant had never left her grandma's neck before tonight. It was certainly not something she would casually set down and walk away. Catching Meredith red handed. It was like a perfectly baited trap, but to what end? Grandma could kick her aunt out at any time. In fact, she had kicked her out too many times to count.

There had to be a reason for this display of odd events tonight. Everleigh tried hard to decipher the clues. It could be something Meredith needed to see in the pendant. Maybe there was something grandma didn't want the others to know yet. The only other place her aunt had to go is the farmhouse. Todd was her only ally in town. It could have been a plan to get her over there, but why?

Grandma Eloise's voice jumped into her thoughts. "Haven't I told you? No sense worrying over what you don't know. All will reveal itself in time."

"Grandma, I didn't see you," Everleigh muttered, throwing her hand to her chest where her heart was beating fast from being startled. It confirmed what she had been thinking. There was more to it than what lay on the surface.

"Obviously," her grandma said wryly.

"I thought you went upstairs," Everleigh told her.

"What? And miss the party?" Grandma waved an arm around the room where everyone's tone had turned serious discussing the news of the Return and Meredith's departure.

Everleigh snickered. "It's certainly one to remember."

"Are they together?"

It was a strange question, and it took a moment for Everleigh to understand who she meant. "Yes, or will be soon if not."

"Good. It won't be long until Jackson learns for himself. He will need her."

"What if she's not there when he finds out?"

Grandma Eloise watched her family and coven members as they tried to work out what the night's events could mean. "We better pray no one is nearby if that happens."

Everleigh's eyes widened hearing it said so directly. It was the one thing she feared most, but she knew her grandma was not wrong.

"I'm going to bed. It's been a long day and an even longer night. You might want to wrap the party up early. I don't think anyone would really mind this year."

"Good night, grandma," Everleigh forced a smile, hugging her.

---

Meredith arrived at the farmhouse and went to the shed where Luke had been living since Eloise forced her to move him out of the attic. No one had ordered him to stay out of the house like this. It was suggested by Luke when they first arrived here asking for help. The house was too crowded already, and it would probably be better all-around for him to keep a little distance from them just to keep everyone calm about their new guest. Luke hadn't been too keen about coming here anyway given past relations between Fire and Air.

Bygones should stay bygones, but it's never easy to forget. It had been an uneventful couple of days for him. Everyone had been pleasant even inviting him inside for meals. It didn't change anything. Luke wanted this over as soon as possible. They had been moving quite often to keep him safe. The plan had originally been to leave after the Return attempt, but with the news Meredith now had, it wouldn't be so easy.

The shed was empty. Meredith called out quietly, but there was no answer. Looking around, it appeared like he had a better deal than the others in the house. At least he had more privacy then the rest of them.

Meredith emerged from the shed, but paused when she recognized a familiar sound. It was Jackson's pickup she heard even though he was probably still at the edge of town. The one item in the vamp's toolbox she was most thankful for besides immortality is heightened senses. She stepped back inside the shed relieved Everleigh had been able to get these two together tonight.

Jackson didn't know yet any of the details about the Return attempt. If he saw her, he'd know it had come to pass already. There'd be no reason for Meredith to not be at Eloise's otherwise. Meredith couldn't risk him asking questions. The boy had trouble keeping control of his emotions on a good day, and the news about Fire and Water would certainly upset him.

The farmhouse would honestly be the best

location for him to lose it now that she considered it. The hoard of Air out of here would be able to contain him. If their psychic strength couldn't do it, then their shapeshifting abilities would allow them to turn into something far fiercer than he could ward off.

Lilah needs to tell him the truth already. It's like ripping off a band aid. Do it and get it over with, so no one has to walk on eggshells any longer. Jackson already knows. He knows exactly who Lilah is and everything about Air. Everyone has to do a song and dance routine around her because Lilah just came into her abilities full strength. Her family is worried about what would happen if she got too upset since she has not yet learned how to control them. All hail, Lilah, the delicate flower.

Jackson pulled up to the house, and it didn't take long before they were on their way. Lilah bounded out the door before he even made it to the steps. Meredith left the cover of the shed and headed to the house sending Everleigh a text as she went. It wouldn't be long before the young lovebirds were at Jackson's house. He needed to learn what happened while Lilah was there. Their connection would keep him subdued.

Meredith didn't have a chance to knock on the door before it swung open.

"Took you long enough," Luke smiled at her. "I was beginning to think you were going to wait in the shed for me all night."

"I wanted to wait until Jackson left, so he didn't ask any questions about the Return," Meredith explained, walking inside.

Luke led her toward the kitchen where he had been chatting with Todd at the table. "Yeah, I heard about Fire and Water."

"There's more to it than that," she said, pulling out a chair to join them.

Both men watched her waiting to hear what she had to say. "What happened?" Luke asked when she didn't volunteer any additional updates.

"Even though Fire didn't show, there were still four people present," she said, nodding at Todd who was hand-signaling to ask if she wanted anything to drink.

Todd poured his guest a glass of tea and set it in front of her. "Four?" he repeated, wanting to make sure he heard right.

"Five if you count Leena," she told him.

The mouths on both of them gaped opened and their eyes widened. Meredith could hear the gasps from the other room where Air was paying close attention to their conversation either eavesdropping or reading Todd's mind. She didn't mind. It would be better for everyone to hear it all at once than have to answer a lot of questions later.

"I don't know who the other person was. I didn't get a good look, but it wasn't anyone I've ever seen."

"Wait. What look? You weren't there, were you?" Luke asked.

"No," Meredith exhaled and leaned back in her chair, tapping her coffee cup with her fingernail. "Eloise left her pendant unattended."

Todd's head jerked sharply. "That's not typical of Eloise."

"I know. That's how I knew she wanted me to look," Meredith agreed. "But she didn't give me enough time before she pretended to catch me and kick me out."

"What did you see?" Luke asked.

Meredith sipped her tea and shook her head. "Only a snippet. I saw Marcus and Leena, Anya, and the one I assume was Water. They were discussing Fire's absence, and Water was angry because there was something that had been kept secret. I'm not sure. Like I said, it was only a quick glance."

"You said there were five people," Todd urged.

"Yeah, that's when the fifth came from nowhere and grabbed Water. Marcus and Leena moved in to help then all four of them disappeared through the same portal leaving Anya on her own. The portal closed before Anya could go through it."

Luke's gaze never left the table, but he tilted his chin toward her. "What happened to Anya? Is she stuck there?"

Meredith and Todd looked at each other knowingly. "Each Element has their own portal," Todd explained.

"That would provide reason for Marcus' absence," Luke thought out loud. "If he went through a different portal, then who knows where he wound up."

"I didn't see what happened because that's when Eloise snatched the pendant from me," Meredith added.

"Then she kicked you out," Todd nodded, "knowing you would come here."

"Exactly. I would come here to update Luke about Fire, and your family about Marcus and Leena," Meredith said softly.

"Thank you, Meredith," Todd crossed his arms on the table. "Unfortunately, this leaves us with more questions than answers."

Luke sat up in his chair, "Hold on. Before we get to the heavy hitting stuff, why was Leena there? I didn't know the Elements could bring guests."

Meredith snickered then bit her lip. His oblivious nature helped to lighten the mood.

Todd sighed and shrugged. "I'm not sure they are allowed, but we've long believed that Leena would want to join Marcus when the Return occurred. That is why she was present, I'm sure."

"The real question is this mystery person. Who

could it possibly be?" Meredith wondered.

"That, and does this have anything to do with the halt of the wolf movement. Did whether Water made the Return or not have anything to do with their plans?" Todd said with conviction.

# Chapter Fifteen

"Now what?" Luke asked, following Meredith onto the porch of the farmhouse later that night.

"We have to find Fire."

Luke nodded slowly and turned his face to her while staring at the road at the end of the driveway. Something had caught his eye, but he couldn't see anything out of place. Probably just an animal. The property was so overrun with wildlife, and the squirrels were almost friendly. "Yes, but how?"

"You can't sense him?"

"No. I'm not from his line."

Meredith stopped and stared at him perplexed. "He is the first vampire to ever actually exist. You're a natural, not created. How can you not be from his line?"

"You know what I mean. I'm too far down the line to be considered a close descendant of his. Biologically speaking, he's like my great times three grandfather. We're too distant."

They walked toward the shed hesitantly. Both feeling the urge to leave and do something to find out more, but neither quite sure as to what.

"Do you think something happened to him?" Meredith asked. It was on everyone's mind. It had to be. Fire had shunned the Return attempts many times before. Maybe he didn't know Water had been found. It wasn't hard to assume Fire just bailed on it again.

"Of course something happened to him. What kind of question is that?" Luke sneered.

Meredith sighed and sat on the hand me down furniture that had been scavenged to make Luke's home in the shed more comfortable. "How sure are you he was planning on attending this year?"

"I talked to him a few days ago. He told me Water had been located. It looked like it was pretty certain Marcus would manage to get Water to the Return. This was to be the year."

Meredith was shocked. He'd never told her about this until now. It almost hurt that he'd keep something so monumental from her.

"Don't look at me like that. Fire made me vow to keep it to myself just in case."

"Just in case?"

Luke walked over to a basket by his mattress, digging through his clothes. Pulling out a sweatshirt, he gave it a sniff and shrugged. It'd have to do. "Yeah," he said, yanking the sweatshirt over his head. The night had grown considerably colder since he went up to the house earlier. "In case the wrong person found out."

It was the worst between the Elementals now than Meredith could remember. No one knew who to trust anymore, but she had a feeling she knew who the wrong person was that Fire meant. No one had any luck in tracking her down yet.

"I'm not saying you would've said anything," Luke told her directly, worried her silence meant she took it personally.

"No, not me," she took his hand. "But people do talk. I would've told Eloise and Everleigh."

"And they would've told others. Well, maybe not Eloise," Luke smiled to ease the mood.

"Let's figure this out then. We know the wolves are involved. There are eye witness accounts from some of the attacks clearly accusing them, but Water was at the Return."

"And Fire wasn't," Luke dug into the dirt floor with his shoe. "What about Jackson?"

She raised her eyebrows. "What about him?" There was no way Luke could think he was behind this.

"Couldn't you do your itchy witchy voodoo on

Fire to find out anything?"

Meredith rolled her eyes so hard she thought she pulled a muscle. It irritated her when he made light of it even after all these years, and even though she knew he was playing around.

Suddenly, she sat up straight. "Wait. You might be on to something."

Luke looked confused. "I am? How? You never completed the transformation. I didn't think it was enough to use your magic on him."

Meredith was already on her feet pacing the shed thinking it over in her mind. It had never been tried before, not exactly like this, but it had to work.

"Are you going to fill me in?"

"Shush. I can't think with you talking so much," Meredith scowled.

He slunk back on his mattress and waited.

If she could get Lilah in on the spell, it might work. She could use Jackson to connect to Lilah's psychic ability. It would be tricky getting it done without tripping over someone's secrets. Lilah was a baby who didn't know much of her own ancestry yet let alone anyone else's, and she certainly didn't know how much her boyfriend knew already.

She sank back down on the used chair about to give up. "Lilah is the key, but how do I use her in a spell?" Meredith asked out loud, more to herself than Luke.

"Use all the Elements," Luke quickly answered.

Meredith sat up straight intrigued. "What?"

Luke rolled to his side and propped up on his elbow. "I'm guessing you want to use the bond she has with Jackson. Bring along me and Everleigh as well. Have all the Elements present."

"Except Lilah doesn't know anything about Jackson yet."

Slowly, Luke sat up and threw his legs over the

edge onto the makeshift plywood flooring covering the dirt floor below his bed. "Yeah, so tell her he represents humans. She doesn't have to know any different."

Biting her lower lip, she was reminded why she loved this man. "I'd need a wolf for her to buy it."

Luke stood up and reached for her, pulling her out of the chair. Wrapping his arms around her waist, he whispered, "And I just happen to know where one is."

Meredith pushed away from him excitedly. "They're here? Already?"

"Only a couple so far, but I'm sure Matt would help us out."

She rubbed her hands together. "Let's do this then."

Luke nodded and pulled out his phone to make a call.

While he was talking, the sound of Jackson's pickup could be heard again. Meredith walked to the shed doors and peaked out. Talk about bad timing. The one person who was most important in the success of this spell besides her was returning home. It was a miracle her family ever let her leave the way they were so overprotective of their kind.

Lilah wasn't out of the pickup before Meredith was on the phone with Everleigh. "Hey, I need a favor."

"Weird. I need one from you too."

Meredith laughed. "Listen. I need you to get your friend Lilah out of the house."

"I did! She's with Jackson."

"Was with Jackson. He just dropped her off. Everleigh, we're going to experiment with magic tonight. All of the Elements will be represented. That's why we need her. Well, one of the reasons anyway."

"I like the sound of that," Everleigh said with glee in her voice.

*'I bet you do,'* Meredith thought. *'That grandma of yours never lets you have fun with it.'*

"It's not going to be easy getting her out of the house again," Meredith warned her. "Sneak her out if you have to and meet me at Jackson's."

"Sure. Where does she live?"

"You know the place. The farmhouse in the country where the coven meets."

There was silence on the other end of the line.

Meredith's eyes closed and slowly rolled up in her head. *'I forgot this girl barely knows more than Lilah. I'll need to come up with an explanation for this before the night is over, or Eloise might just make good on all the threats she's ever slung my way.'*

Ignoring the silence and the questions she knew her niece must have, Meredith went on, "Just make sure you ask her where she lives. You know... Keep up the pretense."

"Okay," Everleigh said.

The tone of her voice had changed drastically, and Meredith knew it was her fault. "What did you need?" she asked, hoping to change her mood.

"Huh?"

"You said you needed a favor."

"Oh, yeah, I wanted to know what was up with the song and dance routine you and grandma pulled with the pendant."

Meredith grinned. This was why she loved her so much. There might be some things kept from her for her own good, but it wasn't an easy task. She was observant and figured things out easily. "Later. I promise I will tell you everything I'm able to."

Everleigh's sigh was audible over the phone. "Fine. I'll see you soon."

Luke was waiting for the call to end. "Matt said he and Rita would be happy to come by and help out. They were hoping to start meeting people soon, but hadn't expected it to be this quick," he laughed.

"Good. I have to stop by Eloise's and pick up something for this to work."

"Do you think she'll give you any trouble?"

"No, I doubt it. The old woman is probably in bed anyway, and if she knows what I'm up to-"

"She does. I bet she knew before you did that you were going to attempt this tonight."

Meredith hung her bag on her shoulder and tried to keep from grinning. "You're not wrong. Eloise is many things and likes to present a rather old school front where the Elements are concerned, but don't cross Fire off her list of ally's. You might be surprised to learn exactly how far she'd go for him."

"Oh, I know they have history, but she wouldn't want Everleigh to suspect a thing."

Meredith opened the door of the shed and stepped out in the moonlight. "That's why we wait until she's gone, and we know she has Lilah safely delivered back to Jackson's house."

They walked to her car and hopped in. Meredith threw it in reverse and carefully backed around the half dozen or so other cars parked around the house. It looked almost like there was a party. "Does Jackson know yet? About the Return?" she asked, putting the car in drive to head down to the road.

Luke inhaled slowly. "It might be good to find that out before we ambush him like this."

"You think?"

Taking their time to drive the short distance to Eloise's house, Luke called Jackson who answered on the first ring.

"Hey, I was just thinking about getting ahold of you."

"You were?" Luke was surprised. He and Jackson were friendly, but they didn't associate much.

"Yeah. You hear about the Return yet?"

Slowly inhaling deeply, Luke said, "I did," fully expecting to be the one to fill Jackson in on all the details. He shot Meredith a look and shook his head letting her know Jackson was still in the dark. It wouldn't be safe to do it on the phone. They'd have to wait until Lilah arrived, and that would create yet another logistical nightmare maneuvering around her in private. He figured this was coming. Jackson's mood was too elevated for him to know the outcome of the Return already.

"Crazy, isn't it? Water finally showing up and all."

"Wait." Luke leaned forward as far as the seat belt would let him. "You mean you've heard? When did you find out?"

"Earlier when Lilah was over. I hadn't been able to get ahold of my dad which made me worry even though it's nothing new. I snuck off to the kitchen to get us drinks and asked Everleigh about it real quick."

'He knows,' Luke mouthed the words to Meredith while Jackson was still talking.

"How's he doing?" she whispered.

Luke shrugged several times and shook his head not knowing how to answer the question. Jackson seemed perfectly fine, but he shouldn't be.

"Alright, well, you're in for more guests. Several of us including your girly friend are on our way. Need to use your house for a spell," Luke chuckled, finding the play on words funnier than it was.

"A spell? An actual spell?"

"Yeah."

"With Lilah?" Jackson's voice deepened and grew louder.

"Got to go. Don't worry. Meredith has

everything covered."

Luke rolled his head back and closed his eyes dropping the phone in his lap. "He had more emotion over Lilah being present for the spell than he did when talking about the Return."

Meredith drove past Eloise's house, but her niece's car was still parked out front. Instead of stopping, she parked farther down the street to stay out of sight until she could sneak in to get what she needed. "I'm not surprised."

"Really? Well, could you explain it to me then?"

"It's an Air thing. Lilah keeps him calm. She grounds him. When he's concerned for her, that's another story. The beast in him will defend her without question."

Everleigh darted out of the house straight to her car unaware of the audience watching her not far away.

"How long do you think this will take?"

Meredith unbuckled and reached for the handle, waiting for Everleigh to drive out of sight before exiting the car. "Not long. Fill Todd in while I'm in here, would you? He should be there too."

"What if Eloise finds out you're here?"

A devilish smile slowly appeared on her face, "She already knows."

Everleigh's car made the turn toward the main road at the end of the street.

Leaning over to give Luke a quick kiss before getting out, Meredith said, "I can sense her watching me."

Luke looked at the house that was dark save for one downstairs light. "Think she'll cause you any grief while you're in there?"

"No," Meredith answered quickly, opening the door.

"How are you so sure?"

Meredith got out and before she shut the door behind her, she said, "Because she's showing me where it is."

---

"Do you think it was smart to let Lilah leave like that? Won't Jackson be a problem without her?" Matt asked, staring out the window waiting for Jackson to return like he had been since they left. "He should be back by now. You don't think he's out looking for Fire on his own, do you?"

"Calm down. Jackson is taking his medication, and I made sure to slip him something extra tonight thinking he may need it," Meredith offered, hoping no one would treat him any differently when he came home which wouldn't be long as she could hear the truck rumbling down the road.

"Lilah's the problem," Luke countered.

Everleigh raised her hand. "I second that."

"Stop. What do you mean, Everleigh? I thought she was your friend?" her aunt asked, wishing they'd drop the topic with Jackson right outside.

"She is a friend. It's just a pain... I mean doesn't anybody see a problem with this? I was excited! I was ready to come in here, guns blazing. Yeah! We're going to do this multi-Elemental spell. I couldn't wait for it to go down. Luckily, right before we got out of the car, she let me know she was worried about Jackson finding out anything. I had to send Jackson a text to make sure we were on the same page with her."

"And we are," Jackson piped in, walking in the door.

Everleigh ignored the interruption unfazed by his heightened hearing. Jackson had been eavesdropping on her conversations since junior high. "Her own uncle had to wait outside for us to sneak him in after she closed her eyes."

"That was Todd's idea," Meredith pointed out.

"That's not the point!" Everleigh jumped to her feet. "Everybody in this room is an Elemental. More than one of you have multiple blood lines. Why can't she just know already?"

No one said anything. Everleigh waited, hoping someone would see it her way. "Would it be so bad if Jackson came clean? Instead of waiting for Lilah to share her secret, let's have Jackson go first. It could work to open her up."

"You didn't tell her yet?" Luke looked at Meredith.

Everleigh crossed her arms and stared down her aunt, "Tell me what?"

"Air is worried, and I don't mean in their typical overprotective way. Lilah's powers have already proven to be much more significant than anyone else's except Marcus."

"I know that much. Their powers usually unfold in a slow progression, but hers came instantly because she met Jackson, right?"

"Yes, there's that, and she doesn't know how to control them yet."

Everleigh sat back down feeling defeated. "There's more, isn't there?"

"Lilah is capable of doing things that it took others of their kind years... I'm talking decades or longer to figure out. Plus some things that the others can't do at all."

"Like what?" Rita joined in, curious to hear more.

"Blocking her family for one thing. It took the rest of them years to learn that. Lilah did it instinctively. It's both natural for her and something she doesn't understand. They had to teach her how to turn it back on, so they could stay connected. Even then, most of the time, it doesn't work. They pretend they can read her to keep her from freaking out, wondering why she's different."

Jackson played with the trim on the edge of the couch. "And there's the cries for help."

"You know about that?" Meredith asked softly, knowing the answer already. It never occurred to her until now how deep their connection might run.

"I hear them too. Sometimes."

Meredith scanned the room and saw the questioning faces on everyone else wondering what cries they were talking about. "All these natural disasters that have been happening. Air can hear cries for help. They can help with a kidnapped child or someone lost in the woods. Lilah is awakened in the middle of the night because the voices of the victims of these disasters all across the globe are so loud in her head. Her own mom can't hear the victims halfway around the world if she focuses all her energy on it."

"They're worried about the strength of her powers. It's not a good time to test them with everything else going on right now. Until they know more, they're trying to be careful around her."

"Speaking of natural disasters," Matt said, looking out the window. "I didn't see this in the forecast. Is this... I don't know. Looks like a tornado could be forming."

Everyone made their way to the windows to watch the storm that sprang up unexpectedly. All but Jackson who continued sitting quietly on the couch. It didn't go unnoticed by Meredith who went to him and quietly asked, "Lilah?"

Looking like he was holding back tears, Jackson nodded.

Meredith sat next to him. "Don't worry,

sweetie. We'll figure it out," she lied. She had already spent many hours discussing Lilah with Todd, and they hadn't been able to come up with anything to help tame her.

# Chapter Sixteen

Daniel's health took a turn for the worse as soon as winter took hold in his sixty-seventh year. Anya worked tirelessly to care for everything especially him. All of the work fell on her because most days he was unable to even leave the bed. She did it without complaint. There were times where she would have liked to have a grandchild or two come stay to aide her in the chores, but she knew her sons required the hands for their own work that needed done.

She would lovingly care for him. Somedays when he was his weakest, she would sit on the bed and feed him. She tried every cure that was known at the time including some of her own. Nothing worked, and she knew they wouldn't before she made each attempt. That didn't stop her from trying. When she touched him, she could see what lay ahead. His days were counting down, but she had to try for his benefit. She would not have him depart this earth thinking she hadn't done everything she could for him.

There was always a line she had to walk. Notices could be sent to her children letting them know that their father was dying, but she didn't know how she would explain it. Daniel insisted on not bothering them because he would be fine. This illness would pass just as every previous one he'd ever had. He told her this each time she mentioned gathering the children for a visit. Every plan she devised to have the family come by or even just one child's family over for a time would be shot down. He wanted to wait until he was recovered. No need in worrying someone when there wasn't anything to worry about is what he would tell her.

Except there was cause for worry only she couldn't express her reasons behind it. She did as she was asked and tended the home and land as best as she could while caring for him under the guise that she too believed any day now he would recover. Humans had done this long before she arrived. They lived knowing the sun would rise and tomorrow would come. They lived believing they would always be here to see it, but it wasn't the case. People would pass on to the spirit world with so much they could have done to prepare for their departure left untouched. And so it was that Daniel would soon cross the veil as well.

Two days before he passed, he was well enough to sit at the table for the first time in a couple weeks. He believed it was proof that he was on his way to full health, and she tried to mirror his certainty. It was only the calm before the storm. There is often a peace before the eventuality of death rears its dark face.

Those two days were remarkable ones filled with laughter and reminiscing about their life together. To anyone who didn't have the foresight she possessed, Daniel indeed looked to be improving and would soon be recovered. Anya would have given anything to have that blind ignorance. Instead she was forced to carry on the ruse while her heart ached to take him into her arms and hold him for the remainder of his hours.

In time, she would learn that many people wished to know the hour a loved one would breathe their last. They think it would make a difference in how they lived the last of their days. Anya would go on to live this reality out over and over during her time in the physical world. The knowledge that the end was near never offered any comfort to her. With Daniel, as well as future lives she would experience, she could never let it be known that she knew what was coming.

All of her secrets had to be kept hidden from those who loved her to keep them safe. Anya rarely worried about what would happen to her if anyone accused her of witchcraft. She could manage to escape. It was her family's survival that concerned her. If her truth were to ever be revealed, the accusations wouldn't stop with her. Many innocent people in her family would suffer the consequences.

Times would change. There would come a day when she wouldn't have to keep her abilities a secret from her loved ones any longer. Even then, this knowledge of the final days would be her burden to bear alone. The truth is people would regret knowing when the last moment will come because it would cast a shadow over those last days. There can be no normal when you know what's going to happen. The person facing their final departure doesn't want their last moments filled with visitors who would not be there for any other reason if not their demise. They want to live their last as they had lived the rest. Anya would learn this lesson the hard way by letting her secret known down the road and watching all the fair weather folks pour in pretending they cared.

The night he died, Anya lay awake by his side holding his hand with her head resting gently on his chest. She listened to each breath knowing soon it would be his last one. A quiet took over him, and she thought he had gone. There was one last ragged, loud, heavy intake after that, and Daniel was gone. She wept. She clung to him and sobbed until sleep finally took her. When she awoke in the morning, she set about the preparations to say goodbye to Daniel and the rest of her family.

Anya had spent all of her years worried about what if something happened to her. She knew one day the Return would be complete, and her family would never have the answers to her disappearance. There was always a chance of someone learning her secret, and what would happen to her family then. They may have been able to escape death, but that was not a guarantee. At best, they would be exiled, but she often wondered if Daniel would still want her after learning she wasn't too far from the tree sprite he had always called her.

She never gave it any thought that she may one day outlive him until he became ill. There were options open to her of course. She could continue this life for a long time if she chose. This winter showed her that she did not want to continue here without him because it would be too painful. There was no assurance the Return this year would be completed, and she didn't want to wait to find out.

Once news of Daniel's death was announced and his body prepared to be laid to rest, her family would be dealt a second blow. They would learn of her demise as well. She felt guilty and selfish for leaving now, but she tried to convince herself it would be easier in the long term for them. It would also ease the burden of having to care for her in her old age. It wouldn't be necessary of course, just a guise she'd have to put on to alleviate questions.

The long winter days were partially spent planning how she would pull off her exit. Parts of it were easy. The potion to return her looks to the youthful beauty she once had was already made and tested. It would be easy to leave and start over afar where no one would recognize her. There were stores of supplies already packed up that would be easy enough to carry since she would have to leave the horse and wagon behind. All evidence of her true self were cleared out and buried save for the grimoire she wanted Isobel to own.

The hard part had been deciding exactly how she would pretend to meet her end. There were a number of spells and potions she could use that would render her in a near death state, but it was all too risky. If she was put into the ground before the enchantment wore off, she would be a prisoner. She knew she couldn't die, but she didn't want to learn how spending an eternity in a grave would feel either. Someday, she would surely be found, but how long would it take?

There was also the option of passing someone off as herself. She toyed with charms that would make others see her persona in the face of a stranger, but even that was tricky. If she were supposed to be a corpse, who would be the one making sure the potion was drunk by those present? She would need a second charm to work on herself to make her unrecognizable and would need a reason why this stranger was in the home of Daniel and Anya.

It also never sat well with her to try to pass another off as herself. Nearby towns were filled with beggars who oft were discovered dead in the passageways from illness, poverty or exposure. It could be easy enough to snag a body that would suit her purposes. These unwanted members of the town were usually piled together in shared graves outside the town's boundaries. Sometimes the holes would lie open filled with rotting corpses for months before someone would fill it with dirt. There was always a need to create less mass graves by piling as many as possible together.

Some people would discard the bodies themselves if they lay unmoved for too long. A few decent folk would dig a grave, but sadly most just dumped the bodies into the river. Anya could ensure one poor soul would at least obtain a proper burial. These beggars already had been dealt a hard lot in life, and she believed it wrong to strip them of the one thing they owned: their identity. Not that a mass grave would be marked, but at least there wouldn't be anyone mistaken who was buried there for someone else.

Perhaps it was because she spent her entire human life worried about her family's pain when she vanished with the Return, but it made more sense to simply disappear. The one thing she needed to see to was that she wouldn't want her family looking for her wrought with worry and hoping she may one day return. She would have to stage an accident, and that's exactly what she prepared to do. They would mourn her never knowing how she secretly rowed away in a boat down the river to begin again anew.

As word traveled about Daniel, Anya left their home late that night to set her plan into motion. She drove the horse and wagon several miles from home opposite of the way her children would arrive. It would appear as though she were headed to the basilica. She guided Daniel's horse to a stop with ease. She was much more skilled then when she first tried to lead Daniel's mare shortly after they met.

Anya unhooked and rubbed him down gently. She could sense the horse understood what she was about to do. Putting her fingers in her mouth, she let out a whistle. The steed raised up on hind legs and came back down hard. She smacked his leg quarter sending him off in a gallop. It would find his way back home, and it would be what sent her children looking for her. They would search north of the house first then the woods where she loved to wander for hours before they turned their attention to the road to the south where they would find the wagon in need of repairs.

She looked along the edge of the roadway and found a large rock which she used to beat a wheel off disabling the wagon. This would make an accident look more believable as well as deter any would be thieves from easily taking the wagon for themselves. In her bag was an old dress. Earlier she had sliced her hand and allowed the blood to drip and spray across the front. She ripped pieces off it and scattered all the bits of cloth, leading whoever investigates the scene on a path into the trees.

Happy with her work, she removed a small vial from the folds of her dress. Knowing her children would believe she had been thrown from the wagon and killed in the fall, she gulped the liquid. They would find her ripped clothing and see it as evidence some form of wild animal carried her remains off into the dense woods. There would be a short scouting mission to try to find what may be left of her, but it would be called off quickly she thought as she felt the wrinkled lines in her face smooth and soften.

It would comfort them knowing she didn't have to continue on long after losing her husband. Touching the side of the wagon, she could picture Young Daniel standing with his brothers as they decided there would be no place their mother would rather be more than reunited with their father. Theirs had been a special type of love that never wavered. It strengthened every day since the night he rescued his tree sprite from the woods near his home.

The bundle of supplies she brought was lightweight and carried easily strapped around her shoulder. A short distance down the road, she entered the tree line to head to the river. There were a couple miles of woods to cut through before she would come upon the boat owned by her love. It was the same boat they used to travel to these parts from their first home. They hadn't used it for years not since their age bested them.

It wouldn't be a problem for her now. All of her aches and pains were gone. Her gait was light and easy over the tree covered ground. She started to spin, looking up through the trees at the moon cutting through the branches above. Even with a heavy heart, she smiled and laughed softly feeling once again at home amongst the tall guardians. If anyone had spied her, they might have believed they just saw a tree sprite with their very own eyes.

# Chapter Seventeen

"Still nothing from Lilah?" Everleigh asked.

"Not since our brief call this afternoon when she told me she just woke up." Jackson's face was filled with worry.

"Alright. Let's do this."

"Are you sure this will work?" Jackson wanted to be hopeful.

Meredith laughed nervously. "In theory, yes, but I've only attempted something like this one other time, and you were there." It should work. If she could use Lilah's psychic connection with Jackson to boost a locator spell, then Jackson should work as a conduit to reach Lilah. They would soon find out if her theory was correct.

The four of them held hands. Meredith, Luke, Everleigh, Jackson and back to Meredith just as she instructed. The two witches between the two men. "Jackson, close your eyes. I need you to focus on Lilah."

"I am."

"I need you to do more than just think about her. Open your mind to me and Everleigh, and try to connect with Lilah at the same time."

Jackson did as he was told not confident this would work. He was not a psychic or a mind reader. He possessed no magic powers like the women in the room held. Lilah was home in bed. Every time he thought of her, that's what he saw. It didn't feel right, but he couldn't push through to learn more than where she was.

Several minutes had passed, and he was just about to let go of their hands when Meredith announced, "That's it. I got her."

He continued to wait not sure if they were

done.

"Something's wrong," Meredith uttered.

That was enough for him. Jackson's eyes tore open. "What's wrong?" he was practically yelling. He yanked his hands away from the others and clasped them on top of his head. Pacing back and forth near the others, he concentrated on controlled deep breaths in and out, but never took his eyes off of Meredith.

"I can't be sure now that our link to her has broken," Meredith stated. There was no missing the irritation in her voice.

"What link?" he asked, working himself up to a full frenzy forgetting his breathing techniques. "I don't understand how this works. I'm not an Air!"

"Breathe," Everleigh stepped in front of him. "It's like Aunt Meredith said. You're her match. The two of you are linked. We can use you to see her."

It still didn't make full sense to him. For years, he'd been told the Elementals were limited in what effect they had on other groups. Now, Meredith had conducted spells twice in a row that worked on other factions. When they learned last night Fire was in town, it almost made sense. Meredith is a witch-vampire hybrid, but no one is supposed to be able to use their powers on an Element. That's why Lilah was needed to help her accomplish it. This was different. It didn't seem possible for Meredith to get a read on Lilah by using their connection, but somehow she managed it.

Jackson started pacing the floor.

"You need to calm down," Everleigh scolded him. "Please, Jackson. You need to keep your emotions under control as hard as it may seem. We can't have you…"

He sucked in a deep breath and exhaled slowly. "Keep me in the loop. I need to know everything if I'm to keep myself under control. You might think it's a bad idea for me to know, but leaving it to my imagination is worse."

The others nodded at him, and Meredith promised, "I won't keep anything from you, Jackson. I want to help."

He walked back to the others and held out his hands. "Let's go again."

No one moved.

He shook his hands toward them. "Come on. Let's do this."

"It won't be necessary. I think I may have seen enough," Meredith told him, grabbing her coat.

"What are we going to do?" Jackson raced to the hall to get his jacket.

"We?" Meredith laughed. "You are staying here."

"No! I'm going with you." Anger rose inside of him, and he was fighting to keep control of his demons.

"I can't have you losing your head and exposing yourself. Take a look in the mirror, would you? You look like your mom," Meredith spat the words at him.

Jackson turned and punched the wall. The others jumped and watched as he retreated to the stairs.

"This is exactly why he's staying here," Meredith sternly told Everleigh in case she was thinking about taking him along anyway.

"Luke and I will go to the house and scout it out. Once I feel it's safe, you will have her leave through the back door," she ordered.

"Alright, I can do that," Everleigh thought it sounded simple.

They headed to the front door near where Jackson still sat quietly halfway up the staircase. "We'll have her here before you know it," Meredith told him gently.

He didn't move a muscle except to ask, "Is she okay?"

Meredith took a deep breath and wasn't sure about answering the question. She despised lying especially after the promise she just made, but he was not in his right mind. The smallest spark could light his fuse, and it was hard to tell who might get hurt in the crossfire.

Jackson noticed her hesitation and looked at her with pleading eyes.

"She will be," she told him. "It's nothing that can't be undone."

With that, the three of them left the house. "I'm going to have to make a stop at home to get something," Meredith informed her niece.

"Since when don't you have everything you need in that bag of yours?" Everleigh said, sounding like she was joking, but she meant it.

"Since Air decided to pump your friend full of sleeping pills," Meredith said flatly.

Everleigh's mouth was still hanging wide open when her aunt drove away. She knew there had to be some reason for Lilah to act as she had been, but she wasn't expecting this. At worst, she thought maybe her family had taken her phone to shut off her contact with them.

She looked up and saw Jackson at the window of the door. She gave him a quick wave then headed to her car before he decided to come out and ask her anything about what her aunt said. Or worse, ask her to bring him along.

---

Meredith left Luke in the car with it running

while she made a quick dash into Eloise's house, hoping she could get in and out without being noticed by her nieces. Opening the front door, she saw Eloise step out from the sunroom in the back, so she walked straight to her as quietly as she could.

"Where are the girls?" she whispered.

"I gave them the day off and sent them to the movies," Eloise answered. "How'd it go?"

"Perfectly," Meredith told her, pulling a small red trinket out of her satchel. "You know when you told me last night to hang on to this until tomorrow, I thought it was because you worried about risking the girls seeing me if I snuck in again so soon. You could've given me the heads up that I'd be needing it again," she said, placing it carefully in Eloise's palm.

"Where's the fun in that?" Eloise asked, tying her treasured rubino pendant around her neck. "Besides, it keeps you on your toes."

Eloise walked into the sunroom, motioning for Meredith to follow. On a table near the door was a small paper bag. "Take this. Mix it with what you have."

"What is it?" Meredith asked, opening the bag to peek.

"Juniper berries. It will help detoxify her."

Meredith dropped her arms to her side. "Why don't you come out and tell us these things? It would've saved us a lot of time, and we could've got to Lilah faster if you had let us know instead of making us go through all this trouble."

Eloise sat in her chair overlooking the garden. "There's time. I would've intervened if it had taken too long. Plus, the lot of you need to learn to work together and trust each other. It's for the good of us all with what's coming."

Opening the bag again, Meredith caught a whiff of something else. "Is that lavender?"

"Of course, it's lavender. Lilah was drugged, wasn't she?"

"You want me to give her a sleeping aid?" Meredith asked perplexed.

"Sleeping never hurt anyone. It will counter the side effects of the pills she has in her system," Eloise looked up at her. "Unless you want to clean up all the mess when she can't get to the bathroom in time."

"Fine. I'll use the lavender."

"I thought so," Eloise's eyes sparkled.

Meredith started to leave, but Eloise stopped her again. "Did anyone find out you had it?"

With her back turned, Meredith grinned, happy the old woman couldn't see her face. "Not a soul."

"Good."

"But Luke suspects."

Eloise was quiet, and Meredith wasn't sure if she was free to go or not. She turned to look at her sitting peacefully in her chair. "I'm sorry," she offered, thinking Eloise must be mad.

"Nonsense. Fire is his kind. It's only right for him to know everything."

"Our kind," Meredith corrected her.

With a troubled sigh, Eloise looked at her niece. "Yes, child. You're right again." She reached up for Meredith's hand and placed several small items in it.

Furrowing her brows, Meredith looked at the wagon wheel shaped objects she was now holding. "Lotus root?"

"You may find yourself in need of some," Eloise said, waving her hand indicating it was time for her to go.

Meredith walked toward the front of the house sticking the lotus root into her satchel. Thinking better of it, she placed one in her pocket just in case. It would be pointless to ask when she would need it or for what in order to be better prepared. The old woman shrouded herself in secrets, loved always having the upper hand, and nothing brought her more joy than watching events unfold just the way she had already foreseen them.

---

It was starting to get dark when the farmhouse came into sight. Everleigh parked her car along the road near the growth covered fence where it would be out of view. She walked a ways down the road past the house until she could use the cover of the trees to get there without being seen. The layout was familiar to her, and she could have found her way blindfolded in the dark. Countless times over the years she had ran the length of the small timber bordering the old house while the coven was busy working. The little red car her aunt drove was coming up the drive when she made it safely to the rear of the home.

All those years, Everleigh had never suspected the farmhouse belonged to a member of Air. It was one of a laundry list of questions she had for her grandma, but knew better than to ask. Considering her grandma had long been adamant against the Elemental groups becoming too close, it surprised Everleigh when she learned that she was friends with someone in Air. Not just friends, but close enough to have free use of their property.

The phone in her pocket buzzed, and she nearly screamed. She pulled it out thinking it was her aunt, but it was Jackson.

"Lilah just called. She said she'd been asleep most of the day. What's going on? I thought you would have her by now."

"I can't talk. I'm outside her house," Everleigh whispered loudly, using as hushed a voice as she could that would allow him to still hear her.

"Good. I told her you were on your way." Jackson hung up. She knew he was still pissed at her for agreeing he should stay behind.

Everleigh watched Matt and Rita get out of her aunt's car. That's new she thought. She sent a text asking where Luke was.

Her aunt stopped to read it. Turning to tell the others to hang on, she called Everleigh. "I dropped him off to keep an eye on Jackson once I learned these two were available to come out here in case things go wrong."

"He didn't say anything about Luke when he called just now."

"What did he want?"

"To tell me Lilah called."

"I had hoped she would be awake. I have something that will help alleviate the effects of what she's been given, but she needs to drink it. Let her know you're here."

Everleigh hung up with her aunt then called her friend. Lilah answered quickly. They talked briefly, and Lilah wanted to use her window to sneak out. She was surprised that Lilah didn't know there were bars on the window. It was even more surprising Jackson didn't tell her when he spoke to Lilah just now. He was behaving as he had promised. Everleigh explained that she would help Lilah sneak out the back door, but she wasn't sure how much of the conversation Lilah understood or would remember.

There was something definitely wrong, and she worried it went beyond sleeping pills. Lilah wasn't acting quite right, and her speech was slurred. It was hard to understand her at times. She needed to buy a little time, so she told her that her Aunt Meredith was on the way, not already here.

They hung up, and she sent another text to her aunt. "Lilah needs us. Now!"

"I'm going to try to sneak upstairs. Sit tight a little bit longer."

Everleigh took a few steps back into the shelter of the trees to wait until she knew what to do next. The air was getting colder, and she shivered in spite of the heavy coat she was wearing. She wanted her friend to be alright no matter what, but for Jackson's sake, she wanted it with every fiber of her being. She could only hope her aunt would be able to help her.

The phone in her pocket wouldn't stop vibrating, and she knew it was Jackson. That poor pup was worried sick. She took a couple more steps back and answered. "I don't have her yet."

"Why the hell not?"

"Calm down. You know what the hell will happen if you lose control."

There was silence on the line except for the sound of his deep breathing, and Everleigh knew he was practicing the techniques she taught him years ago to keep his temper in check.

"Alright. I'm calm. Did you get caught?"

"Nah. She's... I don't know. Something's wrong, but you better keep your cool."

"Do you need me to come out there?" he was obviously upset.

She closed her eyes and scrunched up her face. She knew better. This boy was a walking time bomb. "No. I need you to-"

"Calm down," he huffed.

She heard him take a deep breath and exhale.

"What's the plan?" he asked in a normal voice again.

"I'm waiting to hear from my aunt."

"That's the plan. Waiting."

Everleigh knew he had to be mad, but his voice didn't give it away. "I'm waiting to hear the plan. Just stay on the phone until she texts me, and then you will know as soon as I hear from her."

There was talking in the background. He must be talking to Luke. It was comforting knowing Meredith left him behind, but she wondered if Luke would even be enough to stop Jackson if he got too worked up. If she had to guess, her money would be on Jackson.

"You there? I got a text."

She lowered the phone to check the message. It was time.

"Alright, I have to go. My aunt wants me to sneak up to Lilah's room. She's going to create a diversion."

Murmured voices followed.

"Jackson?" she asked, not wanting to just hang up on him.

"Yeah, I'm here. Hey, Luke is on his way in case you guys need help."

That was the last thing Everleigh wanted to hear.

"Everleigh?" It was Luke's voice on the line.

"He can't be alone. You know that."

"Listen. Either I go or he does. Take your pick. The only thing keeping him sane right now is knowing I'll be there if something goes wrong."

"Fine. But when my aunt is going off on me-"

"I'll take responsibility. Don't worry."

Everleigh gave up. It's not like she really had a choice. She couldn't force him to stay. "I got to go." She hung up.

She walked quietly up to the back porch and waited by the inside door. There was a doorway to the kitchen only a few feet inside. She just needed to make sure no one was around. Any one of them could look down the hall at any time, and she'd be busted.

Just then, her aunt came out of the kitchen doorway. Everleigh sensed it was her. Well, her or Rita, but definitely Earth. She peaked through the side of the window and her aunt motioned for her to come inside.

The door didn't make any sound thankfully. An old farmhouse like this was usually filled with various noises reminding you of its age. She slipped into the kitchen behind her aunt who was slowly walking down the hall to join the group in the living room.

There was only one actual door off the kitchen. The other two entrances were only open doorways. It had to be for the backstairs. Everleigh opened it and closed it softly behind her. She could breathe easy again. She checked the message from her aunt. It said at the top of the stairs, Lilah is the door to the left. Easy enough.

She creeped up the stairs as quietly as she could, but each step groaned under her feet. The family was gathered downstairs and wouldn't be able to detect her because she was Earth. Not that it mattered. They were all in some intense conversation and probably wouldn't pick up on another presence in the house with it being so occupied. It's not like they were Water sniffing out everything in range. If the stairs made much more noise, they might hear something which would tip them off.

Everleigh was in the bedroom in no time. Lilah was asleep. She was sprawled on the bed in what had to be an uncomfortable position. Her face was wet, but Everleigh couldn't tell if it was sweat or something else.

"Hey," she said, speaking as loud as she would venture.

Nothing. Not even a twitch.

She walked up to her and began shaking her

gently. "Wake up."

Still not a movement. It scared her.

"Hey...Hey!" she started becoming frantic, shaking her harder now.

Lilah's eyes blinked open then closed again.

This was going to be harder than she thought it would be. She pulled her upright and tried to figure out the best way to do this. Lilah was out of it. She had no idea what was going on and barely remembered the conversation after they just had it. When she cracked a joke, Everleigh was relieved. Lilah would be okay.

Getting her downstairs might prove to be a challenge. She can't even sit up on her own Everleigh thought as she reached for everything Lilah might need. There would be time for all of this later. For now, she would just drape the coat on Lilah's shoulders and carry the rest.

Everleigh knelt down and explained what they had to do. She wasn't sure Lilah comprehended most of it. It looked like she was already a little better in the few minutes since she found her passed out on the bed. Hopefully Lilah would be able to do some of the walking.

They made it down the stairs, but it was not easy. Lilah could only go one step at a time, and it felt like minutes ticked by before she was finally ready to move on to the next one. The kitchen was clear, so she let her aunt know they were ready.

The two of them stood with barely enough room to breathe while they waited for some kind of diversion that would hopefully give them the opportunity to sneak out the back door. It was risky, and Everleigh hoped she wouldn't find out what would happen if they were seen by anyone. It didn't help that they didn't yet know who was behind what happened to Lilah and whether it was a rogue Air or the family. Worse, there was always the slight chance it was someone from outside the family entirely.

# Chapter Eighteen

Meredith's phone dinged. She didn't have to look at it. It was her niece telling her the girls were ready. The frenzy she caused by walking into the house with Matt in tow was still high. They were comically unprepared to have a wolf in their midst regardless of which side he was on. It wouldn't take much to bring the current argument of whether to trust him to new heights, but she had more devious thoughts on her mind. Luke's unexpected arrival didn't help anyone calm down, especially her. It was made abundantly clear he was to stay behind to keep Jackson in check, but she would have to deal with that later.

Todd was standing in the kitchen doorway nearest the group, but no one would be able to see the girls leave the stairway from where they were gathered. With the three of them in the room and Luke outside until the girls were safely away, it would be unlikely anyone would detect Everleigh sneaking out with Lilah even if they tripped and fell at this point. Their attention was muted and distracted. The girls still needed cover in the hallway. It would only take one look. Just one person to see movement from the corner of their eyes or to happen to glance in that direction, and it would be over. It was the only likely way they'd get caught.

She eyed Todd until he noticed her stare. Her eyes meticulously shifted to the hall and back. If only there had been time to include him in the plan. He was one Air who could always be trusted.

It didn't take long for him to pick up on her signals, and luckily, he never questioned her. He stood up straight from the doorframe he had been leaning against then walked to the entrance of the hallway. One corner of Meredith's mouth turned up to a conniving grin watching him slyly point to the opposite side of the hall and the floor as if to ask where do you want me.

The backdoor was a straight shot down from the main room, and the girls would be less visible behind him. She glanced to the wall that adjoined the kitchen. He leaned into it crossing his arms.

Now for this fight. Shooting Todd one last impish look, she turned her attention back to the argument in progress all around her. "None of you have any room to talk," she told the group loudly.

Their eyes quickly set upon her which is exactly what she wanted. If everyone was focused on her near the front of the house, the girls could slip out easier. "You're going to sit here and act like you're better than the rest of us?"

There were already remarks being fired back at her. This was going perfectly. "Just because Marcus was the saint who didn't eat the forbidden fruit doesn't mean the rest of you get to go your entire lives not being held accountable for your wrong doings."

From the corner of her eye, she saw the stairway door opening. She only needed a couple of minutes. "The southern wolves have been friends with my kind for centuries. They've vowed to help us fight. All of us!"

Several in the room tried to protest they were still wolves, and of course they would be wary. She let them say their piece for a moment before dropping the real bomb on them.

The girls were entering the hallway, and Meredith glanced at them for only a second over Todd's shoulder. He turned to follow her gaze, but she wasn't worried. He would trust she knew what she was doing.

"Enough!" she yelled at everyone. "The real enemy is you!"

An entire room of Air gasped and reeled as though she had smacked all of them in the face simultaneously. Even Todd straightened up at her accusation.

"What kind of person... What kind of family poisons their own daughter?"

Looks were quickly exchanged among them, and it was clear to her they were shocked by her question. It wasn't a family decision as she had suspected. Air does everything with group approval. This was done by only one or maybe a few without the consent of the rest.

Todd started to take a step then checked to see if anyone was behind him before coming into the middle of the group. "My friend," he said to her. "Please explain."

She eyed everyone in the entire room, scanning their faces to see if any would give away their guilt. There was one sitting quietly with his head in his hands. It looked like she found the culprit, but she needed to be sure. Without taking her eyes off of him, she began. "Lilah. That's what I'm talking about."

The girl's name made the man cringe, and Meredith had no more doubts.

"What about Lilah?" her mom asked, jumping from the recliner.

Lilah's dad was making a move for the stairs.

"She's not up there," Meredith said dryly. She needed to keep them in the room as long as possible. The girls still had to get to Jackson's house safely.

"Where is she?" Myles demanded. The tone of his voice suggested he thought Meredith might have some part in whatever happened to his daughter.

"I know you're upset," she told him. "You've

every right to be. The only thing I've done is save your daughter's life."

He joined his wife trying to console her. "Saved her life?" Lilah's mom asked, repeating the words as if they were not making sense.

"She will be fine, Abby. Know that."

Tears fell from Abby's face. It made Meredith twinge a bit with remorse at the way she had broken the news. *'This will be in our favor,'* she thought. *'Once they realize for themselves that they are not above having bad apples in their perfect family, maybe they can see the opposite could be true. That there is a tribe of good wolves out there too.'*

"One of you, however, took it upon yourself to keep her prisoner and controlled for lack of a better way of putting it."

Meredith took a step toward Todd. "Will you go check for yourself? There are bars on the outside of her bedroom window preventing her from leaving unless she walks past her captor."

Todd turned and ran down the back hall to the door. He was outside and back in seconds. It never ceased to amaze Meredith the speed Air had. They couldn't outrun a Water in wolf form, but no mere human would ever catch up to one.

"It's true. There are bars."

Muffled gasps and concerns went through everyone. She let them have a minute to digest the appetizer before she hit them with the big news.

"I'm not saying I approve of this method, but she had been sneaking out a lot which caused her parents to worry," one of the Air family explained.

Meredith nodded and crossed her arms taking a firm stance in front of them. "I can see that. I mean I don't approve either, but I can understand the logic in your statement. Maybe you can help me see the logic in this as well."

She paused again savoring this moment. It

didn't really suit her to be petty, but this family had long disapproved of her friendship with Todd. Lilah's parents were among the few who accepted her which made what happened to Lilah even worse as far as she was concerned. Lilah was almost family to her.

"What would drugging her accomplish?"

There was a loud and unified gasp from the whole room. Shocked expressions on every face. That was except for one. The same man in the back hiding his face in his hands who was now rocking back and forth as this blow was delivered.

Lilah's mom went into a frantic state sobbing and clinging to her husband who had tears streaming down his face as well. It hurt Meredith to cause them pain, and she went to them.

She knelt in front of them and told them gently. "Your daughter will be fine. She's safe now. I saw to it."

They couldn't speak, but Myles reached out and patted her hand. Meredith could feel the words in their heart even though their voices were lost.

Everyone was silent as they processed what they just heard. There was a poetic quality in taking it slow. She needed to buy the girls as much time as she could, and she could savor the once in a lifetime moment of having the upper hand, knowing something they didn't. It could also be said that she was being kind in giving them time to recover before adding insult to injury. It all seemed to click in her favor.

Meredith stood and faced the room again. This time from nearer to the hallway to keep their eyes away from the front of the house. There were curtains draped over each window, but there was nothing wrong with being overly cautious. It was better not to risk someone noticing movement outside.

"I gave her an herbal remedy which will

counter the effects of the drugs in her system. It was a tough call not knowing exactly what she had been given, but it seems to be working."

There were some murmurs going through the crowd now as the relief was sinking in that Lilah would be fine. Meredith could hear a few words of gratitude being aimed at her as well.

"Someone has been drugging her. I know your limits. I know what the only thing is that can bring you death. Lilah could likely survive this on her own, but what if her heart had stopped for too long before she was found."

"Her heart stopped?" Todd asked, choking on his pain.

"She wasn't breathing when I found her," Meredith hadn't been sure if she wanted to omit this piece of news or not, but found herself saying it.

You could have heard a pin drop after the bomb dropped on them. They all sat in silence realizing how close they had been to losing her.

Meredith stood and stared at the man in the back of the room. The man who hadn't looked up for some time now. The man who still hid his face and rocked with his shoulders shaking hard enough to give away the sobs he was hiding. Nothing broke her stare not even when Todd tried to ask her questions, and not even when Luke walked in the house signifying the girls were gone.

Others picked up on it and curiously turned to see who or what she was looking at. One, then another, and another at first. Then everyone joined her. Still the man didn't move. If he had any inclination that he was under scrutiny, he didn't show it.

"Brian!" Myles called for his attention sternly.

The rocking stopped and slowly the man lifted his head. When he saw all eyes upon him, the sobs he had been trying to keep stifled broke free. He didn't say much as his cries grew louder, but he did manage to say, "This wasn't what was supposed to happen."

"Where is she?" Abby asked Meredith after getting herself under control.

"I sent her somewhere safe. She'll be protected."

The words caused Abby to flinch as though it was a direct attack on her.

"She'll be protected from anything that might come our way until she's recovered," Meredith explained gently. Abby had always been an ally, and it would continue to bring her guilt how she had caused this poor woman so much pain tonight.

Voices were starting to rise up all around as the family began demanding the man give them answers for what he had done. Meredith felt like her work here was over, but she wanted to wait a bit longer before leaving. She needed to know the girls were safe.

Todd approached and gave her a hug so tight he might have just as easily been trying to cut her in two with his arms. "I can never repay you for helping my niece. You saved her life."

She placed her hand on his cheek and looked in his eyes, "You have saved me countless times."

"Not like this, Meredith."

"Friends don't keep tabs, Todd. Isn't that what you told me once?"

His face softened a little, and he remarked, "That's what you chose to listen to of everything I've ever tried to teach you?"

They laughed softly. Todd had certainly tried to influence her for the better over the years, but she wouldn't always have it.

He scanned the room and the verbal attacks that were being slung. "This will occupy them for a while," he told her, knowing what she was doing after seeing Lilah leave not long ago with his own eyes.

"That is the hope."

"And you are aware we will all know where she has gone and who she is with?"

"Then you will also know how safe she will be under his protection."

Todd chewed the inside of his cheek. "I imagine there's no place safer."

"I will head out soon once I'm confident the girls are long gone," Meredith told him, feeling like she needed to explain why she was simply watching the show she set in motion.

"They're not going anywhere," Todd said, nodding toward his brother who was being circled like he was at his end, and vultures were awaiting their next meal.

"Why did he do it? Any ideas?"

"I have my suspicions, but it's a ridiculous extreme in any event."

"Agreed," Meredith scoffed. Her family had many disagreements with her over the years especially when she first chose a life with Luke. They had disagreed, fought, and gone periods without speaking, but this is something her family would only do if she were a danger to herself.

It clicked inside her like a cartoon lightbulb that switched on. "Wait. Did she do something? Lilah, I mean."

There was no response, but she watched his shoulders rise and fall with a heavy breath. "There was a… an incident," the words came out slow.

"What kind of incident?"

"It has been observed that our young Lilah is the strongest of us all."

Meredith's mouth fell open. She knew the storms last night had been the young girl's doing, and it had been confided in her that Air thought Lilah's powers were superior among the rest of them. To hear Todd say it like this confirms what had been speculated. There had been numerous times when she saw Todd at the peak of his form. It was more than enough to make her definitively aware that she did not want to ever be at the wrong end of an Air's anger. It was unimaginable that this young little waif of a girl was actually stronger.

"You have to be exaggerating," she told him.

"Sadly, no. We thought...well like how more witches spawned?"

"Maybe Air was increasing in power since you could not increase in numbers as rapidly?"

"Exactly."

"It's not a bad theory."

"No, but it is a debunked theory. We tested it this morning. Even combining our strengths, we are not as powerful."

"Crap," Meredith was stunned. It was mind boggling, and that was without knowing to what extent Lilah was more powerful.

"That's what I said," Todd smiled dryly.

The mob scene was just getting started. The man responsible for what happened was cowering away. The only words he could muster was to apologize over and over.

Meredith clicked her tongue to get Todd's attention and nodded toward the kitchen. She held a finger toward Matt and Rita as she walked by with Luke telling them to hang on.

"You think that's why he did it then? Because of her power?"

"It's the only thing that makes sense."

"Still," Meredith shook her head. "It seems outrageous to me."

"To me as well, but she lost control when she was angry, and you have to admit, there's a lot to get upset about at the moment," he added.

"Yeah, everyone's nerves are fired up," Luke agreed.

Todd glanced over her shoulder toward the fight engulfing his family. "You don't have to tell me that."

"I'm going to take off and see how our little ball of energy we kidnapped is faring. I'll let you know."

"Yes, keep me updated," Todd said, giving her a hug.

"And you get that under control," Meredith turned and pointed toward his family. "Earth and Water are already arriving from the south. By dawn, they should all be settled somewhere."

Todd nodded slowly, but Meredith felt like he didn't really understand. "They're going to want to meet. With all of us," she emphasized.

His head turned toward her then, and his eyes looked old and tired. "I'll be ready."

With that, he headed into the living room and began shouting over the crowd to get everyone's attention. Meredith wasn't waiting to see how it worked out. She motioned to Matt and Rita to follow her, and they all left out the back door.

"That went well," Matt smirked.

"Your speaking skills are amazing," Rita said, joining her husband in teasing her.

"It did go well. The girls are gone, aren't they?"

They hurried to their cars as if they expected an attack to come from the house at any moment. "Jackson's house," she told Matt and Rita, who were driving Luke's car back while he rode with her.

She opened her door then remembered, "Hey!"

Matt and Rita both looked at her.

"I know you are both aware, but just in case, watch what you say when we get there. Jackson still doesn't know," she reminded them, making finger quotes in the air and rolling her eyes.

"What if I forget you told me that and help him find out?" Matt asked, making the air quotes back at Meredith.

"Shush it, Matt," Rita scolded. "Let that girl do things her way."

Matt shook his head annoyed by the pretense he had to keep.

"I'm with you, Matt," Luke told him, "but we have to listen to the women on this one. They outnumber us."

Matt started to object.

"There's Lilah and Everleigh to count," Luke pointed out, beating him to his argument.

Matt threw his hands up in defeat. "Fine, but convince her to do it. This is nuts."

"You think it's bad for you?" Meredith scoffed and folded her arms. "Think about poor Jackson in all of this."

The look on Matt's face showed he hadn't thought about it like that before. He let out a long, lone chuckle then another. Gradually he began laughing harder. "Oh, hell! You're right!"

The four of them got inside the cars and drove down to the main road. Meredith's car was leading the way. "How is our champion Jackson doing?" she asked Luke, not attempting to hide her sarcasm.

"As well as can be expected. He'll be fine once he knows Lilah is safe."

"And you know that because you're there keeping things under control? By things, I mean Jackson," Meredith hissed between gritted teeth.

Luke rolled his head back and exhaled loudly. "I knew you'd be mad, but it wasn't like I had the alternative of waiting until we could discuss it. Have you any idea how hard it is to contain him?"

"I can imagine it's not easy."

"Not easy," Luke huffed, rolling his eyes. "Jackson was hell bent on coming out here to save the day. Either I let him do it, or I had to come out to make sure everything went off without a hitch. Those were the only options. I chose the lesser of the evils."

Meredith opened her mouth to say something.

"And before you try to insist I should have just stayed there and kept him from coming out as was the plan," Luke told her, raising his hand to tell her to wait. "I reasoned with him all I could. It was about to get physical. As old and strong as I am," he shook his head and took a deep breath, "he'd probably finish me off without effort like an afternoon snack."

"That one is a wild card."

Luke sighed, "He always was."

"And this Lilah business isn't helping any."

"It'll be better once all the secrets are out in the open," Luke reminded her.

"I want to respect her wishes on this, but she has to understand that current circumstances require the truth being told," Meredith was frustrated.

"How is she supposed to come to that realization?" Luke snapped. "She is under the impression that Jackson knows a lot less than he really does. That she's keeping him safe somehow."

"And if she knew just how much he knows, she would piece together that he already knows the truth about her," Meredith stretched her neck from side to side. It was a confusing circle.

Luke broke out in a fit of laughter. It kept growing until he was slapping the car door and stomping his feet.

"I don't know how you find any of this to be that hysterical."

"Oh, it is," he cried out, wheezing from laughing so hard and clutching his sides.

"We are in the beginnings of what looks to be a war headed our way. Our very survival is at stake. The last thing we should be concerned with is some girl telling her boyfriend a family secret! And you? You can do nothing but laugh yourself silly."

Luke was gasping now. He tried to compose himself, but the laughing fit came back. "That's not it at all," he barely managed to get the words out before sucking in more air.

Meredith gave him a menacing look waiting for him to explain.

"We are all focused on Lilah needing to be open with Jackson. What about when Lilah finds out?" The laughter returned again much harder.

"One problem at a time," Meredith told him, with a small smile she forced to stay hidden. She had thought about that many times and knew it would be even more worrisome given Lilah's recent outburst.

"I think someone should just slip up intentionally," Luke said, regaining control of his temporary hysteria.

"Don't you dare," Meredith said sternly.

"What? You know as well as I do that Jackson will take the news like a champ."

"But Lilah won't react the same way to her secret being revealed," Meredith said sharply.

"Accidents happen. What're you gonna do?"

"What would she do?" Meredith reiterated, pulling into Jackson's drive. "She would bring the town down around us and quite possibly take all of us out in the process."

Meredith put the car in park and looked at Luke.

"What are you talking about?"

"That girl is like a volatile chemical. You have to proceed with caution around her. If you shake her up, there's no limit to the damage she can cause."

Luke was beyond intrigued. He had to know more. "Did she do something already? Besides the storm, I mean."

Meredith ignored him and turned the car off.

"You can't leave me hanging like that. You have to fill me in on the details."

She opened the door of the car and said as she got out, "There's no time. Just leave it for now."

Luke got out after her and pleaded with his eyes. Meredith ignored him.

Matt and Rita pulled up on the street and joined them on the front walk. "What's on the agenda for the rest of the night?" Rita asked.

"We need to figure out how to convince Lilah to tell Jackson she's an Air, and we need to do it fast." The urgency in Meredith's voice underlined her statement.

They walked up the steps, and Luke suggested, "Have Everleigh do it."

Meredith cocked her head to the side and squinted her eyes at him.

Rita quickly rapped on the door, shivering in the cold.

They waited a moment. "You're freezing," Matt said to Rita, knocking again much harder. The cold didn't bother him so much, but he hated seeing his wife shaking so hard from it.

"Have her convince Lilah. She'll listen to Everleigh before she does the rest of us," Luke went on, ignoring his southern buddies who weren't used to the Midwest temperatures. He didn't much care for the cold either, but he could tolerate it long enough for the door to be answered at least.

"I knew there was a reason I kept you around," Meredith leaned in and kissed him gently.

Luke raised his arm to knock a third time, but Meredith pushed it down. "Allow me."

She stood in front of the door and reached into her pocket. She pulled out something resembling a wagon wheel and placed it on her tongue. "Viam revalare," she said confidently. This probably wasn't what Eloise had in mind, but there was plenty of it to use some to show off now.

The doorknob made a clicking noise as it unlocked.

"Good one," Rita complimented. "I'll have to remember it. Was that lotus root?"

Meredith pulled it out of her mouth showing it to her. "Yes, never leave home without it," she joked, knowing the real reason why she had it on her.

"It's very versatile," Rita said in agreement.

"Alright ladies, can we go in now? It's not getting any warmer out here." Luke's trips to colder climates were typically brief, and he usually only visited them in the warmer months.

"I'm with you," Matt agreed.

The other three all turned to face him surprised. His body was in a constant state of regeneration which required a higher caloric intake for his fast metabolism and resulted in a higher body heat. It stunned them to hear a wolf say anything negative about the cold weather.

"Look, just because I can tolerate it doesn't mean I like it," he answered their stares. "Besides," he said, looking off, "I'm bored."

Meredith opened the door, and they walked in together surprising the three friends who were gathered in the kitchen. She led the others in and helped herself to a hot cocoa that appeared to be waiting for her to arrive. There was a tenseness in the house undoubtedly caused by Lilah's uncertainty over everything barreling around in her muddled mind.

There wasn't a lack of sympathy for the girl that was the problem. Meredith felt for her in waves that would suffocate her if she fed them too long. It was the urgency she felt toward pressing matters that caused her to exhibit some callousness toward Lilah. Basically, she needed to just rip the band aid off quickly and tell Jackson.

Until then, it was difficult to make any moves with her around. On one hand, Meredith could tell that Lilah was going to be a key player in whatever the future held. Till then, she needed to get her out of the way to be able to talk to the others.

It didn't take long before Meredith convinced Lilah to lay down on the couch. With the medication that was in her system and the stress she had been under, the poor girl was out in minutes. Meredith quietly warned everyone at the table they would have to keep their voices down to prevent Lilah from hearing anything if she woke up without them knowing.

"My people are already arriving," Matt began. "In hours, the entire tribe from the south will be in the area."

"My relatives' covens are traveling with them," Rita added.

"I could never thank your tribe enough for coming to our aide," Meredith told him.

"It was your kind who first aided us," Matt reminded her.

"Do you know anything of the northern tribe's plans?" Everleigh asked.

"Nothing new, I'm afraid." Matt sighed. "There is one, a relative of Rita's, who is still in contact with them."

"Can he be trusted?" Meredith's concern was evident.

"Yes. He's trying to gather as much information as possible before they find out he and his tribe are siding with the rest of us."

Luke leaned back and rapped his knuckles on the table. "Playing both sides like that can be risky. Not just for him, but us as well if we trust him."

"I understand what you're saying, but you have my word," Matt told him.

"How can we be sure he's on our side?" Luke asked in a manner that implied there was nothing he could say to convince them wholly.

"Because he's my father," Rita answered with a sly smile.

"Your father?" Everleigh was amused. "I thought the mixing of the blood lines happened centuries ago?"

"It did," Rita's eyes lit up, and she reached out to hold Matt's hand. "But it still continues to this day."

"So you all...." Everleigh's brows lifted in astonishment.

Matt almost choked on an unexpected laugh. "Not all of us. Not like that. It does happen though."

"We need to get this back on track. What do you know, Matt? Anything that hasn't already been discussed?" Meredith asked, irritated by the distraction when there was so much on the line.

"Sadly no, not until they arrive. They'll want to meet."

"I figured as much," Meredith clasped her hands together and rested her chin on her thumbs.

"Are any other covens joining us?" It was Luke asking the same question he had asked many times before, but always hoping for a different answer.

Meredith glared straight ahead to avoid looking at him. "No, Luke. The answer is no just as it was every other time you asked."

"I was hoping it had changed."

"If it did, I would tell you," Meredith growled.

"I was hoping if I bother you enough, you might influence them to come."

"Me? The Earth outcast?" Meredith's voice boomed. Worried, she scanned the front room for any sign she had disturbed Lilah then continued quietly. "They will not lift a finger to help me, Luke. Eloise has been trying to convince them."

"Convince them? Why would they need convincing? It's their lives at stake too," Matt was bewildered.

"Most of the covens have gone into hiding, taking the youngest generation with them even those who haven't yet been called. They're cloaked in protection spells thinking this is how they save their people."

"By hiding?" Matt acted like the words were physically painful to say.

"Don't," Rita told him.

Matt looked at her with questions in his eyes.

"Don't judge their actions. They don't have tribes of wolves and clans of vampires assisting them," she explained.

"We would defend them too," Matt grumbled, acting like it was the most obvious statement he could make.

"Yes, but they would have to travel here. It would be a risk."

"We are all taking a risk," Luke added. "What choice do we have?"

"There's always a choice. Besides, I believe it was your kind who led the way in this game of hide and hope you don't get attacked," Everleigh challenged, growing angry over the insinuations about her people. It would be senseless to die trying to get to Fairview.

"And shouldn't your kind," Luke heavily accented the word, "have learned from our mistakes? Don't they realize the wolves will track them down?" Luke tried to reason.

"They may eventually be found, but not unless we stop them here." Meredith grew weary of always defending her people. It was not met with her approval that they were trying to save themselves at the risk of hurting others, but it was their choice to do so.

"Enough," Rita slapped the table. "Let's

discuss something we can actually do something about."

Meredith walked to the doorway to check on Lilah worried the repeated outbursts may have awakened her. The girl was still out and looked like she hadn't moved since falling asleep. "It's late," she said to everyone when she returned.

They checked the time noting it was still quite early.

"I'm tired. We need our rest for whatever tomorrow may bring," she continued, wanting to deflect any questions about her departure from the group before they could be asked.

"I thought we were going to prepare for the meeting?" Everleigh spoke up.

"Tomorrow. I will have Todd arrive early, and we will all discuss it then."

"What about Jackson?" Luke asked.

Meredith crossed her arms then lifted one hand to her mouth and pulled on her lower lip. "Unfortunately, Jackson can't attend any of our meetings until Lilah does her part."

There were synchronized groans from the table. "I know how you feel," Meredith told them. "Everleigh, I need you to work on her about telling him."

"I'll do my best," she said without looking at her aunt.

"I need you to succeed."

Everleigh closed her eyes wanting to say something, but knowing she shouldn't. It wouldn't be easy. Lilah was set on waiting. She would have to convince her that the truth would come out soon anyway.

Meredith stood and told the group she would see them in the morning. She had business to attend to. Privately.

"Am I the only one concerned about what Fire is up to?" Luke asked, raising his hands and glancing around the room.

In the hallway, Jackson tip toed farther away from the kitchen until Meredith had gone. He would stay there out of sight, but well within ear shot until only Everleigh remained.

# Chapter Nineteen

"Why do we have to move?" Samuel asked. "You said yourself that they're not targeting real witches."

"We do whatever it takes to keep our family safe," his dad answered, rummaging through a drawer.

Samuel looked at his siblings sitting on the edge of the bed they shared. His youngest sister clutched her doll with tears streaming down her face. They had only moved here two years ago after their mom died, but it was the nicest place they had ever lived. They were adapting well to the community and had made real friends.

The only people being accused are ones who posed a business competition. That didn't include them. They weren't connected to any of the prominent families of the town. None of them were even witches. "Father, I don't understand. We have no reason to think any of us will be accused."

"We also have no reason to feel confident we won't be either," he told him. "Your ancestors have seen this type of hysteria before in Europe."

"Won't people be suspicious when we just leave in the middle of the night? It will make us look guilty."

Gideon stopped his haphazard packing and looked at his four children. "It will look like I'm trying to protect you from the witchcraft and sorcery that people believe is running rampant in Salem."

He sat on the edge of the bed and pulled his youngest daughter's head to his chest. He rested his chin on her head. "I know it's hard, and you don't understand. I need you to trust that I'm doing what I feel is best for all of you."

"But we're not even witches, father!"

Gideon looked at Samuel harshly, and his son immediately regretted his outburst.

"They're not hanging witches are they, son? Not being a witch does not mean we are safe."

He got up and walked to the open suitcase on the table and pulled out a grimoire. "Do you see this? This belonged to my mother and will one day belong to one of you."

He slammed the book back into the suitcase. He knows that two of his children are old enough to receive the calling and begin practicing the craft. It's their generation to produce a witch. Any day now one of them could begin the visions, the dreams, and the unexpected magic that always occurred until the new witch learns control. He shook his head thinking what would happen if one of them started to unknowingly affect things around them if front of witnesses. He had already buried his wife. He wasn't going to bury a child as well.

Gideon closed the case and without turning around, he told his family it was time. He lifted it by the handle and walked out the door. He put the case on their tiny wagon and waited by the horse for his children to load in the back with the few possessions they were taking with them. His plan was to head southwest into New York City stopping at his Aunt's house along the way. There was much ground to cover before they got there, and he wanted to get started as soon as possible.

Samuel helped his two brothers and little sister load into the wagon then pulled himself up. He sat to one side with his sister next to him. He slapped the side of the wagon to let his dad know they were ready. There was a jerk, and the wagon began to move out. He watched their small home grow even smaller as his dad directed the horses away.

His sister was taking the move the hardest of them all. She was only five, and this is the only home she remembered. She also couldn't remember their mother at all. "It will be alright, Meredith," he told her. "You'll see."

She clutched her doll a little tighter and tried to stifle a sob. She looked up to him and wanted to believe him. It was just hard to think that anything would be alright ever again.

The wagon rocked and tossed them around making it difficult to find a comfortable position. Eventually all of Samuel's siblings were fast asleep. Meredith had her head on his leg which meant it would be impossible for him to move without waking her. He had to stay still no matter how much he may want to shift around.

Samuel couldn't sleep. He watched as they rode farther and farther from the best home he'd ever had. He was tired of having to move. They had moved around many times when he was very little as they struggled to find a place where his dad could work, and the town's people would be kind to them. The last place they lived before his mother died made it seem like they had finally found somewhere to call home. They only moved away from there because it was too painful for his father to stay.

Salem had seemed like an answer to their prayers. They lived outside the town, so they kept mostly to themselves. When they did interact with the townsfolk, there were never any problems. The people left them alone so long as they weren't hurting anyone, but didn't try to include them much. Their father was a good man who worked hard and always dealt a fair deal. Even so, it didn't help to make them easily accepted in any community.

This one had been a little different. His siblings

had started becoming friendly with the children in town as well. He had even gone to work himself. Now they would have to start over again somewhere new, not knowing what would happen. This was the hardest part of it all. He could still remember some of the places they had been and how the people didn't react well to their presence.

There was nothing he could do. It was up to father to make the decisions for the family, and he was already treading water with the comments and questions he had allowed himself to ask. If he pushed too hard, he would be punished. He was certain of it. His father needed him to be a dutiful son and support him right now even if they didn't see eye to eye. It was hard for him to ignore his own worry to do so, but he made up his mind that he would from this point forward.

It would take them a week to reach his aunt's house in Waterbury near New York. Their plan had been to travel by day and camp at night hoping to run into as few people as possible along their way. They had brought just enough food to last the trip, and weather was on their side. It was summertime, and the rain seemed to be holding off for them to travel. Boredom and worry of what the future held were their only real concerns.

They arrived at their aunt's home late in the evening. She rushed outside to greet them. She had been distant for most of their lives, sending only the occasional letter. She had never cared for the witch business as she called it. No matter what Samuel's dad ever tried to do to convince her that what she's heard about witches, and what his mom truly had been were two different things entirely, she would have nothing to do with him if it weren't for the fact he was the father of her nieces and nephews.

She had often plagued his wife with her thoughts about the life she was setting her kids up for by marrying him. Gideon knew his aunt had not been upset over his mother's death. She had probably been praying for it for years. He couldn't help but feel resentment toward her. This was his father's sister, and they needed a place to stay to rest and gather more supplies for the remainder of their journey. He would be polite and try his hardest to be kind even if it made him feel like he was dishonoring his mother by doing so. He knew his mother would understand, but that wasn't the point.

Samuel had only met his aunt a couple times, and that was long ago. He was surprised when his dad made the turn down a long dirt path that led to a beautiful two story home. His awe was short lived when his dad went past the house and behind the stables to a smaller home in the back.

"Servants quarters," he mumbled aloud, not intending for his father to hear him.

"My father's sister and her husband both work for the estate owner. They live here on the property, but they aren't servants. They are paid help."

He knew that many people lived like this, even back in Salem. He had never known his aunt did as well. He wondered how they would be received as guests on property that was owned by someone else. His dad must have sensed his concern because he added, "Her employer knows we are coming and will be visiting a couple nights as we travel through. We've promised they won't even know we are here."

Samuel's great-aunt came out to greet them. Her smile seemed genuine for the children, but it was obvious she wasn't overjoyed to see them. The smile quickly disappeared when she turned to Gideon.

"Get on inside now, and no noise. I have promised you will all be as quiet as mice while you are here. I expect to keep my promise. Understand?"

They nodded and went inside. It was a small home. There was one large room for the living and kitchen areas with one bedroom in the back. It wasn't much different than the homes they were used to living in except a bit more crowded with the extra people.

There was a stew on the stove waiting for them. The children washed their hands then sat down immediately. They were all sitting on the floor in the living room area while the adults filled the table. They paid no mind as they were famished. They'd had enough to eat on their trip, but nothing like this. Samuel's siblings dug in without reason to think about anything else. He set about his plate at a slower pace being mindful of the adults who were talking.

It was clear his uncle wanted them here even less than his aunt. He was only accommodating them to support his wife's innate sense of family obligation, but if they would leave right now it wouldn't be soon enough.

His uncle and father spoke about plans and deals that had been set in place before they had left their home. His father had brought along furs and supplies to trade for more food and a little money to help them start out in New York. It sounded to Samuel like his dad was being taken advantage of by them, but they really had no choice. His father was set on this move to keep his family safe, and he would do whatever was necessary to see it through.

They were to leave in two days, but Samuel hoped their visit could be cut shorter. The more he eavesdropped on the adults' conversation, the more he didn't want to stay another minute. His aunt despised his grandmother. She felt no real affection for any of the children either since they were connected to her. Her only reason for helping at all stemmed from the love she had for her late brother, and that was obviously not going to account for much itself. His uncle wanted them all gone. It was apparent that he had been quite happy not being a part of their lives up until this point and was quite irritated to have them here now.

After supper, Samuel managed to pull his father aside to talk privately. He wanted to tell him how he felt, but he wasn't sure how to do it without upsetting him even more. He lost his nerve once he got his dad alone and decided to give it a rest. Two nights here couldn't be much worse than the one night they would already be forced to spend. Perhaps things would be better the next day.

His father surprised him by bringing it up himself. "This isn't going the way I had pictured it would."

Samuel looked up at him thankful his father gave him the opening, "This visit with your aunt and uncle?"

"Yes," he said, staring off across the field into the night. "I know she never forgave me for marrying and having children, for passing on the heritage to the next generation. I had thought she would be a bit kinder toward you children given that none of you have been called yet. I should have given more thought to how her husband would treat us."

"How did she find out about grandmother?" Samuel asked. "I thought grandfather never told her."

His father sighed and rubbed his forehead. He was silent for several minutes. Samuel believed he wasn't going to answer.

"It was meant to be kept from her. My father wanted it that way. That's why she was angry about you children when she found out about my mom. She didn't want us to pass on the curse as she called it."

"When you were just a babe, we lived near here. Your aunt had gifted your mom with a marvelous sewing kit when we were married. It continued to be one of her most prized possessions even after we fell out of touch over my aunt's feelings regarding your grandmother. One night, your grandmother was visiting and picked up a needle to set about her embroidery. She connected with your aunt when she touched the loom that had been part of the gift."

"What did she see?"

"Your aunt was alone in the main house and had fallen down the stairs. She was bleeding and unconscious. Your grandmother sent me to fetch help for her."

"And you told her how you knew she was in trouble?"

"Eventually, yes. I thought she might be thankful. Your grandmother saved her life, but instead, she grew hateful and afraid of your grandmother and me. She wanted no more to do with her, me or any of you children."

"I should like to leave earlier if we can," Samuel said the words without thinking.

His father looked at him and nodded. "I had been thinking the same," he told him. "I'm sure they won't mind if we announce an earlier departure. We shall get our business tended to in the morning and leave shortly after we're through."

They went back inside and headed to bed. Samuel's aunt and uncle had made pallets on the floor for all the children while father had decided to spend the night in the wagon outside alone. It was hard for him to drift off. He could hear whisperings coming from the bedroom. He knew his aunt and uncle were discussing them, and he longed to be able to hear what was being said. He couldn't get close enough to listen without disturbing at least one of the other children. He didn't want to bring any attention to himself or what he was trying to do as it would defeat the purpose. Instead, he lay there as still as possible trying to concentrate on their hushed voices hoping to discern a word or two.

He couldn't remember falling asleep and had no idea how late it had become before he did. The wakeup call was definitely loud and rude at its nicest. A noise coming from the direction of the dining table jerked him awake, and he sat up rubbing his eyes trying to see what was happening. The only light was the moon glow through the open window which was partially blocked by trees. He could hear muffled crying from somewhere nearby and knew instantly it was Meredith.

He moved near her and put his arms around her, rocking her gently. He stroked her hair and quietly whispered everything would be alright. More than ever, he wanted to be gone from this place.

His aunt finally lit a candle in the kitchen allowing him to see what was happening. He and Meredith were partially blocked by the furniture as they sat huddled against the wall, but no one was paying attention to any of the children as they woke one by one.

Samuel gathered enough to know that witchcraft accusations were being strewn about and were aimed at Meredith. The aunt had awoken during the night to hear the child chanting in her sleep. She was muttering a spell that would bring the devil upon her home the aunt yelled out.

His father only laughed. If she had bothered to learn anything at all about his mother or his family's beliefs over the years then she would know that the devil isn't even a part of it. His daughter couldn't possibly call upon something she doesn't believe to be real. Not to mention that even if Meredith was to be the one called this generation, it wouldn't happen for at least another ten years. She was much too young to demonstrate any signs yet. He tried to assure his sister that what she heard was merely a small child talking in her sleep, and her own fears made her believe it was anything more than that.

Samuel whispered to Meredith as quietly as he could, and asked, "Do you remember what you were dreaming?'

Meredith nodded. Her crying had stopped, but he could still see the stained tear tracks on her face.

"Can you tell me?" he whispered, putting his finger to his lips to let her know to do it quietly. He leaned down and placed his ear in front of her mouth.

She reached up and grabbed his head, pulling him closer and whispered, "I dreamt about Anya."

He pulled his head back suddenly and turned to the kitchen to make sure no one had noticed them yet. It was safe. The only person paying attention to Meredith was him. Even his half-awake siblings were watching the adults, not them.

"Anya? The first witch?" he asked for clarification.

Meredith nodded. She started to cry again. This time her sobs weren't as hard, but he held her close anyway. "She told me that we needed to leave because trouble was headed our way."

"She said that? In so many words exactly?"

Meredith shook her head no. "She said we need to leave right now. Our lives depend upon it."

Samuel turned his attention back to his father. He didn't know the hour, but he could see it was still awhile till sun up. There had to be a way to convince father to leave as soon as possible.

Samuel was certain it would be Meredith to receive the calling now. If Anya had spoken to her, they would be wise to heed the message. They shouldn't wait for dawn.

The aunt was still insisting that she knew what she heard. It was chanting in a tongue she had never heard before, and the child was spelling her family and casting a curse.

His father slammed his fist against the wall and yelled, "Enough!"

Everyone stopped at that moment and focused their full attention on him. "I might be a guest in your home Delilah, but remember your place. Need I remind you that you owe me your life? In more ways than one? You would not have met your husband if I hadn't introduced you. Neither of you would have been employed by the owners of this estate that allowed you to live comfortably while you raised your own children if it weren't for me putting my name, my reputation on the line for you. You would do well to remember that."

He turned to his children and told them to get dressed. They would be leaving immediately. This seemed to calm his aunt and uncle down at once. They tried to apologize for their error and convince them to stay, but his father would not hear any more of their weak attempt to make things right.

"You didn't like my mother. If you choose not to like my children, that's your own unfortunate misguidance. You didn't have to agree to take us in and help us when I wrote you, but you did. I am and always will be your nephew. I thought you would at least extend the curtesy one might show a stranger they pass on the street, but you have done nothing except make us feel as unwelcome as possible. And now you awaken everyone in the middle of the night with these horridly absurd accusations. I'll be damned if we stay here a moment longer."

The children jumped to their feet and quickly grabbed their meager belongings before rushing to the door. No one had to be told twice to leave. In fact, everyone would depart gladly even with the sleep disturbing scene.

Samuel's aunt and uncle followed them outside trying to convince them to wait until morning. Gideon ignored them completely except for one instance where his uncle got too close to the wagon. "You would be wise to step back, Vincent." He held a tone in his voice that could not be confused for anything other than what it was, pure unadulterated rage.

They quickly loaded up and departed. Samuel sat by his father as he was now too awake to try to lay down with his siblings. Plus, he needed the chance to tell him about Meredith's dream. He sat in silence until they were miles down the road and the sun had risen behind them.

"How long until we reach New York?" he asked, when he felt his father's temper had calmed.

"Less than a week before we get to the city. I would say five days, four if we push hard."

Silence followed. Samuel had so much to discuss, but he wasn't sure if his father was ready. He didn't want to upset him more, but he knew there would never be a right time. He had resigned himself to waiting until that evening when they stopped for the night to eat and rest. After the younger ones had fallen asleep, he would try to approach him.

These thoughts were interrupted by a small chuckle from his father. Samuel looked up trying to figure out what had amused him. Nothing about what happened in the last couple of days was humorous. His father saw the puzzled look on his face and laughed even harder.

"What is it?" he asked his father.

"I shouldn't be laughing, son. I have only now

realized what a terrible thing I've done."

Samuel was even more confused. How could it have taken his father this long to realize that going to an aunt's home who hated his family was a bad idea? As if reading his mind, his father shook his head.

"No, son, it's not that. I knew almost as soon as we arrived that we never should have gone there."

His father then explained that he had taken their talk the night before to heart. After Samuel went to join the others and go to sleep, he had gone into the shed and loaded the meat and other previously agreed to items into the wagon. He pulled the trunk of furs and other supplies to the edge of the wagon where it could be easily handed over to his aunt and uncle in the morning.

"I was going to have us leave right after breakfast. I had everything ready. In the midst of the argument, I had forgotten all about my preparations."

"You didn't leave the trunk for them?"

"No, son. I've never thought of myself as a thief, and part of me is saying I should turn around without delay and give them what is rightfully theirs." He sighed and looked off distant. "I don't know. What do you suggest?"

Samuel felt vitally regarded because his father had asked for his opinion. "There's something I haven't told you yet because I wasn't sure when to bring it up. Send them something when we get to New York to ease your mind over what you took, but do not turn around. We can't go back."

He went on to tell his father about what Meredith had told him. He described how she said Anya came to her in a dream advising they leave at once.

His father laughed again. "So my dear aunt was right after all? My daughter was chanting in her sleep. Imagine that."

Samuel was happy his father took the news so well, but it was a little unnerving just how high spirited his father reacted. He had expected some concern over Meredith receiving a vision at her young age, or what would they do if the trouble followed them wherever they went.

It would take a couple years before they knew it, but New York would turn out to be the best hope for their family. Father wouldn't have to work from sunup till sundown like he had all his life. He would find employment tending the horses and driving the carriage of a wealthy businessman who treated everyone kindly. He and his children would live in a wing of the estate with a few of the other help. They would grow up being well provided for as this man's heart was as generous as his waist was wide.

Father had sent a package to his aunt and uncle repaying them for what he unintentionally stole. The package was returned to him some while later. It had never been opened. Father took it to mean that his aunt had finally cut him out of her life and for good this time. His conscious was still clear as he had attempted to make amends for his wrong doings.

Not long after they settled into their new life, Meredith would receive her calling. It would begin with prophetic dreams and visions. Soon it would grow stronger until she learned to harness her power gracefully. Father had worried about how to help whichever of his children were called since their ancestors had passed on leaving no one to help with the training. He also worried that if his employer suspected her of witchcraft, they would be tossed onto the streets if not reported to authorities and hung.

His employer died unexpectedly one afternoon leaving a greatly distressed widow who would wander the halls of the estate aimlessly at night in her grief. The widow stumbled upon Meredith practicing the craft one night, but she was not frightened. The woman had long held a secret fascination with the occult and had privately visited psychics, fortune tellers, and so called witches many times throughout her life. She was eager to learn that there was a real witch hidden amongst the children who shared her home. In fact, she did everything she could to encourage her studies including finding rare and ancient texts and grimoires, supplies for spelling, anything the girl could want. In return, she only requested to use her powers to communicate with her deceased husband nightly. Meredith did this gladly.

It was during this time that they learned the truth about the package, and why their aunt had opened her home to his family that fateful night. Delilah had turned them in for witchcraft. When she talked to her employer about her nephew's request for a visit, she told him about the witchcraft in the children's blood. The employer being a greedy man turned them in for a small reward. Hours after they fled the sister's home, the authorities showed up to bring them into custody.

Finding the family gone, the aunt's employer was left feeling humiliated in front of the crowd that had gathered to watch. He was also forced to repay the reward he had already received. Money he had already begun to spend. His embarrassment turned to anger, and he fired both the sister and her husband on the spot even accusing the husband of theft. He was arrested and died in jail. The property owner set fire to the small house they had lived in for over twenty years before Delilah could remove any of her belongings, or the little money they had stashed away.

She was turned out penniless with no family to help her after she had so carelessly discarded her nephew. Her husband was gone, and their children steered clear of her, not wanting the ill affects the association would bring them. They learned to do that from her and her treatment of her own family. She was seen for a time living on the streets in Waterbury where she was often tripped, tricked and ridiculed publicly for having no one and no home. Eventually, she wandered off on her own hoping to find better favor in another town. She was never seen or heard from again.

Meanwhile, Samuel and his family's esteem continued to grow. A new maid at the estate where they lived was coincidently an Earth as well named Gaia. She taught Meredith so much more than she would learn from books in a lifetime. She also taught her about her heritage as an Elemental.

Their kinship continued to grow and was believed by many to be an act of fate that they would find each other as Gaia had never married or had children of her own. She took Meredith under her wing like she was her own daughter. Nothing came between them until Meredith met Luke.

Gaia disapproved of him immediately while father liked the boy's spirit. Gaia warned Meredith from the onset to keep clear of him as he was nothing but trouble who would bring heartache to her family. Her warnings fell on deaf ears. Meredith fell hopelessly in love.

Meredith soon learned the meaning behind Gaia's warnings, and the sacrifice she would have to make to be with Luke. It was still worth it to her to be with her one true love. Meredith was working out how to break the news to father when the widow woman passed away. She had left her family enough money to be able to start over again on their own feet after having to leave the estate. It was no doubt a thankful tribute for the help she received from Meredith over the years to speak to her departed husband.

Once Meredith knew that her father would not suffer for her choices, she fled with Luke. She never saw her family again, and they blamed Gaia for driving her away. Her family lived long and happy lives, but died not knowing what happened to Meredith. It was the only way she could be with Luke.

They never knew it, but she visited them often. Meredith would stay in the shadows or be one of many faces in the crowd. She often left small gifts or surprises for them when she could. Only once did anyone suspect it was her. She had purchased a whittled figurine of two children huddled together at a small shop during her travels. She snuck into Samuel's home one day long after his own children were grown and left it atop his dresser.

# Chapter Twenty

Everleigh went upstairs to the room where her aunt had slept last night after rescuing Lilah from her uncle. Voices could be heard in the hallway, but they weren't argumentative at least. She quietly rapped on the door. Nothing. She knocked again louder.

The door opened a crack. It was Luke. "I knew you'd miss me."

She glared at him. "Where's my aunt? I need to talk to her."

Luke opened the door for her then flung himself back on the bed hard enough to bounce acting like a child.

"Is something wrong?" Todd asked.

"No, I just wanted to tell you guys not to come downstairs for a little while."

"She's telling him then?" her aunt was pleased, and you could hear it in her voice as well as see it on her face.

"Soon. She's going to take a little glance into the future first."

"What?" Todd was visibly shaken. "That is too dangerous for her to do without someone nearby in case it goes badly."

"I know the risks, but it was the only way she'd tell him. She had to see for herself first that Jackson would take the news well."

"I'm going down there," Todd headed for the door.

"She has already started," Everleigh stopped him, not sure if it was true. Lilah would be doing it soon at any rate.

Todd shook his head in frustration and began pacing the floor like a madman with his hands on his hips. "Do you have any idea what could happen?"

"I do," Everleigh said annoyed. She wanted to leave him to his panic attack and jump in the shower like she told her friends downstairs.

"It could be severely damaging for her. There's no limit to the injuries that could result."

"She is well aware of this. She's only going to see into the future as far as this conversation. Lilah's told me she's looked farther than that before."

"With one of her parents on guard!"

"On guard?"

"You know what I mean. Someone to help if things go wrong."

"And things only go wrong if she gets sucked down the rabbit hole, right?"

"That's right."

"Which only happens if she tries to see too far ahead? Not just one simple conversation?"

"You don't understand, Everleigh. You haven't seen the adverse effect it could have on us."

"I do understand the risks, but I also know Lilah wouldn't do anything to tempt that fate. Stop treating her like a child and trust she knows what to do." Everleigh said angrily, growing tired of the eggshells that everyone had to walk on around Lilah. Let her live and learn already.

"Even the strongest of us have slipped down that slope. It's easier than you realize."

That was enough pointless arguing for Everleigh. It was a futile argument. Lilah was already on her vision quest and could even be finished by now. No arguing could change it. They insisted she convince Lilah to tell Jackson the truth as soon as humanly possible. Mission accomplished. If they don't like her methods, maybe they should have put someone else up to the task.

"I'm going to take a shower," she said to her aunt. "I'll check on things downstairs when I'm done and let you know."

Meredith mouthed the words thank you at her niece, and focused on Todd to try to assure him everything would be fine.

Everleigh walked down the hall to the room she had shared with Matt and Rita, sneaking in slowly not wanting to wake them. It was a good thing Jackson's dad was out of town, or they'd have run out of room for people to sleep. She grabbed her overnight bag and headed back out, but noticed Rita's eyes had opened.

Kneeling down by the bed, she whispered quietly what was happening downstairs. If anyone walked in while Lilah was talking to Jackson, she would lose her nerve. Everleigh was as certain of that as she was her own name.

Now that everyone had been informed, she headed to the bathroom. It needed to be as believable as possible for Lilah's sake which means there could be no questioning by either of them what she had been doing upstairs if not taking a shower like she had told them she was going to do. There would be a hell of a storm to contend with if that girl found out Jackson already knew her truth. It was sure to come out one day and likely soon, but there was hope Lilah would be able to handle it by that time.

The hot water felt great running down her body and maybe she needed this more than she realized. There had been day after day of stressful news and preparations without a break for far too long now. A ten minute escape was more than warranted.

Something caught her attention, and she yelled out from the shower. There had been a loud rumbling in the hallway almost like a herd of cattle ran past the door. There was no reply. Turning the water off to hear better, she thought she heard a loud thud coming from the downstairs. Everleigh yelled again only louder this time. No one answered.

She wrapped a towel around herself and peeked out the door. There was silence. "Hello?" she called.

The room she had slept in last night with Matt and Rita was across the hall. The door was wide open, and it was easy to see it was empty. She tiptoed down the hall to the room where her aunt had stayed with Luke. No one was there either.

She started to panic that something had happened with Lilah. It must have gone horribly wrong. Whether it was the seeing into the future or the actual conversation, she had no way of knowing. She made it back to the bathroom as quick as she could and threw her clothes on even faster.

Everleigh ran to the stairs carrying her bag and shoes. There was no sign of anyone anywhere. The kitchen was empty, and one chair was toppled on the floor. *'That must be the noise I heard,'* she thought. She went to the door and looked out the window. The only car still there was hers.

The panic escalated. Lilah had to have ran away. It's the only thing that would explain it. She searched her bag for her phone, but couldn't find it.

"What the hell?" she yelled to an empty house, trying to remember when she last used it. It had to be in the kitchen.

She surveyed the room and saw a soft flashing red light hit the backsplash behind a box of pancake mix. That was it. There was only one message, and it was from her aunt.

"Farmhouse! Now!"

Everleigh didn't need a second nudge to move her along. She hopped toward the front door, putting her shoes on as she went. Something awful must've happened between Lilah and Jackson. There is probably a tornado getting ready to bear down on the family of Air that have congregated out in the country. She only hoped she could get there in time and talk some sense into her friend before it got too bad.

The drive took forever in her mind even as she pushed her little car as hard as she dared with the new snow that covered the roads. The farmhouse appeared in the distance, and it didn't take long to see she had been wrong. There was no storm beating down on the old structure. Lilah wasn't out of control. This urgency still had to be tied to Lilah's news. There was nothing else that could have happened as far as she knew.

The northern wolves hadn't arrived yet. There were updates on their locations sent out that Meredith relayed to her. The wolf movement had stopped. It seemed they were setting up a new base to prepare for their next move. They had time before the threat reached them.

She turned into the drive a little too fast and fishtailed a good way. It scared her, but going off road and getting stuck now would not be a problem. The rest of the driveway could be run in minutes. Parking was non-existent at this point. She turned her car around and parked it on the side of the drive facing the road. It would be better if she had to leave fast, and she also wouldn't have to move her car for someone else because she wasn't blocking anyone.

The house's aura vibrated brightly. The indigo shade that followed Air wherever they went was all but lost in the bright pulsating red and dark green. They were angry and pointing fingers at everyone except themselves. She knew she was headed into a frenzy parallel to a lion's den at feeding time.

At the door, she debated about knocking. Voices could be heard, but she couldn't tell what was being said. It sounded controlled like they were having a successful, albeit emotional, discussion. She rapped on the door lightly.

It quickly swung open. Jackson beamed at her. "Hello," then added "Lee-Lee," quietly afterward.

There was no time to yell at him, and he knew it. Everleigh pushed him out of the way and entered the house.

Lilah looked genuinely surprised to see that she was just arriving.

"I was in the shower," she explained.

"That's right. I didn't realize you weren't with the others when we left. Everything happened so fast."

"No worries. Just get me up to speed."

Before Lilah could say a word, the group continued their discussion.

"It isn't an issue of how he came to be in his current predicament," the elder Joseph said, his tone implying it's not the first time he's made this argument. "We need to concentrate on what to do to help him."

Todd had been pacing and stopped to face his brother. "It matters because if one of us turned him out to the wolves, that person might have knowledge that could be helpful to us."

"Whoa. What did I miss?" Everleigh asked more to herself than anyone in particular.

Jackson leaned over to her and whispered. "Brian drugged Lilah. Went outside. Disappeared. The northern wolves have him."

"Thanks," she said, without taking her eyes off the brothers who were now yelling at each other.

Lilah gave Jackson a slight nod, and he let out a shrill whistle that made Everleigh jump.

"He's been our referee," Lilah told her.

"Listen. There's an easy way to settle this," Meredith walked to the middle of the room.

Everyone turned to look at her. "Unblock

yourselves."

There were glances throughout the group as they both knew what she was suggesting, but unsure it was a fool proof plan.

"Pick one of you to read the rest then someone else will do their reading. It's simple. Time consuming, but simple. In the interim, we can start to work out a plan to help him." The last words rolled off her tongue with a bitter taste as she couldn't fathom why they would want to save that man after what he did to one of their own.

"I'll do it," Joseph volunteered.

The room filled with groans. "No," said Todd. "I think it would be best for Lilah to do it."

"Lilah," Joseph laughed. "She has no reason to want to successfully help her uncle."

"That I don't doubt, but when I read her at the end, I will know if she withheld anything from us."

Joseph stayed adamantly against it, but everyone else agreed. Lilah set to work on her family one at a time while the rest tried to work out a plan.

"What do we know?" Everleigh asked.

Meredith looked at her strangely before remembering she hadn't been here but a few minutes.

"When Brian didn't return last night, they thought he left of his own accord. This morning, Abby had a massive migraine."

"Air doesn't get migraines, not like that anyway," Everleigh said apprehensively, looking up from under her lids at her aunt. One of the biggest traits of Air was their health.

"Exactly," her aunt nodded. "It raised concerns. The migraines also cut off her ability to use her powers."

"So then what?"

Meredith raised her eyebrows, "Somehow they determined the solution was for Abby to not only unblock herself in the hopes the others could help, but to concentrate her energy on whatever was blocking her abilities."

"It worked? Brian was trying to communicate?" Everleigh was following what her aunt was telling her easily, but it didn't make sense. Air's gift was psychic thought. Their telepathic communication shouldn't be difficult if they were unblocked.

"Yes. Whenever she gets a headache now, they know it's because he's trying to contact her."

Lilah approached Meredith for a moment giving Everleigh's mind plenty of time to wander. As soon as Lilah began working with her family to see if anyone knew more about the situation then they let on, her aunt saw the look on Everleigh's face and grew concerned.

"What is it?" Aunt Meredith asked.

"It doesn't make sense."

Her aunt narrowed her eyes and waited for Everleigh to continue.

"The intermittent headaches. Brian is obviously unable to contact her continuously, and there are many different possible explanations. But why does she have to focus so hard. Shouldn't he be able to communicate freely? And why Lilah's mom?"

Aunt Meredith nodded slowly and eyed the room. She pulled Everleigh off to the side as much as she could and lowered her voice. "Good points. These concerns have been raised already. Air has been worried that whoever is behind this might be able to block their communication. No one here has brought it up since the headaches started with Abby, but Todd and I have discussed it before."

"Is it possible? Could they be blocked?"

Deep concern filled her aunt's already troubled eyes. "I don't think it's a question of if it can be done anymore. I think the focus should be on how it was accomplished."

Everleigh looked at her friend who was still moving through the room trying to determine if any of her family had secrets to divulge. Whatever was happening was constantly growing into something bigger than she expected. If the vampires could be controlled and the shifters communication could be blocked, there would be no limit to the confines that could be put on the witches to impair their ability to defend themselves.

There had been a dance with fear that spun around inside her since the day she looked into her grandma's pendant months ago. Sometimes the fear would lead, but most of the time Everleigh was in control of it. It firmly rooted in her mind as she realized the true nature of the situation all the Elementals were in and slowly spread through her body like the cold blast of icy air that hits when you first step outside. Each beat of her heart echoed in her ears like the ticking of a clock that was counting down, and they were running out of time.

# Chapter Twenty-One

Everleigh went home while her friends gathered for the meeting of Elementals. No one would have minded if she stayed, but there were things she needed to do herself. She walked in and felt almost like a stranger. It seemed like an eternity since life was more carefree without the daily conversations about impending doom.

In the kitchen, her grandmother and cousins gathered round the island discussing herbs. This is what she should be focused on right now. Helping the newly called learn and prepare for whatever may come. She went into the kitchen and asked, "Need me to do anything?"

Eloise was smiling before she came into Everleigh's view. Somehow her grandmother always knew what she was going to do before she did it. It impressed her and made her wonder if her abilities would ever be that strong.

"I'm glad you came," her grandmother smiled, leaning over allowing Everleigh to kiss her on the cheek.

"I was starting to think you decided to move in with the rest of that crew," Amber's voice was stained with anger. It wasn't easy always being left out of the group. Everleigh had been in her shoes once when she was first called and learning the ropes.

"Someone has to keep Meredith in line," Eloise remarked.

Same old grandma she thought. Meredith had spent half her life away from her familial line because of the decision she made with Luke. It took a long time for anyone to accept her again. Even then, it took a long time for her to be able to form good bonds and strong relations with her witch kin. Things had improved for her over the last century or so, but grandma had always made her feelings known. Meredith was born to be a witch, but chose to be a vampire. It didn't matter that she had the abilities of both. In grandma's mind, she chose against her heritage. Grandma would tolerate her, but could never fully accept her.

"I'm just saying I wouldn't mind being a part of things too," Amber whined.

"It's not that I don't want you to be a part of things," Everleigh tried to tell her.

"Then next time, you take me with you."

"Take you where?" Eloise asked.

Amber shrugged. "I don't know. Jackson's? The café? Wherever it is she's going."

"Why are you certain you would want to be a part of something when you don't even know what it is?" Eloise had never allowed jealous attitudes in her home.

"I don't like feeling left out," Amber answered honestly, which Eloise would no doubt appreciate.

Eloise had a small mischievous grin, "You are not left out, child. You have been called."

"I know, but-"

"No but's. You are included. You have been given this gift that if not for these abnormal times, you would not otherwise have had. It's time now to put in the work to learn how to use it well." Eloise always spoke about the craft as a birthright that should always be respected.

Their numbers were growing, and not just because of the calling. What began with Anya in one family many years ago had grown to countless covens all across the globe. They would normally never meet most of these witches or learn anything about them, but if any one of them was ever in need, Everleigh had no doubt her grandma would be on the next flight to aide them.

"Tell you what, Amber," Everleigh offered, remembering how it felt to still be learning the craft but being limited in what you were allowed to do. "Later, I'm supposed to be meeting up with some of them. Maybe you can come if you're done here for the day."

Grandma raised an eyebrow at her knowing it wasn't a full truth she had told. Everleigh was going to see if there was a way she could include Amber for a while, but really had no idea it was even possible.

"Sure," Amber said, trying not to sound happy about the offer because she didn't want to be reminded of the importance the work she was learning held.

"I'll be gone this afternoon," Eloise told her granddaughter.

Everleigh said nothing. She had already learned who the chosen Earth representatives were.

"Maybe your friend could come here, and everyone could have a break while I'm gone."

The four girls were sitting around the island and looked up hopeful. Everleigh wasn't near as close to the other three cousins as she was with Amber. She lived nearby, and they were close enough in age to have run into each other at school. It would be a chance to get to know them a little better as well.

"I think that sounds wonderful, Grandma. Thanks," Everleigh told her, relieved to have been saved from the hopeful promise she made Amber.

"You could even teach that friend of yours a few helpful tricks they can use without the power of magic," Grandma added.

"Oh, like magic for dummies?" Amber asked.

The kitchen filled with laughter.

"Something like that. Just make sure to

include some flying ointment when you do it," Grandma suggested.

"Why that one?" Everleigh stared wide eyed at her grandma not understanding why she should be introducing something so dangerous to anyone so inexperienced.

"It's a handy tool for anyone to have. Wouldn't you think?"

It made absolutely no sense to Everleigh. That was one that had virtually no real-life applications in today's age. The hallucinogenic and astral projection effects of it could be produced in much less dangerous manners. It was used quite often for various purposes in the dark ages, but as with most everything in the history of witchcraft, its actual use was exaggerated for the purposes of persecution. It was odd her grandma would mention it.

"You will cover that one, then?"

"Yes, Grandma," Everleigh knew not to argue. "I will."

"Good," she turned to the rest of the girls. "Remind her if she somehow forgets. She can teach all of you as well as her friend how to produce a successful flying ointment in my absence."

Grandma Eloise leaned in closer to her and said quietly, "Make sure they are all given a sample to keep, yourself included. Tell them they will know when to use it, and not to touch it until then."

Everleigh nodded even more upset than she had been. *Why give these girls something so dangerous? It could kill them if they played around with it.*

"Oh, and make sure Jackson gets some as well," her grandma smiled at her with that familiar knowing gleam in her eyes.

They looked just as confused as Everleigh, but they agreed to make sure it was covered. Eloise was unmistakably up to something, but no one knew exactly what it could be. *'She's probably just giving me a simple test. It's the only logical reason. Not only that I remember how it's done and execute it with accuracy, but to see if I'm capable of teaching others as well. It might be harder to teach a non-magical person,'* she assumed. *'Maybe this was another of her lessons. Preparing me to teach my own granddaughter one day.'*

"I'm going to go prepare myself now," Eloise announced, kissing her granddaughter on the forehead. "This is herbal review. Make sure they are preparing the plants correctly, would you?"

"Of course, Grandma."

Everleigh scanned the island and the kitchen counters. There were baskets of dried plants everywhere. The young witches were bottling them for both kitchen and spell use.

It's like when children help their mom who is busy baking. They always wind up wiping counters and drying dishes. That's how they learn. They do the grunt work and watch the adult who knows how things are done. This is the method her grandma applied to teaching witches who have been called too.

They will do the hands on work of planting, harvesting, drying, and preparing the herbs while Grandma gets the use out of them. It's not all bad. She knew her grandma would provide each girl with some to keep. Everleigh had already been through this herself.

"Alright," Everleigh began, figuring she should do something besides just watch them. "Which of these is beneficial to plant near other herbs who may be struggling?"

"Chamomile," Kiara answered excitedly, confident she was correct.

"Good."

*'That was an easy one,'* Everleigh thought. "Of the ones in front of you, which one will be most

used during Yule?"

"Rosemary," Jasmin answered as though bored.

"I wouldn't let our grandma hear that tone," Everleigh scolded.

Jasmin simply shrugged and continued her work.

It was obvious the girls had been at it for hours already and needed a break. "Okay. Two more questions for Amber and Grace. If you answer both correctly, I'll teach you a few quick fun things you can do with these herbs."

That caught their attention. All of the girls seemed to perk up a bit.

"When would you harvest Yarrow for magical purposes?"

"Midsummer's Day," Amber replied quickly.

"That leaves Grace. Let me think," Everleigh knew it would be unfair to make it a hard question as the rest of the girls got off easy, but she didn't want to make it too easy either. "Which of these goes by the nickname of Bruisewort?"

Grace looked at the plants covering all surface areas of the kitchen. "Mugwort!" she shouted. "No, wait. That's not it. Can I change my answer?"

Everleigh nodded.

"It's Comfrey," she said timidly.

"Are you sure?" Everleigh tested her.

She looked around hesitant. "Yeah, I'm sure," she said, but she didn't sound like she believed it.

"That's right."

There was a heavy sigh of relief.

Amber stopped what she was doing, and eyed Everleigh. "What are you teaching us then?"

Everleigh picked up a chamomile flower and a lavender bud and placed them in a sieve over a cup. With the Keurig on the counter, she filled the cup with hot water and let it steep for two minutes. She removed the sieve and chanted quietly over the cup, "The dark of night... Make her mind... Dream of things to come... And things desired... Sleep... Sleep now... Awake refreshed... So mote it be."

She placed the cup on the island and asked who was brave enough to try it.

"I'm not even the tiniest bit tired," Amber declared. Her eyes challenged Everleigh as she took the cup.

"Go on then," Everleigh smirked.

Amber took a sip. "See? Nothing."

Everleigh only watched as Amber continued to sip the tea. It wouldn't take long for the effect to hit. As Amber lifted it to her lips again, her eyes began to close. Everleigh walked around and grabbed both the cup and Amber before they hit the floor.

"Kiara, help me move her," she instructed.

The two of them struggled, but were able to move Amber to the couch.

"That was amazing!" Grace cried out when Everleigh returned to the kitchen. "How long will she be out?"

"It depends on how tired her body was and how much she drank. I would think not long. An hour, tops."

"Show us something else," Kiara pleaded.

This time Everleigh picked up a handful of basil leaves and breathed in the scent, but set them back down. She left the room and returned in a minute with a candle. "I will show you this one, but whoever casts this must put something good out into the universe to replace the positive energy bestowed to them."

Jasmin raised her hand weakly. "I'll do it."

"This is a candle that's been infused with basil. Look closely, and you can see pieces of the leaves throughout."

She turned the candle over in her hands then passed it down for the other girls to look as well.

Kiara was the last to look at it, and she handed it back to Everleigh.

"You are going to light this candle, draw in the light to protect you, and then repeat the chant I give you. Then blow it out."

"That's it?" Jasmin asked.

"Simple and effective. This is the chant." Everleigh said it to her slowly, allowing her time to repeat it to make sure she had it. "The moon... The sun... The skies... The ground... The waters... The Stars... Gather your luck... Flow through me... We will unite... We will shine bright."

Jasmin repeated it a couple more times under her breath before lighting the candle. She uttered the chant confidently. At the end when she said, "We will shine bright," the candle flame shot several feet high then extinguished on its own.

"Perfect," Everleigh smiled. "It's a short term spell. The effects will wear off soon."

"What is it for? Good luck?"

"Yes," Everleigh told her.

"How will she know it worked?" Kiara asked.

"Oh," Everleigh chuckled. "She will."

The girls exchanged doubtful glances. "If it works," Grace began, "what's to stop a witch from using this spell all the time?"

"Abuse of power," Everleigh stated. "I'm sure that was one of your first lessons."

"Yeah, but-" Kiara started.

"No but's. A witch must always exhibit caution when using their magic to their own benefit or to extremes, and you must always replace what nature gives you in some way."

"What if we don't?" Jasmin asked, but Everleigh wasn't sure if she was genuinely curious or trying to find a way to beat the system.

Before she could answer, Jasmin's phone rang.

"Hello?" She didn't say anything else for a

couple minutes, but her eyes widened in surprise. "I will. Thank you!"

The rest of the ladies waited for her to say something.

"You know that Halloween party we went to last weekend? I filled out a form and won a gift certificate to the restaurant."

"There's your luck," Everleigh winked at her.

It was clear by the look on her face that Jasmin wasn't convinced. "I probably would've won that anyway."

"Maybe," Everleigh told her, "But you never know."

Before she finished speaking, Jasmin's phone rang again. The entire group gasped collectively.

"Hello?" This time she stared at Everleigh throughout the entire call and started shaking her head by the time it was over. "Wow. Thanks. That's amazing."

Everleigh crossed her arms and waited for her to spill the news.

"Um, it appears I also won the costume contest."

"What did you win?" Kiara asked.

"A two hundred dollar Visa gift card."

"Holy hell!" Grace shouted.

"Still think it's a coincidence?" Everleigh asked.

"No, I shouldn't have won that."

"Why do you say?"

"Her costume was horrible," Kiara snickered.

"What was it?" Everleigh was really intrigued.

"I went as a witch."

"Well, I don't think that's horrible," Everleigh told her, but Kiara was in the middle of a laughing fit at this point. Everleigh looked back and forth between them wondering what she was missing.

"Her costume," Kiara gasped. "It was just the dress and hat. Cheap looking."

Jasmin's face flushed. "I decided to go last minute, and they insisted I dress up. I grabbed it as I ran out the door. It wasn't like I knew there was a costume contest or anything."

Everleigh got a chuckle picturing Jasmin dressed up in a cheesy low quality costume without any makeup or accessories. "So what do you think of the spell now?"

"That one was definitely the spell. It had to be. There were so many really good costumes at that party."

"Think about what you won. You have to replace these good vibes somehow, or it will be taken from you in another way." Everleigh explained.

"What do you mean taken?" Jasmin was confused.

"It's like karma," Grace told her.

Everleigh bobbed her head from side to side contemplating the comparison. "A little like karma, yeah. That's one way of saying it."

"Except times three," Kiara chimed.

"Exactly. The rule of three," Everleigh said decisively.

"So what do I have to do?" Jasmin looked worried.

"Do something good for others. Something unexpected and without them asking for it," Everleigh told her. "We should always be putting that good out into the world anyway, but you especially need to now."

"I'm just going to donate it. I didn't deserve to win it anyway," Jasmin decided. "But I'm keeping the restaurant one."

"I think that will do it," Everleigh smiled in approval. It was exactly what she would have done in Jasmin's shoes.

Eloise walked into the room and looked around before spying Amber lightly snoring on the couch.

"Teaching those fun spells, I see," she said, not necessarily approving.

"It was a reward for getting all the answers correct to questions I asked about these herbs," Everleigh explained.

Her grandma's attitude changed hearing that, and she nodded favorably. "Did you teach them about flying ointment yet?"

"No, but I will when Amber comes around."

"Good. Don't forget."

There was a knock on the door which opened right after it. Meredith's voice could be heard down the hall, "Knock, knock. It's me!"

She appeared in the kitchen moments later and groaned. "I feel for all of you. I hated this part of magic training."

"It's not training, Meredith. Its life knowledge," Eloise was easily agitated by her.

"To-may-to, to-mah-to," Meredith quirked. "Everleigh, why are you doing this? I thought you would be long past Intro to Witchy Plants 101."

"I'm helping out since Grandma will be gone for the afternoon."

"Oh," Meredith raised her eyebrows and pursed her lips. "I'm impressed. Eloise doesn't trust the education of newly called witches to just anyone."

"Enough of your mouth," Eloise snapped.

Everleigh stood back out of the crossfire. It still amazed her that her grandma agreed to ride with her aunt. It would be an awkward ride for both of them given how Grandma felt about the vampire side of Aunt Meredith.

"I'll be good," Meredith acted innocent. "I promise," she said, crossing her fingers in plain sight for all to see.

A couple of the girls snickered which brought sharp glances their way from Grandma Eloise.

"Let's get going," she told Meredith. "You know

how I hate arriving late."

Meredith's eyes widened, and she looked at her watch. She mouthed the words, "I'm early!" to Everleigh as Eloise left the room to grab her coat.

Everleigh instinctively slapped her hand over her smile even though her grandma couldn't see her anymore.

"Meredith!" Eloise called from the doorway. "Time doesn't stop for anyone, least of all you!"

She balled her fists and scrunched up her face with eyes her closed tight. Moving closer to Everleigh, she whispered, "You better cast a spell for us while you're at it. We're gonna need the help."

With that, she called out, "Right behind you, Eloise," and hurried toward the door. In seconds, the door shut behind them.

All of the ladies in the kitchen burst into laughter at once. They laughed until they cried. They were so loud Amber woke up, and in a confused state wondered aloud how she wound up in the next room asleep. This only added to their outburst. It was several long minutes before continuing any spell work was considered.

Jackson arrived not long after that. It was time. The idea of producing a flying ointment made Everleigh nervous. Jackson would no doubt be careful with it, but some of her cousins might decide to play around. One in particular caused her alarm over the possibility.

"What exactly is a flying ointment?" Jackson raised an eyebrow at the herbs spread out before everyone.

"It gives witches the ability to fly," Grace answered.

Jackson pulled back the corners of his mouth and shrugged. "I wondered if it was that simple."

"Not exactly," Everleigh countered, cutting a sharp look at Grace. This is why she didn't think they were ready for such learning. They didn't even understand what they were creating.

"Go on," Jackson encouraged.

Everleigh grabbed a box of medical grade plastic gloves to pass around. "These herbs are deadly if not handled properly. I'm not taking any risks," she told the group.

"Flying ointment is a salve that has been around in one form or another long before the term witch was coined. Back around the medieval times, it got its name because it was believed to give a witch the ability to fly on her broomstick," Everleigh rolled her eyes. It never ceased to disturb her the untold horrors and often comical accusations her ancestors had been dealt.

"When applied, it will cause hallucinations before sending the user into a comatose state. Anyone who discovered your body would believe you to be dead. There would be no detectable heart rate or respirations. Meanwhile, you will be in the midst of an out of body experience."

Jasmin's eyes lit up. "Astral projection?"

Everleigh nodded. "Before you get too excited, you must use extreme caution. These herbs we're working with and the salve itself can, and will, kill you if you don't know what you're doing."

The atmosphere in the room changed as Everleigh spoke the words which is exactly what she needed. This work demanded respect. It was hard to say which unnerved her the most.

Teaching these novices how to make flying ointment would allow them to try to recreate it on their own, sending them off with their own sample to be responsible for safe keeping when they barely revered the craft. There was also the glaring certainty that there would be a need for them to use it because it's the only reason her grandma would have asked her to complete this task.

Measuring out the belladonna, devil's weed and mandrake kept her cousins solemnly in line. Jackson was the one who needed to be informed of the harsh consequences of the herbs. Everleigh did most of the work not wanting to risk any accidents on her watch. It took longer than she'd have liked to finish up, but everyone was equipped with a balm tin of flying ointment when she was done.

Amber was the first one to ask how to use it which didn't come as a surprise. "Just rub it on your skin or something? How much? All of it?"

Everleigh closed her eyes and swallowed hard. The one person she would expect to play around with the ointment was Amber. The girl had developed very little respect for the craft yet. It was becoming clearer by the day why she hadn't been the original one to receive the calling. Witchcraft really didn't suit her insubordinate ways. This was a lifestyle you had to take on as your own. It wasn't something you could control and amend to your own needs. It was something you had to obey and honor.

"Ask Grandma to give you the directions," Everleigh said, opening her eyes. The ingredients on the table were all dangerous on their own, and she hurriedly began collecting everything to store them away.

"You showed us how to make it and gave it to us, but you're not going to tell us how to use it?" Amber seethed with irritation.

That's another reason why the calling should have skipped her. She was quick to anger. One needed to keep a cool head about themselves in this line of work. "That was all Grandma asked me to do. If she wants you to use it, she will tell you how."

Amber was about to object again. The irritation was growing into something more, and that rage could be felt by everyone in the room.

*'Let her get as angry as she wants. I'm not telling her what to do with it just so we can find her lifeless body in the morning.'*

Before either of them could speak again, the front door burst open, and Grandma Eloise's voice could be heard yelling through the house. They were all needed and whatever was going on sounded urgent.

"Jackson, wait a minute," Everleigh told him, sneaking to look out of the sunroom.

Matt, Rita and Luke were walking in the front door. There'd be alarm over Luke's presence except it looked like everyone from the meeting was showing up. "Where's your truck?" she asked.

"Way ahead of you, Lee-Lee," Jackson smiled. "I walked over here because I suspected something like this might happen."

Everleigh was so relieved she almost let the use of the nickname slide without retaliation. "How about that?" she said slowly.

Jackson squinted his eyes wondering what she was getting at.

"You do have a brain in that thick head of yours! Who knew?"

She caught the box of medical gloves Jackson whipped at her head. Everleigh held a finger to her mouth telling him to be quiet and nodded toward the hall. "Use the back door. Go back home and get your truck. I'll let you know when it's safe to show up if Lilah doesn't get ahold of you first."

Everleigh waited for Jackson to disappear through the backyard before checking to see what all the commotion in the front of the house was about.

## Chapter Twenty-Two

Eloise and Meredith came rushing into the house together startling the friends who were busy finishing up the work left for them to do. "Girls!" Eloise called from the front room. "Come now."

They filed in to see what was so urgent with Everleigh taking her time joining them. They had been waiting to hear the news of the meeting, but this looked too urgent to bring it up.

"There is important work to be done," Grandma Eloise informed them.

A knock on the door was answered by Grace. It was Rita, Matt and Luke.

The girls held their breath and waited for the fireworks to begin. It was beyond anyone's comprehension that Luke would just waltz in the front door knowing Eloise was at home and knowing how much she despised him.

"Boys," Eloise called out. "Move this furniture post-haste. We need a place to work."

Luke and Matt immediately set to work clearing all of the furniture from the front room until it was empty. All that remained were the framed prints on the walls.

This was surreal like a twilight zone experience. Everleigh walked in on Luke offering a helping hand like he was one of the family. She had questions and more were developing at lightning speed. What had happened to convince her grandma to work with the others like this was her main concern. Something forced this change.

Todd and Lilah soon joined the group as well. It wouldn't have surprised her at this point if the southern tribe leader walked through the door. *'That actually wouldn't be too bad,'* she thought.

She was overly curious to meet him, but he was the one representative who didn't make an appearance.

"Alright, girls," Grandma Eloise said, directing her attention to the four newly called witches. "We are in need of a coven. You will partake in this as well. Now, gather what we need to cast a circle."

The girls excitedly ran from the room gathering everything that was needed. There was much rambling coming from them as they marveled in the idea of doing real spell work for a change and to be a part of a coven with their grandma. It didn't matter what spell was being cast. They did not concern themselves with any more details. They were finally being included as equals.

"How many of us are there?" Grandma counted off the witches. "Four," she said, looking toward the directions the girls had just went. Then she counted Everleigh, Rita and Meredith in that order. "Five, six, seven, and I make eight. That won't do. We need at least nine."

Amber and Grace walked into the room with their arms full of candle boxes and holders. Meredith and Rita helped them unload then sent them back for more supplies. Kiara was making one trip after another bringing chalices and herbs. She didn't even know what would be needed, so she grabbed everything she could find. No one instructed her different. Jasmin came in bearing salt and chalk not sure which they'd use for the circle.

Meredith smiled at her and took what she brought. These girls were doing their best to be helpful, but in their hurry they were creating a lot more work for the rest.

Everleigh scanned through everyone she knew in her mind trying to see who was the closest to them as time certainly appeared to be of the essence. "There's Aunt May," she told her grandma. It would take about an hour for her to get here allowing her time to get ready to leave. That shouldn't delay them too long.

"Not necessary," her grandma told her.

*'There's no one closer to us than Aunt May,'* she thought as she searched her mind a second time trying to figure out who she missed.

"Matt," Eloise called.

"Yes, Ma'am."

"You will be the ninth member, and Todd?"

"Yes, Eloise," Todd answered immediately as if he'd been waiting for his instructions. He moved with superhuman speed to her side.

"You and Lilah will amplify the effects of the spell. You know what to do?"

"Yes, Eloise," Todd told her. He had done this very thing many times in the past with Meredith.

"Me?" Matt questioned, looking at everybody in the room with surprise. "I can't be the ninth."

"And why not?" Eloise asked tartly. "Do you have better plans for your time?"

"No," his eyes darted away. Eloise could intimidate the strongest of men. "I'm a wolf. I'm not an Earth."

"I know that, dear," Eloise said, sounding irritated and looking at him like he had just called her an idiot. "I also am well aware of who was your great-grandmother. Am I wrong to believe that Earth blood resides in your veins just the same as Water's blood runs through them?" she asked.

Matt nodded at her. "That's enough?"

Eloise put her arm around him. Everleigh was setting up the candles around the floor while Meredith and Rita drew the star, but she paused to watch. She knew her grandma was about to explain to Matt that anyone could fill the position, magical or not. It just wouldn't do with only eight people. Having a trace of Earth blood was better than none at all, but in a pinch, a non-descendant would've worked. Everyone in the house was distracted from their tasks before her grandma could say a word.

A loud sudden noise from the hallway caused everyone to jump. Everleigh turned to see Lilah collapsed on the floor on her side, clutching her chest and struggling to breathe. Todd went to her and held her head still between his hands on his lap.

"Look at me, Lilah!" he yelled at her. "That's it. Directly in my eyes. You are at the home of Eloise Campbell, remember? We have gathered here to aid the witches. Focus!"

Everleigh walked to the doorway with her mouth gaped open. The beating of her heart was so loud and fast beneath her sweater she was sure everyone could hear it. They had all worn blinders while working on the setup. She hadn't seen anything happen to Lilah. She didn't know what it was that had affected her like this or who.

"Breathe, Lilah," Todd instructed her again, as she continued to fight for air.

Lilah was slowly improving. Whatever had happened to leave her like this had to be strong, but it was clear that she would soon be alright.

Todd continued to hold her face and didn't break his eye contact with her, but he spoke to someone else. Perhaps it was directed solely to Eloise. Perhaps it was for the group. Everleigh wasn't sure who he was talking to, but everyone could hear him. "I assumed she was helping with something like the rest of us. I didn't pay any attention to her."

She stared right at him listening to his instructions. Utter terror shown in her eyes. Everleigh had no idea what was going on, but the effect it had on her friend made her extremely nervous. She had never seen that level of fright on anyone's face.

"What happened?" Matt muttered, more to himself than a question he expected anyone to answer.

"She was in a trance," Todd answered, without breaking eye contact with his niece. "It can be dangerous when you're new to them, and I didn't realize it was happening."

"Why...How?" Rita stepped forward curious.

Todd looked baffled. "It's not something that just happens normally. We prepare for this. That's why I didn't think to watch her," he explained, growing more upset.

"She's going to be fine, Todd," Meredith put her hand on his shoulder and gave him a gentle squeeze. "Look at her. You can see it."

"Amber, go get Lilah a glass of juice." Eloise was quickly taking control of the situation.

"Juice?" Amber asked.

"Anything sugary," Eloise further explained.

"Everleigh?"

"Yes, Grandma."

"Fetch a blanket. Her body temperature will have dropped."

Everleigh sprinted from the room wanting to return as quickly as possible.

Eloise looked around. "Boys, where did you move the couch?" She'd no sooner said the words before she spied it. It was on top of other furniture piled in the hallway that ran along the stairs. "Set it back down. She will need to rest."

Matt and Luke easily moved the couch to the doorway of the front room, blocking the path to the door. It jutted into the room, but wouldn't interfere with the space they needed to work.

Todd told Lilah, "I'm going to carry you to the couch now. You ready?"

Everleigh and Amber returned at the same time with the items Grandma Eloise had requested. She held a hand up informing them to wait.

Todd started to lift Lilah, and she panicked. Her arms flailed against him, so he stopped moving her.

Everleigh had been studying her face every moment she was near her since her friend collapsed, unable to look away from the terror Lilah appeared to be going through. When Todd attempted to move her, she saw the change. The recognition came back to Lilah's eyes. It was then that she returned to this house and her surroundings. Everleigh wondered if anyone else realized Lilah hadn't been in her body the entire time she was being tended to.

"They have Fire!" The words burst from her mouth so fast no one could be sure they heard her right.

Luke bent over and took a step backward like the words punched him in the gut. Meredith put her arms around him to steady him.

"What did you say?" Her uncle's face was frozen in alarm.

"Fire! They have him," Lilah repeated, tears breaking free from the corners of her eyes.

"Who has him, dear?" Eloise asked.

Lilah looked like she was searching for the answer, but it couldn't be found. "I don't know," she finally said.

"Let's make her comfortable," Eloise told Todd.

"Okay, Lilah. I'm going to move you now." He picked her up and set her on the couch that had been placed behind her.

Eloise nodded at the girls, and they rushed to her. Everleigh draped the blanket over Lilah and fought the urge to sit next to her, assuming that her uncle would probably want to stay by her side. She was right. As soon as she stepped away, Todd sat on the edge of the cushion, his body angled toward her.

Amber brought over a glass of yellowish liquid. "It's pineapple. All we had," she told Lilah. "My grandma said you need to drink it."

Lilah took the glass and sipped.

"What happened, Lilah? Why did you go into a trance without assistance?"

"I didn't. I mean... It just happened," she said quietly.

Todd shot Meredith a look that implied this isn't right. "What do you remember? Anything?'

Lilah shook her head and took another sip. "There was a white room."

Everyone hung on her every word filled with curiosity and hoping to learn what had happened to Fire.

Eloise walked to the side and leaned against the arm of the couch. She leaned down toward Lilah and softly spoke, "You said you saw Fire. What did you mean?"

Lilah's eyes looked at the floor, but they darted quickly around like she was watching something no one else could see. "They have him," she said, becoming agitated again.

"He's being held against his will," she started.

"By who?" Todd asked.

"I don't know. There were two women," Lilah told him. Her eyes were still displaying the rapid fire movement as she spoke. "But they talked about someone else."

"Were they wolves?" Eloise inquired.

"No," Lilah swallowed. "I mean I don't know. There was a witch."

"Witches?" Meredith cried out in disbelief.

"One of them, yes. There was a spell."

"She's not making any sense," Rita murmured, trying to quietly tell Matt. Everyone heard it.

"There can be some confusion when you emerge from a trance." Eloise explained without taking her eyes off of Lilah. "Your mind is muddled like waking from a dream. Sometimes only fragments remain. Sometimes you remember every detail vividly. Give her time."

"Where is he?" Luke's voice was wrought with agony.

Lilah didn't answer. She stared at the floor clutching her empty glass tightly with her eyes flitting as if they were out of control. It was almost as if she hadn't heard him.

She handed her glass off to her uncle and rubbed her palms over her legs before finally looking around at the group that had collected to learn more. She glanced at the faces until she found Luke then looked back at the floor. "Is there..." she didn't finish her thought.

"What, Lilah? Is there what?" Todd encouraged her.

"It was a white room," she repeated.

Todd looked at Eloise frustrated. A white room wouldn't help them find him.

"Lilah, honey. I want you to remember the white room. What was in it with him? Anything you can remember will help us," Eloise coaxed.

The movement in Lilah's eyes increased again, and as if for the first time, Todd took notice. He leaned his face forward until it was inches from hers staring into her eyes watching the movements. "Lilah, close your eyes."

She did as she was told, but the movement was still there behind her lids. "It looks like a meat locker. Some kind of butcher shop."

"How far away?" he asked.

"It's here."

A collective gasp filled the room.

"Here? In Fairview?"

"Yes," she answered, pointing across the front room in the direction she had traveled astrally.

"Is there a place like that in town?" Todd

scanned the group waiting for anyone to answer.

"Yes," Eloise answered him. "On the back side of town no more than a mile from here there's a meat locker."

"Lilah, try to remember did you see anyone else there with him?" Todd asked.

"Yes, there were two women," she replied.

"Women? What were they doing?"

"They were examining him. Draining his blood."

Todd glanced at Luke before continuing to see how he was handling the news. "Okay. Do you remember anything else? Anything they might've said or did? Anything that may help us?"

"They're coming back."

"What do you mean back? Where did they go?"

"I don't know. They left the room, but before they did, they talked about coming back. Things they needed or needed to do. I don't remember."

"That's good. You're doing great, Lilah."

"One of them is a witch," Lilah blurted out again, forgetting she had already mentioned it.

Everleigh felt lost watching her friend and not knowing how to help. Whatever had happened left her out of sorts. It wasn't long ago she had encouraged her to intentionally enter a different type of trance to see the future. The warnings were well known, but Everleigh had been confident Air was being too soft and coddling Lilah. When she caught Lilah looking at her, she had to look away. The guilt she was feeling for what she could have put Lilah through was forming in her gut. Todd hadn't been exaggerating about the effects it had on them. This trance couldn't have lasted more than a few minutes, and the recovery was already taking several times longer.

"How do you know its Fire? Did they say something that alluded to that?" Uncle Todd asked.

Lilah shook her head.

"What did he look like? Can you describe him for me?"

"Uh, dark hair. Really dark. Blue eyes."

"You were that close to him?" Luke inched closer.

Lilah's breathing quickened, remembering the fright she had when the man's eyes flew open. "Only briefly."

"Take it slow and drink," Eloise instructed.

She continued to sip her drink until the glass was empty while she filled everyone in on what she remembered about him. "He looked fit. I'm sorry I don't remember more."

Luke clasped his hands over the top of his head. It wasn't enough. It could be anyone. "How tall was he would you say?"

Lilah closed her eyes and opened them several times. "He was sitting down."

"Any marks or anything that stand out?" Meredith asked.

There wasn't anything that she remembered seeing, but vampires wouldn't have any. Wounds heal leaving no trace behind. Not even tattoos last long on their skin. Lilah slyly smiled without realizing it.

"What?" Luke asked.

She looked at him not sure what he meant.

"That smile. What were you thinking just now?"

Her cheeks flushed a deep red as everyone's eyes bore on her waiting to hear her every word. "Nothing. Just...I was thinking he was quite handsome."

The young witches started murmuring wondering if they would ever get to see him in person.

"Anything else?" Uncle Todd wanted to know.

She looked at him then shifted her eyes away. "One thing, but I know it's impossible."

"Go on," he gently instructed.

"I ... Somehow I felt like..." Lilah looked at everyone fixated on her, wishing they'd leave. "It was like he knew I was there."

"Has to be Fire then," Uncle Todd told the group, looking at Luke.

Luke nodded and exhaled the relief of knowing Fire had been located while the panic of how he came to be in his current predicament started to build. "He's the only one of us who might, and I repeat might, be able to detect the presence of another Elemental."

"In an astral state?" Grace asked bewildered, and promptly slapped her hand over her mouth.

"Even in an astral state," Todd nodded. "The Elements have far more power than any of us."

Eloise tilted her head to the side, "How are you certain one of the two women is a witch?"

"There was a spell on the door when they unlocked it."

"A spell? Did you hear it?"

Lilah nodded. "I heard her say something. It was in a different language. I didn't recognize any of it."

Meredith straightened up and crossed her arms. "Some spells can only be undone by the witch who cast them. If she's using it to keep him in the room, and to keep others out, it's likely she has to be the one to perform it."

"That won't be a problem," Todd stated. "Luke," he said, already developing a plan.

Luke walked over to him. His fists were clenched, and the veins were bulging in his neck. Centuries of practicing and strengthening his self-control was the only thing preventing him from snapping.

"I need you to get Jackson over here now,"

Todd instructed. "Eloise, call Irving. I'm sure he'll want to know about this."

They were on their phones in seconds doing as Todd ordered.

Todd reached into his pocket and took out his phone.

"What are you planning?" Meredith asked him.

"I know how I can get in there. I just have to make a call."

"I want to be a part of this." Meredith told him in a way that conveyed she wouldn't be told to stay behind.

"And don't think I'm not coming," Luke hissed.

"Actually for what we're going to do, I will probably need all of you," he reassured them.

Eloise looked at Everleigh and said, "Dear, I need you to stay with your cousins and Lilah. Keep an eye on everything."

Todd was already on the phone talking to someone saying there was no time to explain, but be ready to be picked up in ten minutes. When he ended the call, he turned to Everleigh and said, "Please take care of her. She will be extremely weakened and will need to rest a while longer. When she is better, take her to the farmhouse and wait for us to return."

Todd looked away and called out, "Luke?"

Luke appeared again, and Todd pulled him into the living room out of ear shot from the group gathered around Lilah, and asked quietly, "Do you know what we need from Jackson?"

"I'm on it," Luke answered.

"Good. Eloise, what about Irving?" He asked loud enough for all to hear.

"He's waiting for us to pick him up."

"I've got a stop to make. The rest of you pick up Irving and meet me at the meat locker in 20 minutes."

Tires could be heard squealing down the street when Todd opened the door to leave. Jackson ran inside a couple minutes later rushing to Lilah's side, but Luke quickly pulled him off into a different part of the house to fill him in on what happened. Jackson immediately returned to the couch that still sat awkwardly cutting between rooms.

"You're bleeding," Lilah noticed, pointing to the sleeve of his shirt where blood was soaking through the fabric.

"It's nothing. Looks worse than it is."

"What happened?"

"When Luke called me, I ran out of the house so fast, I fell down the steps. Scraped my arm. That's all," he assured her.

It looked a lot worse than a scrape, but there was too much activity around her that made her head spin. The cut was forgotten almost instantly.

Meredith spoke to the younger witches explaining that there would still be spell work for them to partake in later. For now, she needed them to help pack their elders for the trip. Meredith and Eloise would soon be departing with Everleigh to recruit other covens. "Listen to her," she said, pointing to Everleigh. "She will inform you what to gather."

Within minutes, the only ones left in the house with Jackson and Lilah were the witches. They were hurriedly set to work on tasks including Everleigh who had her own packing to do. Once Lilah showed some improvement, the two friends loaded into Jackson's truck and drove to the farmhouse where they waited for the others to return. They waited to learn of Fire's fate.

Arriving at the farmhouse, the mood was light for the first time since outside Elementals started gathering in Fairview. For a few brief minutes, the fate of their worlds was forgotten while Abby showed Everleigh how they can manipulate the temperature around them. Sometime from now, she would look back and remember laughing with Abby as they stayed warm while spinning circles in the yard watching the snow fall around them. It would be the last time any of them smiled and laughed so carefree for months.

Everything changed once the distress call came in from Todd. No one knew what happened, and worse, no one knew who needed emergency help until Matt carried Rita's lifeless body into the house.

Everleigh sank to her knees in front of them sobbing uncontrollably. Somewhere deep down she had to have known there was a risk involved in what they were undertaking. Anyone strong and organized enough to detain Fire would have to be a powerful enemy to go up against. It had never crossed her mind that one of them might not make it back.

"Is she...?" Jackson asked.

The room was silent save for scattered sounds of crying. No one answered him.

"Not yet," Matt finally spoke.

Everleigh's eyes shot open, and she took a closer look. Rita's jacket was covered in blood. A gaping hole in her neck was proof the attack came from a member of Fire or Water. They were the only ones to savagely attack like animals. She wanted to scream, "Save her! Why isn't anyone doing anything?"

*'Where was Luke? Why wasn't he offering his blood to heal her?'* She spotted Luke holding Meredith in his arms right by where Matt sat, and was about to demand he save Rita.

"Not completely," Matt continued. "Soon she will awaken and have to make the choice."

Everleigh gasped, and she looked at everyone in turn. They all seemed to know already. Even Jackson didn't appear surprised to hear it. *'How does he know? Maybe Lilah. Telepathically, of course.'*

"Where's Todd?" Luke asked. "He should be here by now. He left right after us."

"He's almost here," Abby sighed with tears in her eyes. "Taking his time because...well, you know why."

"Yeah, to make sure we weren't followed," Luke thought out loud.

"That, and to bring Irving to his car. He's going to put the locker under surveillance tonight hoping for some activity that might give us useful information. He needs to be mobile just in case."

"You alright?" Jackson asked her.

She nodded. It was a lie. She wasn't alright. Nothing was right about this whole situation.

"I'm going to check on Lilah then," Jackson told her, before walking out the front door.

"I'm coming with you," Abby said, following him out.

Everleigh fell back off her knees and sat in front of the couch. Her eyes were open wide, but she saw nothing. *'This can't be happening.'*

"Hey," her aunt called to her, gently rubbing her shoulder. "You sure you're alright."

"No," Everleigh sputtered loudly, crying again.

Aunt Meredith squatted next to her and put her arm around her. "It's a lot. I know. Once the others get here, we'll find a chance to talk more, but first I want to make sure everyone is safe. Love you."

"I love you too," she said between choked sobs.

Everleigh stared at the floor wondering what she would do. The war of the Elementals had barely begun, and already they had their first potential casualty. If she had to choose between dying and transitioning into a vampire, would she choose death? It's what her grandma would expect her to choose. She didn't think she could. Only created vampires were actually dead with no pulse to speak of, so she couldn't really say it would still be a life. It had to be better than no existence at all.

There was a sharp intake of breath, and Everleigh lifted her head to look at Rita as hard as it was to bring herself to do. The blood remained, but her neck appeared flawless having healed completely. Rita's eyes fluttered open, and Matt smiled at her through his tears.

Privacy wasn't an option in a home where so many were staying. Even so, most had wandered off to other parts of the house. The ones who lingered had the good sense to stick to the shadows in the corners giving some semblance of leaving the couple alone. It was what she should do as well.

Everleigh opened the front door of the farmhouse to an even more frightening sight. Directly in front of her, Grandma Eloise and the others were approaching the house. Lilah was at the top of the steps, bent over in agonizing pain, but from what? Her mom and another woman were holding her up on her feet. She wanted to ask what happened, but when she looked to Abby, she saw Lilah's mom was distracted by something else.

She followed Abby's gaze across the porch where something was in the midst of changing form. Air might be used to it. Both shape shifting themselves and watching their kind change. Everleigh was not. The grotesque half animal, half humanoid form was straight from a slasher movie. Everleigh ran to the far side of the porch from it and vomited over the rail.

As she straightened herself and wiped her mouth on her sleeve, she heard two voices behind her. One she recognized and one she didn't. Both saying the same name, "Leena."

Marcus' match. *'Could it be?'* Everleigh wondered. She turned and gazed upon the man opposite the porch from her who was draped in robes that had to be centuries old. *'An Element? Here? In front of me.'* The thought made her heart rate quicken, and she grabbed the rail for support.

"Lilah," Todd said gravely.

Everleigh looked to see her friend reaching for the face of a wolf. Reaching to touch her boyfriend Jackson. With Matt inside, Jackson was the only known wolf there, but even Everleigh wouldn't recognize him now if it weren't for his slightly torn clothes.

It was the first time she'd seen him like this. He'd transitioned many times over the years. Judd would take him on so-called camping trips to allow him the freedom to explore his true identity. There had been pictures. Not of Jackson, but of others. It couldn't prepare her for seeing her friend masked under the guise of a wolf.

His hands and feet were longer, distorted too somehow. Jackson's entire body was more filled out. He had been muscular as it was, but now everything seemed more pronounced. Larger. Hairier too, but it wasn't fur like she expected. But his face. It scared her, yet she couldn't look away. His ears were larger and pointed. His mouth and nose protruded as you would expect a muzzle to look. Jackson's mouth was closed. The teeth couldn't be seen, but Everleigh knew they could tear the strongest man to shreds with little effort. Nothing on his face was human anymore. It was that of a nightmare induced beast, and her friend was staring lovingly into its eyes.

"Lilah!" Todd yelled, just before her hand could reach his face.

It broke through to her this time, and Lilah looked confused to see him. Moments later she passed out with Jackson's abnormally construed hands catching her before she hit the floor.

"So," a voice in the darkness said, clapping his hands. "What did I miss?"

Everleigh couldn't get a good look at the man on the steps between Todd and her grandma before everyone piled in gathering around Lilah. The time for gawking would come later. There was only one person it could be, and that was Fire. More important was how none of them appeared to be afraid of the beast gently lifting Lilah and carrying her to the swing. Jackson had been her best friend for as long as she could remember, but she was fighting hard against the urge to run away.

"Are you going to drink that?" Meredith asked.

Eloise smiled with a twinkle in her eye. "I already have," she said, looking down at the vial in her hand.

Little by little, the wrinkles on Eloise's face began to soften. The gray in her hair darkened slowly at first, then finished the change almost at once.

Marcus walked over to her and gripped both of her shoulders with his hands. "You will soon have the face of the Anya I remember from our first meeting."

"Do we keep up the pretense?" Meredith asked. "Or shall I call you grandma now?"

The years were slowly rewinding on her grandma's face right before her eyes. Everleigh couldn't look away. Her mouth fell open wide as she realized while she was looking at the woman she'd always known as grandma, she was also looking at the woman known to her kind as Mother Earth.

# Fire
## The Elementals: Book Three
## Available August 2021

These people were crazy. It was beyond his comprehension why Water wanted to go on this quest of exploring earth in the flesh. There was no reason or logic to the maddening way they constructed their society. Across the water, starving people were killed for hunting in the King's forest. If you could not afford to pay and were caught, the punishment was public mutilation and murder. And for what? A wild hare?

The vicious acts were well known before any of them came to this land. Whether or not any of them agreed with what was happening wasn't their place to say. Still knowing how these miserable creatures went about their lives couldn't prepare him for being there to see it. It's not the same when you are watching from worlds away. Only the big picture can be seen from beyond the veil, not the details. The small bits are what makes the acts so vile.

Public executions are not for the purposes of punishment at all. That's only a guise to make right their actions. It's for sport! These heathens gather and cheer on the executioners. No manner of crime received a proper sentence. Stealing a loaf to feed your family could land you with your entrails wrapped around your neck while your fellow countrymen shout and throw rotten food your way. The very people who were your friends and neighbors would be there in the crowds hollering in delight as the sword cuts through your flesh.

The one he witnessed soon after arriving cut